I0722263

Hold on to your seat! *The Eternal Struggle* immediately draws the reader into the action. The dire situations of the two main characters—Valoretta, Queen of Mira, and Arnacin of Enchantress Island—are clearly portrayed as the action alternates between their evolving parallel perils.

Wallace is a solid storyteller. Her ability to maintain the period dialogue adds charm to the reading that frames the action in an unusual fantasy world of old. The characters peopling this world are clearly drawn and compelling.

— Andrea O'Connor, author of
The Gaby Quinn Mystery series

The Savage War is an ingeniously plotted novel that is fast-paced and filled with action and focused scenes. There is a kind of ritual that opens the narrative, establishing a custom that is passed from father to son, allowing readers an idea of a tradition that reflects the setting in which the story takes place. Arnacin is a young protagonist who grows in wisdom, but he is a character that has internal battles of his own. I loved the way the author allows his humanity to come out in the narrative, a personality that is characterized by "humility, compassion, and intense feeling of responsibility" and these are the values at the center of the internal conflict when he has to make difficult choices. *The Savage War* is well written with a vivid setting; deft and balanced, and featuring characters that are interesting and real.

— **Readers' Favorite, 5-star review**

The Savage War is definitely packed. (But do buckle in for the long ride, because it is definitely worth it.) There is a lot going on by way of story, themes and thought-provoking moments. I especially love Arnacin's willingness to see the conflict from all sides, to ask the hard questions, and do what he feels is right despite opposition.

— M

The characters in *The Savage War* were well thought out with unique personalities. The protagonist was wise with sharp instincts and values honor above all else. The reader can feel how torn he is when he has to make those hard decisions.

— Eileen K. Copeland

The Savage War is ideal for fans of G.A. Henty and R.A. Ballantyne. It's intentionally written in an older style, evoking classic adventure/fantasy authors. The characters are charming and the imagery evocative.

— CT Reader

Many books of epic medieval fantasy clamor for attention in the market today. But few of them manage to retain a balance of majestic tragedy with the themes of honor and nobility, a balance which characterized similar novels of a bygone era. [In *The Savage War*,] Author Esther Wallace tells a story about a young man who feels called to an adventure away from his idyllic homeland, where he eventually discovers a nation torn by war. Arnacin's sense of honor compels him to take part in the conflict that, over time, threatens to crush his spirit... Snippets where Arnacin and Princess Valoretta are teasing each other are genuinely touching while heroics on the battlefield stir the soul with excitement.

In short, this is a great novel for anyone craving realistic fantasy with a dose of spirituality. It is awash with battles, drama, political intrigue, and raw human emotion. Just make sure to save some room on your bookshelf for Esther's next entry!

— Amazon Customer

THE ISLAND SIEGE

Other Books by the Author
THE BLACK PHANTOM CHRONICLES
The Savage War
The Eternal Struggle
The Island Siege
The Final Drive (*forthcoming*)

THE ISLAND SIEGE

THE BLACK PHANTOM CHRONICLES

BOOK THREE

BY

ESTHER WALLACE

EMERALD LAKE BOOKS

Sherman, Connecticut

The Island Siege
The Black Phantom Chronicles (Book 3)

Copyright © 2022 Esther Wallace

Cover design by Mark Gerber

Cover illustration copyright © 2022 Mark Gerber

Books published by Emerald Lake Books may be ordered through your favorite booksellers or by visiting emeraldlakebooks.com.

Library of Congress Cataloging-in-Publication Data

Names: Wallace, Esther, author.

Title: The island siege / by Esther Wallace.

Description: Sherman, Connecticut : Emerald Lake Books, [2022] | Series: The black phantom chronicles ; book three

Identifiers: LCCN 2022035991 (print) | LCCN 2022035992 (ebook) | ISBN 9781945847646 (trade paperback) | ISBN 9781945847653 (epub)

Subjects: CYAC: Kings, queens, rulers, etc.--Fiction. | Orphans--Fiction. | Horses--Fiction. | LCGFT: Novels.

Classification: LCC PZ7.1.W3527 Is 2022 (print) | LCC PZ7.1.W3527 (ebook) | DDC [Fic]--dc23

LC record available at https://lccn.loc.gov/2022035991
LC ebook record available at https://lccn.loc.gov/2022035992

To Dad,
for your endless support of and faith in our aspirations.
Until we meet again...

Cast of Characters

Alexander Maxwell . The older brother of Evan Maxwell and heir to the throne of Ansky while he lived.

Andrew Dalacort . . The cousin of Evan Maxwell, son of Wilber and Lorene Dalacort, and heir to the throne of Evfel.

Arnacin . . . . Our islander. Son of Bozzic and Lady Talliaha and brother of Charlotte and William.

Barth . . . . An island shepherd boy from the northwest coast of the island and the younger brother of Tahan.

Bounen . . . . An islander from Arnacin's village, who was one of the group of boys that used to play with Arnacin when they were children.

Bozzic . . . . The father of Arnacin and Charlotte and husband of Lady Talliaha.

Channing, Brother . A refugee from Baulis, now living in Nomacir.

Charlotte . . . . . . The sister of Arnacin and William and daughter of Bozzic and Talliaha.

Clare . . . . Queen Lorene's handmaiden.

Darkfire . . . . Stallion of the Ice Woods.

Evan Maxwell . . . . A prince and heir to the throne of Ansky after the death of Prince Alexander.

Reginold, Duke . . . A duke and regent of Evfel.

Talliaha, Lady . . . . The mother of Arnacin, Charlotte and William and widow of Bozzic.

Tenacius . . . . The son of Arnacin and Valoretta.

Tevin . . . . An islander from Arnacin's village and one of the group of boys that used to play with Arnacin when they were children.

Tyron, Lord . . . . . The Anskonian lord of Fortress Tyhoronous.

Valoretta, Queen . . The dethroned queen of Mira, wife of Arnacin, and mother of Tenacius.

Vilo . . . . An islander from Arnacin's village, known for his skill with music.

Wilber Dalacort. . . The king of Evfel, husband of Lorene, father of Andrew, and uncle to Evan Maxwell.

Contents

IN ENCHANTRESS ISLAND'S FORTY-SEVENTH YEAR, Arnacin sailed away from home and found civil war on Mira. Now, four years later, he still hasn't returned home and the threat of neighboring Elcan's warring kingdoms looms over the island's freedom.

Unbeknownst to his family and friends, Arnacin wants almost nothing more than to return home. But when spring comes and Elcan's journey toward the island begins, Arnacin is a prisoner of pirates on an island called Baulis.

Soon, islanders will voyage to Elcan for the first time. Meanwhile, their presumed-dead islander leads Valoretta, Queen of Mira, through Ursa's woods to a small town called Boarderwood. It will be another eleven months before he comes home.

But for now, this is the story of Elcan and Enchantress Island...

Prologue

WILBER DALACORT, king of the most powerful monarchy in all of Elcan, paused in his personal chamber's doorway. Queen Lorene stood at the window; her golden hair streaked with red in the evening light.

Straightening, she wiped her cheeks before regally turning around. Her eyes were shimmering too brightly to fool the king, but he said nothing as she asked, "Do you intend for us to go to Ansky?"

Wilber's gaze briefly dropped to the letter she held crumpled in her fist—no doubt private condolences. He kissed her forehead sadly before sighing, "I see no alternatives, unless their foolish ruling council would take on their rightful duty."

"That would be horrible!" the queen gasped. "Even disregarding the potential jealousies they wish to avoid, a councilor acting as king would disrupt the entire foundation of Ansky. They need an actual king as their counterbalance."

With some satisfaction, Wilber lightly mocked, "Can you not trust an entire council to rule fairly?"

Seeing the sarcasm in his raised eyebrows, Lorene shook her head. "Ansky balances power through their double rule. Why must you ridicule them just because you rule Evfel absolutely?"

Smiling, the king buried his nose in his wife's shoulder. "Remind me how king and councilors can share power without creating chaos."

Quietly, Lorene admitted, "I never fully understood it, but by working together, they stop tyranny."

"Insanity," Wilber whispered, running a hand down the back of his head. "Even without needing the approval of a king, councils spend forever just bickering. By the time they decide on a resolution, it is too late."

"It also goes the other way. The king must have the agreement of the council."

"That makes it worse. If a king cannot act on his own strength, his land is doomed."

Lorene dropped her gaze back to the letter, then unfolded it, smoothing it against her bulging stomach. "Perhaps you are right. This circumstance would never have arisen without that system."

"Do you mean the absurd circumstance that your brother's dying wish was to have his children raised by ignorant peasants?"

"And the council thinks as you do—that Phillip's wish was foolishness." Fresh tears shimmered in the corners of the queen's eyes. She swiftly turned back to the window, but her attempt to disguise her pain failed as she burst into sobs. "Wilber, the last I saw him was before our marriage!"

"Lorene," the king sighed, wrapping his arms around her. "The fault lies entirely with him. He disowned you, and his letter of apology only arrived a month ago. There was nothing you could have done."

Stroking her hair as she continued to cry, Wilber sighed. Ansky was offering a compromise, where he, as the closest male relative, could raise their prince, spending some time in Ansky and the rest in Evfel. That way, he would not need to worry as much about a regent during his absence. But he cared little for Phillip's offspring. If it wasn't for the Sanguinea Peace Treaty, he would declare war on Ansky, and he would win.

If it wasn't for… Why had he not thought of it before? True, he could hardly kill their heir under the treaty, but if he raised him into the worst sort of king Ansky could ever imagine…

Wilber shifted. No, if he took the child to Evfel even once, out of their watch for any length of time, they would suspect manipulation. But if he appointed the right regent for Evfel and stayed in Ansky until the day arrived for their prince's reign, playing his game well, the willful country would, at last, belong to Evfel.

With that thought, he nodded. "Come next spring, we will leave for Ansky. You can raise Evan Maxwell to be the Anskonian king."

"But I am with child. If you intend to bring Evan back to Evfel, I can stay here for the time being."

"No. They are willing now, but with their distrust of us, it would be better to let them always see we treat him well. If you wish to stay here until you feel our child is ready to travel, I will go alone for now."

"Who will be regent of Evfel while we are the regents of Ansky?"

"Duke Reginold."

"But you have never trusted him!"

"No, but he has no backbone, Lorene. He knows that if he commits treason, he will effectively crush the dam that stands only through my renowned strength. If he tries, every noble in Evfel will fight for their right as king. Reginold knows he will never win. For that reason, we can trust him in this instance."

"If you trust him," Lorene whispered, "then do raise Evan for kingship. It spares Ansky from a political feud."

Wilber merely nodded. For her, he would pretend to raise the prince of Ansky. And if Evan Maxwell became a failure of a king, his dream would still come true.

Chapter 1

A Dysfunctional Family

Eleven Years Later

Brushing down the gelding, Dedalo, Evan Maxwell briefly rested his head against the steed's side. With a nicker, Dedalo nipped the prince's brown hair.

"Stop rebuking me," Evan whispered, pushing the thick head away. "As it is, Uncle Wilber will drag me out by my ear if he knows I am 'acting like a lowly stable boy.'"

Dedalo snorted, as if in protest. Smiling slightly, the prince threw a saddle blanket over the horse's back.

Footsteps approached him from behind, but he ignored them. After a moment, the husky voice of one of the handlers asked, "Tell me again why we keep these horses? Without you standing by, they refuse to carry our knights or to do so much as plow. By all rights, we should slaughter them and use their meat to feed the dogs."

"Dare you speak so?" Evan snapped, whirling toward the offender. "These are my father's horses! Give them the respect owed them as faithful servants of your king!"

Hastily, the handler bowed. "Pardon my rambling tongue, Prince Maxwell. These horses are precious beyond gold, as your father always said."

Turning back to finish tacking the steed, the prince muttered, "More faithful, indeed, than everyone else." How he hated the court! Not a single person spared a thought for him, outside of their wish to force him onto the throne to avoid Dalacort rule. They were a self-centered bunch, caring only for their petty comforts. No one had ever considered trying to fill in for the lack of a proper family in Evan's life. Nor did they open their eyes enough to realize the Dalacorts would never do so.

Very well. Evan could return the favor and despise them too. If only his conscience would stop pricking him...

"Prince Maxwell, may I assist with anything before your uncle finds you?" the handler asked cautiously.

"When I finish here, you may take him out of the gates. I will follow shortly."

"Why follow? You may go with me. Or has he also outlawed riding?"

"You may not ask," Evan said without turning around in an attempt to hide his reddening face. "Your task is to obey without question."

"May I at least know where you intend to go?"

Snorting under his breath, the prince muttered, "To the Calmar Mountains. I will disappear to raise horses in peace."

Even at a low whisper, Evan heard the stablehand's reply. "Fine by us."

He had no desire to answer. Not that he had fooled the stablehand, anyway. The lack of supplies on the steed would have revealed his wishful sarcasm.

Once Dedalo was tacked, the prince stepped aside for the handler. As the man led the horse out of the stable, Evan pulled his hood over his head. If he looked solitary, it was because he was friendless in a suffocating world.

Outside, he dismissed the stablehand. Barely had he mounted and turned Dedalo toward the main road of the town before a middle-aged woman, facially scarred and already stooped despite her relatively young age, stepped out of her doorway into the horse's path.

Dedalo reared. The woman screamed, dropping her basket. Stockings scattered through the mud.

Quickly, the prince dismounted, helping the woman in her scramble to rescue the wayward articles. A raspy wail erupted from her. "Oh, my merchandise is ruined!" Her lower lip trembled.

Now in the freedom of the valley, Evan felt responsibility and shame prick him. "I could buy them," he mumbled, bashfully handing her his armload of muddy stockings. A crafty smile quirked at the woman's mouth. She could cheat him by charging double what the socks were worth, then wash them and sell them again.

King Wilber would have ordered any noble to leave her rather than appear so foolish. Still, Evan could not just ride away. He was now responsible for ruining her livelihood. He had a duty to either help her wash them or pay for them. Not that he had ever washed a thing—it would be less humiliating to allow her to cheat him.

Crone and prince appraised each other. Although the crone's eyes remained pale blue, they seemed to have abruptly gained a piercing quality. Before those eyes, Evan felt bare, not just of clothes, but of skin and tissue. Hesitantly, he stepped back.

The crone bowed. "No one would expect generosity from you, my prince. At best, they say you are aloof and scornful by nature."

"I am, rather." Swallowing, Evan shrugged. "I startled you. Tell me your price and where to leave it, and I will do so this evening when I return."

A laugh, harsh and croaking, poured forth from the crone. "Most would consider that a sweet way to swindle the unfortunate, but I know you speak truly." Again, she bowed. Her voice changed, lost its coarseness as it grew gentler. "Never mind, Prince Maxwell. I confess to stepping out on purpose. Thus, *catching* people is a trait of mine."

Evan stared, his heart thumping.

Nodding to herself, the woman shoved her muddy stockings back into her basket. She paused, looking up again. "Prepare yourself, my prince. Your birthright is at hand. Hide no longer as the resentful orphan. Though not an act, it shields your deep kindness from others' eyes. For Ansky, you must forget the scorn, the wild, hurtful speculations of those around you, and your uncle's manipulations. True life cannot come without love, my prince. Step into the crossroads with this knowledge." With that, she slipped into the alley between two buildings and disappeared.

For another second, the prince stood there, dumbfounded. Then, hastily, he remounted and kicked Dedalo into flight. Light snow flurries swirled about them as they temporarily escaped for the wild.

Sir Quincy heard that, in Evfel, knights were too highly regarded for guard duty. Not so in Ansky, where forces were much fewer. Pulling his cloak closer against the snow flurries, the knight turned back along the ramparts to continue on his patrol. Not ten paces away, he spotted Prince Andrew Dalacort leaning against the parapet, staring down.

The knight stopped beside the younger of the rival princes. Below, a cloaked rider trotted away to the east.

"If he thinks he hides among the commoners in that maroon cloak, he lacks all brains," Andrew muttered without lifting his red head from his arms.

Smiling as he noted Andrew's tasseled blue cloak, Quincy asked, "Did your tutor excuse you?"

"Silence. I want to know only one thing. How is it that Evan Maxwell can go riding as he pleases when I have history, geography, mathematics, the study of strategy and so on, with a tutor to ram it down my throat?" He cast a glance sideways at the knight. "If you think the reason is his future kingship, remember, I am also heir to a throne."

"I think the reason is that you have a father, while your cousin refuses his assistance."

The younger prince's scoffing snort was cut off as his tutor, Father Magdalon, joined them. "Pouting is hardly suitable for a king's heir, Your Highness."

"Great," Andrew murmured, without straightening or turning. "Who sent you here?"

"King Wilber." Leaning against the parapet himself, the tutor added, "He also gave me permission to drag you back to your books, should the need arise. Your laziness is hardly promising for your kingdom."

"Not another word," the boy warned.

Lips quirking slightly, the tutor reached for Andrew's ear. "Very well, Your Highness. Your father did permit the use of force."

As far as Quincy knew, most ten-year-olds—even those who were almost eleven—would squeal when their ear was seized and twisted. Not this one. Yanking away from his tutor with only a slight wince, Andrew smoothed down his cloak with a single, huffy swipe. "I will go if Father insists, but you had best keep your fingers away." Head high, he whirled toward the battlement stairs. Like a defiant captive on the way to execution, he led the way while his tutor followed on his heels.

Shaking his head, Quincy turned back to where Prince Maxwell was shrinking into the snowy distance. Evan Maxwell, Ansky's future king. At that thought, the knight's smile faded. A sigh escaped him, and he resumed his patrol.

Not two steps later, he ran into Sir Radnor, who was also patrolling. "No, Quincy, you must remain in Ansky."

"Pardon?"

With hair the color of iron, Sir Radnor was the oldest of the Anskonian knights, yet still hale enough for duty. All the other knights took his word as law, though Quincy refused to view mere age as of greater value than reason. Still, Radnor did know many things.

"When you fondly shake your head while looking toward Prince Andrew and then sigh as you look toward Prince Maxwell, what can I assume but that you desire to escape to Evfel?"

"Hardly!" Quincy laughed. "I am and always will be Anskonian. However..." His gaze wandered back to Evan, now a shrinking black dot. "As impudent as Andrew is, he has time to change. At fifteen, Prince Maxwell is already old enough for the council to force him onto the throne—but no one wants him. Everyone is happy to wait until he calls that doom upon us."

A long breath filled Radnor's chest as he also turned east. "Aye. If only King Phillip still lived."

Snorting, Quincy resumed his patrol. "Phillip was completely selfish. Had he even once thought of anyone besides himself, he would have protected himself against the plague like a proper king. If his queen insisted, as a physician's daughter, that she knew secrets the monks lacked for treating the sick, he should have locked her out of the castle until the disease was past."

"You only say that because you were but nine years old at the time," Radnor said, walking alongside him. "Those of us who were older know there was nothing in all of history more beautiful than our queen leaving her home to help the dying. When she returned sick, King Phillip carried her across the bailey, up to their room. There he stayed by her side, locking his boys out to keep them safe from the plague. Sadly, it was too late for Prince Alexander."

His voice dropped in defeat. "Little could he have known what came of his love... Yet no king ever gave a truer gift or example."

Stubbornly, Quincy folded his arms. "Regardless, you must admit he condemned us. If we allowed the Dalacorts to rule, all our customs, all the freedoms we value, would die. But Evan Maxwell? He will use his reign to exact vengeance on the world for his family's death."

"I hear the people's speculation in that."

Disregarding the older knight's comment, Quincy could not prevent himself from glancing toward the distant rider—the rider who, he was sure, would forever change Ansky for the worst.

For the past three years, Andrew had made a habit of waking around midnight to skulk through the castle's stone corridors. He had learned at the age of seven that his cousin was usually awake and wandering sometime over the next four hours. It was up to him to see that nothing terrible ever befell his family because of it.

That night, he came across his quarry where the north passage met the middle corridor. Evan meandered toward the crossing, his gaze on the floor, an unclasped cloak hanging over his shoulders. With no one near, he was a specter wandering the world alone.

"Where were you?" Andrew scoffed. "Moping about with the horses?"

True to his expectations, Evan's head jerked up, his shoulders straightened, his blue eyes narrowed. He was now every inch the picture of disdain. Yet contrary to expectations, he brushed by wordlessly, his cloak slapping against the younger prince.

"Hey!" Stepping closer, Andrew drew himself to his full height. "No one may turn his back on a Dalacort! I asked you a question!"

Evan halted abruptly, though he continued to face away. "Unless you refuse to answer me because you were finally enacting your plan of destroying us?" Andrew continued.

"Andrew," the older prince growled, slowly turning. "I suggest you return to bed and cease trying to make this into a problem of nationality. In that case, you will lose. You stand, after all, on Anskonian soil."

Glaring, Andrew assessed his cousin. Evan was taller and more muscular than the younger prince, but he was small for his age. His growth spurt had not yet come, and he still appeared very much a boy.

Andrew himself was thin, all up and down, the top of his red head only reaching Evan's shoulder. But he refused to think himself beaten by such odds. "Would I? Do you still refuse to answer? Is it because you were, in fact, off moaning about your dead family? Ah, poor Evan, all alone."

Evan turned red. His eyes burned. However, beneath his brown hair, that only made the blue of his irises shine more brightly, seemingly glowing. Andrew's lips curled upward, and he cocked his head. "It was their own folly that kil—"

His words ended in a yelp as Evan punched him in the jaw. His own eyes flashing, Andrew pounced, swinging high. When his cousin moved to block, Andrew's other fist landed beneath his ribs.

Gasping, the older prince doubled over. As Evan's cloak slid to the floor, Andrew jumped on his back, but he had claimed victory too early. Twisting, Evan threw his cousin to the floor, dropped on top of him, and wrapped his fingers around Andrew's throat. "Take it back, Andrew!"

"You would not dare!"

Tightening his grip, Evan growled, "Do you wish to risk your life on that?"

Struggling to breathe, Andrew warned, "Father would... see you... flayed to death."

"See if I ca—"

A shriek echoed down the corridor. Both boys looked toward the sound of running feet. Shawl bouncing over her shoulders, the queen rushed toward them. Her favorite handmaiden, Clare, was at her elbow.

In moments, Clare had yanked Evan off. Sinking to the floor, Queen Lorene wrapped her son in her arms, stroking his hair. Trying to hide his laughter, Andrew buried his face in her embrace.

"What do you think you were doing?" the queen snapped, glaring at her nephew.

Gasping, but somehow managing to stand erect, Evan replied, "Holding my own against your brat." As Clare shook his arm, he pulled free.

Pursing her lips, the queen pulled back slightly and dropped her gaze to her son, who quickly lowered his eyes. "You will both apologize to each other! Immediately!"

Without looking up, Andrew muttered, "Sorry, Evan." Swiftly, he sucked in his lips to control his grin.

Evan himself remained silent and glowering until Clare reached for him again. "My apologies."

Yanking her shawl back over her shoulders, the queen ordered, "Now go to bed! I do not know what possessed you to be up at this hour. Thankfully, Clare heard you, but this is enough! If there is any more of this behavior…"

She left her threat hanging. Tearing his cloak free from beneath Andrew's legs, Evan nodded. Then, bowing, he stormed away.

With a sigh, the queen turned back to her son. "Andrew, what were you thinking? Evan is four and a half years older than you."

Folding his arms, the younger prince huffed, "I could best him."

The queen's lips compressed before she continued. "I am fetching your tutor. He will make sure you are well. I will also ask him to sleep outside your door for the rest of the night. Understand?"

His smile vanishing, Andrew demanded, "Why do you saddle *me* with a jailer? Evan—"

"Does not fight without someone forcing him."

Ducking his head, Andrew found no words to say. So, he allowed his mother to help him to his feet, endured the kiss planted atop his head, and turned to start down the corridor toward his room, knowing his mother was watching him.

"Stop!"

His uncle's order brought Evan to a halt just as his wooden practice sword struck against Andrew's ribs.

"How is it, Andrew," Wilber continued, "that you lose every time? Can you not see the signs? This is all the same basic concept—feints."

Tossing his sword to the hard-packed snow at their feet, Andrew folded his arms. "He changes his attack every time!"

"As is proper. It is the only way to learn or tea—"

An unearthly noise rent the air—a stallion's clarion call, but unlike any horse Evan had ever heard. Prouder, colder, more commanding, it was a call to war that caused the winter air itself to freeze in fear.

"That must be the stallion from Fortress Tyhoronous," Wilber muttered, turning toward the sound. "It appears practice is unfortunately over for the day."

As the king made his way to the commotion coming from the gates, Andrew kicked at his sword. "Practice is unfortunately over for the day."

"You have nothing to complain about," Evan commented, following his uncle. "Your father will take you secretly out tonight to drill you until you drop, even as he continues to pretend he cares about training me. As if he does! He waited until I was ten, while you were only six when you started."

"You alone would think of that as caring, pampered brat."

Evan simply continued onward. He could hear his cousin following amid the growing sound of shouts as they neared the gatehouse, but the sight just inside the passage stole his breath.

Four stablehands and six knights struggled to pull a massive rearing stallion through the gatehouse tunnel. Ropes trailed through the trampled snow from the horse's head, neck and girth, but his handlers could not subdue him. Death and fire seemed to flicker from his eyes and run through every motion, lighting his many whip marks, sparking throughout his thick mane and flashing hooves.

The thud of the gates closing brought another scream from the stallion. With an abrupt lunge, he broke free of his captors and bounded up the rampart stairs. At the top, he looked neither left nor right, but simply jumped over the battlements.

Even Andrew gasped in the seconds during which time seemed to freeze as several knights grabbed at the ropes whipping past their feet and hastily wrapped them around the closest crenellation, arresting the stallion's fall.

The interrupted sound of a strangled whinny followed. Evan sprinted toward the gates. "Open!"

Before more than a crack had appeared, the prince was outside, running along the inner curtain to where the stallion dangled by his head and shoulders. "Let him down!" he shouted.

Despite its predicament, the stallion's hooves lashed out at Evan's head as the knights lowered the horse to the ground. The prince swiftly ducked back. Then the horse stood gasping, hanging his head as his body trembled.

Removing one glove, the prince cautiously approached. He brushed bare fingers through the thick, reddish coat on the stallion's shoulder. It was not black, as he had first thought—but it was not a dark roan either.

Fire again sparked in the eye watching him, but the stallion's only sign of resistance was a flinch of skin as Evan's hand brushed against him—as if his fingers were flies. From that hate-filled look, he knew the surrender was temporary. Moving slowly, the prince slid his hand down to the trailing ropes.

"Fight later, boy," he breathed. "You need water first."

One shaking leg after another gradually followed Evan's retreating steps, but the stallion's eyes remained a bonfire. With any other horse, the prince would have assumed that last spurt of pain had defeated it, but this one... He wondered if it had merely relented to the truth of his words.

Refraining from making the stallion pass once more beneath the murder holes and the portcullis's heavy spikes, the prince took him to what many deemed the weak point in the defenses—the outer doorway of his father's barn, which cut through the inner curtain without even a door to close. Head hanging, the stallion trailed him inside.

There they were met by Wilber, Andrew and the horse master. Stunned expressions were fixed on the faces of the latter two, while Wilber seemed as stoic as ever. None, however, spoke until Evan led the stallion quietly into a stall. Then the horse master shook his head. "How you do it, Your Highness, is a wonder. If only you had that effect on people."

"Bring water," was Evan's cool response. Carefully, he unknotted the many ropes hanging from the stallion. His jaw clenched as he loosened the rope bridle sawing into the back of the horse's ears and mouth before slipping it off.

For a second, he thought he saw the stallion's eyes close, as if in relief—an extremely human expression. But it was only momentary.

When the stall door creaked open, someone pushed a water bucket in and shoved something soft into Evan's hand. "A blindfold," the voice of the horse master hissed. "Put it on now, while he lacks the strength to fight or he will break loose."

"Let him."

"This beast was given to King Wilber, not you, and this is his order."

As a cold lump hardened in Evan's stomach, his fingers clenched the cloth. For now, the stallion remained unmoving, only coughing in coarse breaths—but he fixed his eyes challengingly on the prince.

Once the stallion's strength returned, it was unlikely anyone could ever stand so close again and, if Evan obeyed his uncle's order, that chance was even less. Yet the stallion had been given to Wilber. Should the king fail to tame him, he would not escape before he was slaughtered.

Crouching to check the water temperature, Evan brought himself level to the stallion's head. Hot air snorted from blowing nostrils, tickling the prince's neck. Slowly, he brushed the long, crimped forelock off the animal's head.

The stallion's muzzle twitched threateningly, revealing his teeth, and the prince moved in abruptly, binding the cloth around the stallion's head as he reared. He somehow evaded the flashing hooves, then ducked out of the stall. The blindfold would fall off soon, but perhaps his gentleness would be noted before the handlers began their pathetic attempts to tame this noble creature.

Andrew's eyes widened as he watched the stallion's fury. "Would it not be prudent to allow it to wear itself out and then to break it?"

"Fool!" Evan snapped. "You try that, and you will kill his very soul! Only hatred will remain, if that has not happened already. Do you not see the whip marks, all the ropes hanging off him when he arrived? Someone has already tried and failed!"

"Which is perhaps why they offered it to me," Wilber muttered.

"Are you suggesting someone wants you dead?" the horse master gasped.

The king's gaze never left the raging stallion. "I doubt the knights of Ansky would dare try to kill me, when they know such a move could lead to war—particularly since their stronghold sits on the edge of the Ice Woods, and they cannot afford a two-fronted assault."

A shudder passed through everyone except the king, who only lifted a shoulder slightly in dismissal. "It is more likely they thought Evfel's king was a trainer of last resort."

"Only if you want a demon," Evan muttered, rankling at the idea that they would consider *Evfel's* king the foremost expert on horses.

Turning to the princes, Wilber dropped a hand on Andrew's shoulder. "You boys have studies to attend to. When the stallion calms, the horse master will deal with it his way."

"You mean Andrew has studies." With that, Evan strode back through the trampled snow to the keep. "I study on my own time!" As he reached the castle steps, he muttered to himself, "You never bothered to find me a tutor, remember?"

Despite his bitter protests, Evan tried to study Anskonian history for a few hours. That granted him the seclusion of his room, if nothing else. But his mind constantly wandered back to the stallion. Tracing his fingers over an illustration of Castle Ansky, he sighed.

"Ansky," he whispered, as if the drawing could hear him. "What simpletons you were to build your castle and town to keep Evfel out, only to surrender your princess to them. And if you failed to secure your doom then, you certainly did so when you invited their king as regent."

Tossing the book aside, the prince rolled off his bed and shuffled across the room to his window. Below, the barn his father had built with his own two hands to drive away the frustrations of the day—King Phillip's barn, with its rearing horse doorposts—stood quiet and motionless. Hopefully, the stallion had surrendered slightly, and his silence had not been imposed by force.

It was a pointless wish, however. The stallion would forever refuse any normal means of training, and the fool of a horse master would never know where to go from there. That wild spirit was already dead.

If only Evan had not been wholly overlooked! Was it so hard to acknowledge his skill with horses and let him tame the untamable? He would have proven them all inept—especially Wilber, whom they thought so masterful.

A sharp rap interrupted his peace. "Prince Maxwell! It is supper-time, Your Highness."

When Evan only sighed without reply, another call followed. "You know your aunt always insists you eat with them."

Oh, he knew. She did indeed insist, if only to make him feel even more alone while she, her husband and her son acted like a family. Once or twice, he had successfully missed the meal by saddling up a horse and disappearing. Under the circumstances, he was inclined to try that again, despite it only having worked when he left long before the meal. Yet, as he thought of the horses in the barn, he reconsidered.

"You may tell them I am coming."

"I was instructed to wait for you."

Huffing, Evan straightened before following the page down the hall.

In Ansky, the royal family ate in private whenever they did not have members of the council or Evfelian guests visiting. Evfel had never had such privacy, but even Wilber confessed to enjoying the time with his family. Having been raised in Ansky, Andrew never knew the difference.

Since the private dining room of Ansky's royal family had been mostly unfurnished, Evfel's monarchs carted an ornate chandelier and chairs with them at Lorene's request. Although Evan hardly remembered how the tower room had looked before the regency, he recognized the foreign products of Evfel, with or without the stories that circulated. This recognition lay in the items' stuffiness—like the chairs with red cushions rimmed in gold braid on the seat and backrest.

His family's hard wooden chairs with horse heads on the ends of the armrests had been moved to storage long ago. Occasionally, Evan would slip into the storage room to run his hands along the furniture hidden away there. He wondered if he was capable of failing his parents, who had succumbed to the plague, and his older brother, Alexander, who died not long after them on his coronation day. Could he allow Ansky's standard itself to join the other representations of their emblem? Surely it would if he continued to do nothing. Already, Evfel's golden lion hung as one of the flags in the throne room. It waited only to sit behind the throne itself.

Yet he could not make himself care if they did take over... At least, not much. The truth was, he only remained in the castle because a portion of him refused to flee.

Once they neared the dining room, the page slipped down the tower stairs to the buttery. Evan paused briefly to prepare for their presence and for his request.

"Evan." Lorene acknowledged the prince as he entered and wordlessly took the empty chair. Wilber and Andrew, however, never paused in their conversation.

"...it seems a failure already," Andrew commented.

Thoughtfully, Wilber ran his knife between his thumb and index finger. "They did manage to drag it across the valley, somehow. They must have known some trick to subdue it."

"They hobbled it with a war bridle attached to one of its legs."

Everyone stared at Andrew in surprise. Without looking up from his plate, the younger prince shrugged. "In the first place, it had those ropes trailing from its sides. In the second, I asked the gatekeepers how it came in. Apparently, some fool of a handler released its feet, thinking it had suffered enough. After that, they lost all control."

"I thought your father told you to study," Lorene reminded him. "When were you able to learn all of this?"

"That slave driver of a tutor could spare me a few moments to discover why the stallion became so unreasonable *after* they succeeded in bringing it here. It sounded like an attempt to make Father look foolish to me, and I was not laughing."

Sighing, Lorene lifted Andrew's chin. "Does your tutor teach you such suspicion, son?"

For a moment, Andrew's eyes locked challengingly with Evan's. They both knew he was about to say his cousin had taught him suspicion. But instead, Andrew merely pulled away and shrugged.

Evan turned to his uncle. Wilber, however, only stared vacantly across the room, seemingly not having noticed anything of the past few moments. Breaking the silence that followed Andrew's wordless shrug, though, he said, "The stallion is inconsequential. If the handlers fail to tame it, it dies. Leave it there, Andrew. You have far more important things to do."

"But if there is any possibility of ill intent..." his son insisted.

"I doubt it. But if there is even the slightest bit, the plot will fail when the beast dies. I doubt it is tamable."

"Unless you allow me to train him," Evan whispered without looking up from the food he was pushing around his plate.

"What!?" Wilber's knife clattered onto the table. "Never! You will keep your hands off..."

Lorene touched her husband's arm, although her gaze fixed on her nephew. "That is pride speaking, Evan. It was weak today. That was the only reason you came so close. Most likely, if you continue to approach it, you will die sooner rather than later."

For a long moment, Evan glared at her. "When was the last time you cared whether I lived?" Before she could reply, he continued, "There has never been a horse I fail to understand. I would not approach it at once. I would wait and watch. In time, I would know what it needs." He looked sharply at Wilber. "Then you, Uncle, could have your precious war horse without fear for your neck."

The scrape of a chair announced Andrew shooting to his feet even as the king's eyes flashed. For a long moment, Wilber said nothing. Then, sighing, he pulled his son back down. "That horse is too much of an asset to be killed if it can be trained. You truly do have a way with horses. I give you my permission."

"Wilber!" Lorene screeched. "You condemn Evan to death! He—"

"Has a way with horses," he finished for his wife. Turning back to his nephew, though, Wilber leveled his knife meaningfully. "However, if I cannot touch it by the middle of this spring, I will have it destroyed."

Nothing more was said. The meal finished in silence, but Evan's heart raced with excitement.

Chapter 2

Mound Dragons and a Horse

Before the sun rose the next morning, Evan pulled on his cloak and slipped out to his father's barn. Walking between the doorframe's carved horses sometimes brought memories of his father lifting him onto a high fur-covered back. Prince Alexander had been afraid of the height, but Evan could not remember any fear of sitting so far above the ground, particularly not when such loving, strong hands held him.

But those memories grew fainter by the day, more like a dream of a dream. This was now, not then. King Wilber of Evfel had come to Ansky, and Evan had his superior knowledge of horses to prove.

The stablehand, Henry, was already about, feeding horses, refilling water troughs, and cleaning stalls. He paused when the prince entered. "What may I do for you today, my prince?" His sigh was only barely controlled.

"How is the stallion?"

"Well, he refuses to eat, but he did sleep some last night."

"Have you tried giving him anything besides hay?"

"In winter? Your Highness, your question is insane!"

His eyes flashing, Evan growled, "Hay is cut and dried. If he lived in the wild, he foraged for dead grass, maybe bark. Go find some."

Sighing, the stablehand bowed and trudged away with a shovel and bucket.

With a shake of his head, Evan let his breath out. Why was the castle filled with empty-headed horse handlers? They failed to train, failed to comfort, and now even failed to feed their charges. True, most horses would yield to the feeding system. Yet this one...

Looking over at the stallion, the prince noticed the horse was watching him, ears back, disdain clear in the cock of his head. To some degree, it was almost like looking in a mirror—assuming Evan had been a horse.

With that guilty thought, the prince sighed. "Why do you refuse food, boy?"

The stallion made no move, but the fire in its eyes appeared to intensify. At that moment, however, Henry returned with a bucket half-full of dead grass and roots, as well as snow. "This is for His Highness, the stallion," he huffed, plunking the bucket at Evan's feet. "May he eat now."

Meeting the man's vexed expression, the prince nodded. "Thank you, Henry." The soft reply was forced from his throat by the prick of his conscience.

Brief surprise passed over the stablehand's face, and some of his frustration dissipated. "Are you going to chuck everything into the stall?"

"Is that what you did?"

"Well, no one can step near without being attacked. If you wish to try, be it on your own head."

Exhaling, Evan hefted the bucket and stepped over to the stall. He ignored Henry's sharp inhale and locked gazes with the stallion. "I know you hate it here. I do too, believe it or not."

With each soft word, he inched closer. The stallion had not moved. "But what do you gain by quitting?" Reaching the door, Evan cautiously opened it.

Abruptly, the stallion lunged, slamming his weight into the prince. Sharp pain raced up Evan's left arm. Through the haze of agony, he felt the bucket bounce off his feet, saw hooves rear above his head, and stared at the red eyes of the stallion as his natural weapons descended. Dodging the attack was impossible.

Fingers seized him by his right arm, jerking him back onto the floor outside the stall. The door slammed into the stallion's nose. Sounding a furious clarion call, the animal reared again—but with the walls higher than his shoulder and not enough room to jump, he could no longer attack.

"Shh," Evan croaked. "Good boy."

"What?!" The exclamation came in the voice of Queen Lorene. Turning slightly, Evan saw he was laying against her chest, her fingers clamped around his arm. "This is enough, Evan! That beast must be destroyed!"

"No..." His protest was naught but a low gasp. His aunt ignored him, sliding free from his weight. As she bumped his left shoulder, however, pain such as Evan had never known brought darkness swooping in on black wings. The last thing he saw was a whipping mane as the stallion tossed its head.

As Evan slumped to the floor, Lorene snapped at the stablehand, standing dumbly against the stall door. "Quick! Do something!"

Huffing, Henry threw the unconscious prince over his shoulder and stumped off toward the keep. Lorene brushed the hay off her skirts, then strode after them. Wilber would hear of this.

The king met them in the entranceway, as hurriedly dressed as his queen. "Is he alive?"

"I think so," Lorene gasped.

"He is," Henry grunted as he shifted the prince's weight on his neck. "His heartbeat is quite normal; I can tell you that."

"Pass him to me," Wilber ordered. "Then go wake Father Magdalon and tell him to meet us in Evan's room with his medical supplies."

Lorene waited only until the stablehand was just out of sight before hissing, "The stallion did this. You must order its death."

Wilber said nothing as he carried his nephew up several staircases, down corridors, and into the prince's room. Then, laying his burden on the bed, the king sighed. "Look at him, Lorene.

He lives in bitterness except around a horse—and that horse in particular. If I am to have it destroyed, Evan needs to agree that there are no alternatives."

"Do you not understand?" Lorene implored. "All the hearts of the Maxwell men beat to the sound of hooves. Do you think it chance that Ansky's emblem is the rearing horse? If you ask any of the olden kings, they would tell you it was chosen for its valor and wisdom, without having the savagery of a hunting beast. But some now say the emblem cursed its kings with an obsession for horses. And each has the disease worse than his predecessor.

"Whatever the history, Evan will allow that stallion to bash his skull before he submits to wisdom. I know you hated Phillip, but if only for your own word, keep his son alive."

For a long moment, Wilber just stood there, staring at his nephew, his thoughts hidden beneath his somber expression. Finally, his fingers tapped once at his thigh. "Did you notice he came to dinner last night without shuffling? The stallion, in just the day it has been here, has brought a new purpose to Evan Maxwell. He has a reason to live. Take that away without his consent, and you will bring further injury to his heart."

Defeated, Lorene brushed her hand over her eyes. She could not deny Evan's sorry need for something to return his empathy to him before he and Andrew murdered each other.

Father Magdalon insisted the break in the prince's upper left arm would heal well, though he ordered a full day of bed rest to allow it time to begin healing. After that, Evan could return to his usual routine—as long as he was cautious and wore a sling. Yet there was nothing resembling caution in his sword practice against Andrew, regardless of the sling.

Excitement glimmering in his eyes, Wilber suggested that Evan not practice until his arm was healed, but the king's nephew stubbornly moved into position, grasping a light practice sword. The prince knew they would have loved an excuse to increase

Andrew's skills alone, but they could keep dreaming. "I never use my left in sword practice," he insisted with a proud lift of his chin.

The king said nothing. Sighing, Andrew stepped into position.

Regardless, even Evan's precautions failed him when Andrew locked blades with him and, in that split second, punched Evan's left arm. As the older prince cried out, his cousin whacked his sword out of his loose fingers.

"Well done, Andrew!" Wilber exclaimed, clapping his son on the shoulder. Andrew himself beamed, meeting Evan's stony expression with a victorious grin.

"I won, cousin. How do you like losing for a change?"

Wincing as his arm throbbed, Evan refrained from grabbing it. "The only thing you proved, Andrew, is your tremendous courage against invalids."

As Andrew flushed, Wilber stepped between them. "Enough for today, Evan. You must sit out the rest of our practice. Do you want Father Magdalon to look at your arm?"

Staring into Wilber's unconcerned gaze beneath his furrowed brow, the prince pulled away from the hand on his good shoulder. "No," he hissed.

"Rest all the same." Then, dropping his arm over his son's shoulders, Wilber rubbed his red head. "You did the right thing, Andrew. On a proper field of battle, you use every advantage you find or you may not live. Very well done."

Without another glance at Evan, father and son walked away a few feet to resume Andrew's practice—alone. Taking a ragged breath, Evan pulled his cloak close about his injured arm as his eyes dropped to the muddy ground.

For a long moment, he stood unmoving, but at last, he wandered away. Involuntarily, his feet took him to his father's barn and the stallion's stall.

At his approach, the stallion's head jerked up above the wall. Evan hardly noticed, but his subconscious recognized the lack of hot fire in the deep-set eyes.

"Have you eaten, boy?" he asked, swallowing his hollow pain. Those eyes seemed to probe him. Leaning against the stall, Evan confessed, "I know it makes no difference to you, but I lost..." Trailing off, he pushed the scattered hay around with his toe. "I lost any imagined fancies I could trick myself into believing. Any illusion that I could ever be part of this family. My uncle just revealed the truth. Only Andrew matters."

In a flash of temper, he swept the floor clear with his foot. "Well, I hate them, too!"

It abruptly occurred to him he was leaning against the wall everyone was too afraid to step within five feet of. He glanced up into the one eye trained on him. Although cold, it lacked aggression. With a quick inhale, Evan stepped near the door, watching. Danger or no danger, he had to try. He had seen deep into the stallion's gaze. His arrogant reasons for taming the horse had been snuffed out by the mirrored reflection of the stallion's pride.

Questions brushed through his thoughts. Was this the choice the old crone with the stocking had spoken about? A time another being would need him to think beyond his own desires? But there was no way she would have known in reality. Still, the fact was plain. Should he fail to train the horse, he would silently set him free. Since Wilber technically owned it, releasing it could be seen as one king's theft from another, which could easily lead to war. But what choice was there? He could never allow his uncle to kill this animal.

As the prince slipped into the stall, holding his breath, the stallion's only movement was a backward twitch of the ears. For a long moment, Evan remained there, holding the door slightly ajar in case he needed a swift exit.

A second ticked by, then another. No attack came. His heart hammering, the prince closed his escape route.

Separated by only a few feet, they continued to study each other. Then, shaking his head, the stallion dropped his nose to the roots and dead grasses about his feet. Could Evan chance it?

Did he dare? Without thinking about it, the prince reached out and stepped toward the horse.

Almost at once, the stallion's ears flattened. His teeth flashed at Evan. Taking two hasty steps back, the prince retreated to the wall. There he remained while the horse returned to his meal.

For a long time, Evan dared not lower his guard. Instead, he stood there, watching every flinch of skin across powerful muscles. After all, the stallion might only be waiting until his attack was least expected, to guarantee he would kill his victim. And yet, there was no watchful alertness in his eyes.

After half an hour, Evan slipped to the floor and drew his knees to himself. Even then, the stallion left him alone.

Over the month and a half during which the fracture in Evan's arm continued to heal, he refrained from practicing swordplay against Andrew again. His cousin instead trained with King Wilber. Knowing he had fallen behind, Evan doubled his lessons once he recovered, ordering Anskonian knights to duel him.

Meanwhile, he made no further progress in his attempts to tame the stallion, even though the prince spent all his time in the stall, hoping the horse would come to accept him. He took his studies there, sometimes reading aloud, sometimes quietly flipping pages. With each passing day, he became increasingly concerned—for it was one day less that the stallion had to breathe if he refused to submit.

As early spring blew its first breath across Ansky's valley, Evan's heart slowed in despair. The stallion still refused his touch, and spring was only three weeks away, which was all the time they had left to overcome the wildness before Wilber put the horse to death.

Within Ansky's portion of the Calmar Mountains, its council met in private to discuss other concerns. The hometown of Cardinal

Kernan, Woodell, boasted of their fine monastery. Those statue-girded walls had long housed the meeting place of Ansky's council, safely away from the king's hearing. That spring, they were particularly relieved their kingdom's laws forbade all monarchs from venturing within earshot.

Once the nine chairs around the oblong table filled, middle-aged Brother Marcus stood. Despite being a member of the council himself, one of the council's four monks, he also served as its secretary. "Thank you for coming, gentleman." His voice echoed around the frescoed room. "We shall now commence our three hundredth spring meeting since the founding of Ansky. Unless some unforeseen emergency draws us to gather—heaven forbid—we will not meet again until fall. Therefore, be bold in your opinions and concerns for Ansky. The primary interest in this gathering is of our intended king, Evan Maxwell."

Ears buzzed in the ensuing silence. Then mutters rose from the seven councilors on either side of the cardinal and Brother Marcus, but it was the voice of the dark-haired, bearded noble, Lord Fobson, that rose above the rest as he slammed his fist on the table. "Evan Maxwell is hardly in a state of mind to claim his title! He told Lord Tyron's man last year that he refuses our right to force him on the throne! If he has no respect—"

Soothingly, the cardinal raised his hands, as lined as his careworn face. "He is too old now to deny us. By the end of this year, he will turn sixteen. More importantly, I feel it is time to end Evfel's regency. With every year that Evan grows older, we find ourselves in more danger of becoming a part of that kingdom. If we fail to act now, within one more year, there may be Evfel spies in this very room."

Most nodded their agreement, but Fobson spat.

"If Evan Maxwell takes his crown, I can guarantee he will claim sole dictatorship for himself. He will burn this building if he must."

Crossing his arms, the Lord Tyron of Fortress Tyhoronous sighed. "Is that not an exaggeration?"

"From the boy who acts so utterly dismissive of this body? Yes, he is our other half. Without his approval, we cannot act on anything. But it is in our laws that the king must heed our decision, if we are unanimous. Two years ago, we all agreed Wilber had spent too long in this valley. Prince Maxwell ignored us, claiming he was still too untrained. I was willing to believe him then, but he best abdicate as he acts like he intends to—the traitor!—so we can find a better king before we have no say in the matter. If he chooses not to do so, then he must claim the throne now, instead of playing this stalling game of his."

"I agree with Fobson," another lord, Jerah, voiced. "Prince Maxwell should abdicate, if he feels any duty at all."

"Does his stalling not prove that he wants to abdicate, yet feels some responsibility?" the cardinal asked.

Fobson shook his head. "I have no idea what it proves, if anything. However, as I mentioned, he has no care for our authority. When he claims the throne, he will remove our bicameral system. While in other times, the people might have revolted in support of us, their current fear of the Ice Woods in our valley has weakened that spirit. They want a strong, working government to stand against that threat. Many actually believe our system will weaken our ability to unite in the face of its evil when it emerges. It is prime time for a dictator to make his claim."

Tyron raised a finger. "Are you certain Evan is a dictator?"

Fobson waved his hand in dismissal. "Certain people swear he is, and his disregard of Ansky rules—that he must accept our unanimous vote as law—proves it. I need not remind anyone that there were signs of this long before now. The day he met Queen Lorene, his aunt, he tried to scratch her the first time she held him."

"He was five."

"True, but I think any sane five-year-old would sink into love. The emotional scars from his family's deaths have turned into pure hatred."

One of the monks spoke up. "Perhaps he had cause. Lorene had only just arrived in Ansky, four months after Wilber had arrived to serve as regent."

"It was *anger*," Fobson pressed. "Not shyness, not fear. Anger."

Opening his hands, Tyron said, "The Dalacorts teach self-defense as soon as their sons can stand. At least, they did so with Andrew. How do we not know that Wilber started training Prince Maxwell as soon as he set foot in Ansky, so by the time Lorene arrived, his fear sparked a different reaction?"

Impatiently, Fobson drummed his fingers. "Wilber was there before his queen, and he says Evan was the same with him."

"Wilber would say that regardless of the truth," Brother Marcus reminded all of them.

Still, Fobson had an argument. "The servants also swear to the story. They tell us he has remained the same. Remember the handler our prince drove away because there was a horse that no one could stop from biting people, and he caught the fellow slapping the beast's nose?"

At last, the cardinal intervened. "We all know the rumors, but he has matured."

Fobson glared at their spiritual leader as if accusing him of arguing simply for the sake of arguing. "I think we would be safer as part of Evfel than if we accept Evan Maxwell as king."

Sighing, the cardinal folded his hands into his lap. "I fear the danger of our thoughts. I cannot argue against the rumors coming from our own people and our council's informants dwelling in the capital. They have no reason to lie, though I pray they lack a full understanding of what goes on in the royal family."

Contemplatively, Fobson pressed his fingers together. Then he sighed. "Tyron, you have repeatedly voiced your concerns about the Ice Woods. I believe Evfel is the only strength we can trust to stand against it. In the turmoil Evan's reign will bring, one way or another, the woods are sure to attack us—and win. They wait only for that moment."

"Then perhaps our aim should be to convince Wilber to attack it now," Brother Marcus muttered.

Choking on a laugh, Tyron asked, "Attack it? No one can enter."

"If we fling fire into the woods, the ice will melt enough to cross."

"Perhaps," Tyron agreed, while around him monk and noble nodded in concert.

Soon, word came to the castle that the council's messenger was on his way. Evan was first aware of it when, just entering the barn for the evening, he met Lord Tyron's knight, Sir Klement, passing his steed off to a handler.

"Prince Maxwell." The Anskonian knight bowed, but Evan stiffened upon hearing the formal address, lacking his given name, which all knew to mean "rightful heir to the throne." Most people used the formal title without even thinking about it. But there was something in Sir Klement's eyes and tone indicating he meant every word. After the council's insistence over the past two years, Evan could guess why.

As the prince remained silent, the knight stepped closer. "The council wishes to know when you intend to claim your crown."

An image flashed through Evan's mind of walls collapsing around him, and he raised his chin in defiance. "When I feel ready and not before."

Unperturbed at the cool response, Sir Klement lowered his voice. "The most important reason the council has sent word this time has nothing to do with the regency. They wish to remind you that by next winter, you will be twice the age your brother was when the council demanded he ascend the throne."

"Outside of our local priest, you lacked a regent then—and tried everything you could to avoid one. In any case, Alexander was eight at the time, so you had more right to choose for him. I am not eight, Sir Klement. I alone will decide on the timing."

"Prince Maxwell..." The knight sighed. "Since he was eight, he was too young to have an equal voice. But you are old enough to understand that we also have one. The council fears you will move too late. Evfel may act any day to merge our kingdoms. Eleven years already gives them time enough to set a coup in motion. Each new day only makes it worse. Two years have passed since we decided unanimously—it is your duty to accept our judgment."

For a long moment, Evan was silent as his gaze drifted to the stallion, whose head rested on the stall wall as it sometimes did while staring outside. Yet this time, he seemed to be watching the knight and the prince. If so, the horse was the only one paying attention. A single stablehand was working at the other end, rubbing down Sir Klement's horse, and Sir Radnor was leading in his own steed for a handler to take. Both were out of hearing distance.

At last, the prince whispered, "If you were honest, you would admit you fear my reign, as does everyone here. I refuse to be pushed."

Shifting his weight, the knight dipped his head to the side. "Were honesty not treason in this matter, my prince, I would admit to that, but also tell you most of the council fears Evfel that much more. And I would suggest that your repeated refusal is an abdication of the throne."

Again, the prince remained silent. As it was, living in the castle as the heir was prison enough. If he accepted the council's ruling, he would be tossing what little freedom he had; the key to his current cell that allowed him to flee when he chose. He had no desire to accept the strain of ruling, let alone the emptiness of a kingdom that detested him more than he scorned them.

He whirled toward the stallion's stall. "The council shall receive no answer. I have every right to reject anything they suggest, knowing I am not ready, even if they will not acknowledge it. King Wilber awaits the rest of your news. I will see you at supper."

"It is only an hour from now. Do you wish to join us?"

Without turning around, Evan repeated, "I will see you at supper."

Like most everything in a kingdom where the rulers spent money on their people rather than their comfort, Castle Ansky remained a barren military fortress, its halls of unadorned stone used to the tramp of purposeful feet.

"Your Majesty." Sir Klement bowed to King Wilber, meeting him in the entryway. "Is all well with you?"

"Of course." Wilber's tone was curt.

The knight turned to the boy at the king's elbow. "Prince Andrew, I offer my best wishes for your upcoming birthday. Eleven is a large number."

"Hardly," the prince muttered, as sullen and undignified as always, despite his father's reprimanding glare. Since Dalacorts had never been known for being spoiled, with their rigorous training and discipline, one could only assume it was the Maxwell in him. Klement smiled at the irony. Everyone knew the "spoiled" Maxwell princes, who often had more freedom and gentleness, had long turned out better in the end. Perhaps there was hope for Andrew, though it was far more likely his father would eventually turn him into a traditional Dalacort.

"A large number or not, Your Highness, the birthday of a prince is always an important event in Ansky. Who would miss the chance for a holiday?"

"You honor Evfel, Sir Klement," the king growled, "but I have never seen much merrymaking on Andrew's birthday, unlike the last month of the year."

Shifting as his senses pricked, the knight nodded. "I cannot speak for this town, Your Majesty, only for the north."

"Do you actually celebrate Andrew's birthday or is this mere flattery?"

"We do, but you can hardly blame anyone if Prince Maxwell's birthday is more celebrated. He is our future king. The holiday is mandatory for us. Moreover, his birthday falls at a more convenient time. In the first third of winter, supplies are plentiful enough to keep the food flowing, and we have fewer responsibilities than in spring."

Nodding regally, Wilber turned the conversation to happenings in northern Ansky and to the council. As they spoke of these subjects, he led Sir Klement and Andrew to the great hall where they would eat that evening.

They were seated at the table, discussing the Ice Woods when Evan entered, head high and expression closed—the Dalacort that Andrew was not. As the room stilled, Klement briefly wondered if someone had swapped the princes. However, it was clear Evan was older. Furthermore, no one could mistake the Maxwell-blue eyes for the Dalacort green of Wilber's son.

No, Evan was a Maxwell, though he had chosen the Dalacorts' aloof regality.

Or had he?

As Evan neared, the knight asked softly, before he could be overheard, "Your Majesty, is your nephew always so... impenetrable?"

Evan's head lowered an inch, his eyes darkening as he glared at the twosome.

Klement dropped his gaze. To his surprise, Wilber answered. "Sadly, yes." The king's eyes pierced his nephew's. While their stone faces revealed an equal dislike, Andrew smiled victoriously. Perhaps there was more to Evan's aloofness than it appeared. Or perhaps not.

"We were discussing the dangers of the Ice Woods, Sir Klement," the king reminded the knight at last. The tenseness in the air altered. "Another fool died trying to enter, you say?"

As Evan took a seat at the small table, the knight nodded. "Yes, but the council wishes you to attack the woods for other reasons."

"What, pray tell, do they fear?"

"The activity in the woods is growing."

Andrew froze, his bread stopping in midair. "How so?"

"When I was born, the woods were already there. Lord Tyron remembers the day they appeared on the horizon, but for myself, watching them has been as much a part of life as breathing. For years, they just sat there. A few of its storms were large enough to sweep snow and ice onto our valley's grass, even in the summer, for short periods of time, but there was no other change, morning or evening. The woods provided a light in the night and stood cold and frozen by day.

"Then, nine years ago, it was as if the sun fell upon us. First the shadows vanished, and then everything was so bright..." Klement stumbled for words, then pressed on. "It was brief, but it took hours for the knights on watch to see clearly again. Since then, we have seen many birds rising from the trees, some black and others glowing. Some say they have seen red eyes watching them from the blackness, others that steam rises from its entrance in the morning. Still more claim a black creature has crawled out at times to scour the plains.

"When we tried to tame the stallion, I had wondered if it had been mistaken for the creature from everyone's fearful imaginings. After seeing it in King Phillip's barn, though, I realize it is just a horse."

"Yes. Why did you not destroy it when you failed to tame it?" A low growl filled Wilber's voice.

Glancing at Evan, Klement replied, "Because we knew you could tame it. Has it given you trouble?"

"None." Evan's word forbade inquiry, and the knight noted that his meal remained untouched.

"I thought no one could enter the Ice Woods," Andrew commented, returning the conversation to its track. "How would we be able to attack it?"

"There is little need at present, I think," Wilber answered. "Once whatever lurks in there comes out, it will be in our lands. We will have the advantage, and since all the sightings of steam and creatures have been due to overactive imaginations, I doubt there is any real danger."

Klement sighed. "You must agree, Your Majesty, that the Ice Woods are filled with magic of a most devious design. It is said that when the dragons—and worse—were finished with the island to the north, they came this way. Here, deep inside the woods, they have gathered servants of every kind—humans that have allowed themselves to be altered beyond recognition, animals that have wandered into the creatures' paths. Eventually, it will act against us. It has already been there for forty years. Do you wish to allow it the perfect choice of time?"

Instead of directly answering the question, the king asked, "Do you think you would win with your current ignorance of the woods and its occupants? Wait, bide your time, build your strength. Make it come to you. Destroy it at your defenses."

Evan stood abruptly. "Your pardon." Bowing, he strode out before anyone could respond.

"*Bide your time*," Evan grumbled to Dedalo as he angrily brushed the gelding's shedding coat. "*Evfel is so strong.* Just wait until that magic lights up the sky over him."

What could almost have passed as a laugh escaped the horse as it bobbed its head up and down, enjoying the grooming. "You are so unconcerned, boy, but this is serious. Not that I disagree with his opinion on launching an attack."

"Pray tell, what do you think should be done?"

Dropping the brush in surprise, the prince turned. Sir Klement was leaning against the barn's doorway. Coolly, Evan retrieved the brush, returning to his task in silence.

"At your age, Prince Maxwell, the choice is yours alone—and yours is the word the council awaits."

The swish of the horse brush filled the expectant pause.

At last, the knight sighed. "I do apologize for my unkindness regarding you earlier. I wanted to know your uncle's response, whether he would lie for you." The sound of his feet approached. "I must admit, because I owe you my honesty, that I know of many who fear your reign. All of Ansky loved your father, my prince, and for him, we will serve you. For him, the council will yield to you—if you will claim your authority now."

His feet stopped just behind the prince. "My report on your decision will lead us to another meeting, however. Some think we should yield to Wilber, but most will decide to choose a new king from among our nobles. That debate will take months. Must we wait for Evfel to step in without our consent or for the woods to attack?

"I have heard others wish Phillip still lived." A soft sigh sounded in Klement's tone as he continued. "As proud as he was, he followed his conscience no matter the cost. No man could tell him to do otherwise. All we ask is that you show us some compassion. I know we are all fools, but the time is now."

The air filled with anticipation, pulsing with impatience. Evan's breath snagged in his throat. The barn grew suffocating.

At his shoulder, Klement bowed at last. "Should you decide to assert your right, we will halt our search and claim you. But for now, my prince, I ride with word of your unofficial abdication."

Evan did not move. Eventually, he heard the knight mount and ride away, unanswered.

Chapter 3

THE PRISON OF DUTY

SPRING CAME TO ENCHANTRESS ISLAND as it always had—with strong winds blowing in from the ocean, initially cold before the warmth came inland. Dropping another mollusk into her bucket, Charlotte shook the water from her red fingers before wrapping them tightly in her skirt.

Beside her, Lady Talliaha arched her back, pressing a hand against it. "I'm sorry, Charlotte. It's probably too early in the season for this."

Trying to push her long hair away from her face despite the prevailing wind, Charlotte smiled wickedly. "You wanted an excuse to wander the beach, Mother. This is your reward."

"I never said that. I wanted something different for dinner."

With a grim laugh, the maiden glanced into her bucket. "We have enough for the two of us, unless you wish to share with someone."

As she turned inland, her mother breathed, "What a glorious sunset."

Charlotte dropped her gaze to the many shells and rocks beneath her feet. She could easily picture the brilliant pinks and purples painted in the sky, reflected onto the water and beach at low tide. Every wet rock, shell and wave threw back the light. Exhaling, she took another step toward the rise that marked the actual shoreline. "I promised myself I'd never look."

After a second, she heard her mother turn back toward her. "Then what do you do on your favorite outlook on the mountain?"

Halting, the maiden whispered, "At least in the *village*, I never look."

"We're not in the village." Talliaha's amusement sounded in her voice, quiet in its way.

Charlotte found herself laughing in return. "I'm not on the mountain, either."

Placing a hand on her daughter's shoulder as she neared, Talliaha advised, "Never fear showing hurt, Charlotte. There is strength in a shameless expression of pain."

"*Women* cry, Mother. I don't."

"I doubt you would cry."

Pulling away, the maiden strode forward again. "I know what you want, Mother, but it's impossible. Leave it at that."

"When you do look, Charlotte, what do you see?"

The quiet plea in Talliaha's tone caused her daughter to pause. She sighed. "I should ask what it is you see. It's said mothers sense the spirits of their offspring."

"Are you asking if I think Arnacin lives?"

"Never would I ask that. I don't wish to hear the answer. The truth is, I fear I will reveal my false hope by looking out to sea."

When only the wind and waves replied, Charlotte turned around. Talliaha stood with her face toward the ocean. Sunset glowed against her skin and shimmered through the silver and black hair that the wind loosened from under her kerchief. Now, in her seventies, she retained the beauty of the sprite she was, the heritage she had passed on to her children.

"Then you also trick yourself into seeing a sail on the horizon sometimes," her mother finally breathed.

"You already know, Mother. I've no need to answer."

"Please."

Shrugging, Charlotte once again turned inland. "I see an empty ocean, void of ship or sailor, wailing its loneliness to the shore. Even as it gorges itself on unwary vessels, it cries that its longing is altered not at all." Closing her eyes, she whispered, "And my heart swells in time with it... Then, sometimes, I see the sea beneath the moonlight, the stars shining on a lone sail as it's shrinking, ever shrinking, into the distance."

The soft crunch of shells announced her mother stepping near, but the maiden did not look up as an arm slipped through hers. "It's been four years, Charlotte. Will you now tell me of his farewell?"

"Do you honestly expect there was one? He feared farewells so terribly, he left like a burglar in the night."

"I don't think it was fear that begat his escape."

"Could you call it irresponsibility?"

"No." Talliaha sighed. "No one could ever call Arnacin irresponsible."

With a tight-lipped smile, Charlotte led them back to the village surrounding the large pond dubbed Alleluia Lake.

Long after the village had fallen asleep for the night, Charlotte sat awake, looking through the records of their flocks: each sheep's name and the quality of its wool, its breeding records, and the quantity from each year's shearing. Soon, after they sheared the sheep for this year, she would add another entry.

Yet it was not the yearly variations in production that absorbed her thoughts as she turned each page. It was the entries written in years gone by, first in her father's light hand and then in Arnacin's meticulous one.

With a sigh, she finally snapped the ledger closed, her gaze falling on her sleeping mother. Ever since her brother, William, had died last year, her mother had seemed ever older. Now, perpetually exhausted, she rarely stayed awake for more than an hour past dinner. Perhaps her age was simply catching up to her.

In lonely silence, Charlotte decided to complete whatever needed finishing for the day. Snuffing out the candle, she crept across to her mother. There, she pulled the blanket higher over the old woman's shoulder and bent down to place a light kiss on her high forehead. "I'll be back later."

Talliaha barely stirred, and Charlotte slipped outside to the blazing stars. Even though their house stood toward the back of the village, it was lit by the moonlight reflected in the large bodies of water.

"You've been restless lately," came a soft whisper from above. Charlotte knew the voice. Their neighbor, Raymond, sat on the edge of his roof, one leg dangling over a ladder. A pile of small planks lay beside him, but he seemed not to have moved for some time. His gaze was turned toward the ocean.

"What gives you that notion?" Charlotte growled, turning away from him, toward the woods and mountain.

"Your mother told me."

Pausing, the maiden fell silent, but only for a moment. "You appear restless yourself. The sun set three hours ago, and there you remain by your unfinished task."

Dismissal laced Raymond's tone as he replied, "There wasn't time during the day to fix the leaks in my roof, so I brought a lantern. With it and the moonlight, I can see well enough, but I was mostly cleaning up when you came out."

Without reply, the maiden started off. She could hear the young man hastening down his ladder. "Charlotte, wait!"

He caught her elbow at the edge of the stream from the woods to Alleluia Lake. "Charlotte, please. We both wish to know what's wrong. I know there's pain, but it's time to live."

Ripping her arm out of his grasp, Charlotte snapped, "What difference would it make if I told you? You're a failure as a provider, Raymond. Had it not been for you, William would still live and... Arnacin would have stayed."

"That's not fair, Charlotte, and you know it! I admit to providing the food the night William died. I'll never forgive myself, but was it not you who told me you feared Arnacin would die if he didn't go to sea? Did we not both decide to ensure everyone's needs were handled? True, if I hadn't thought myself more capable than I am, he might have stayed. In fact, we both know he would have stayed—but don't think that would mean he'd be alive now."

In the ensuing silence, he added, "And admit it, you haven't allowed me to be a provider since..." Raymond let his breath hiss out as Charlotte's chin rose sharply. "Believe me, Charlotte, I never had any desire to imprison you."

"No, your problem all along is you don't think. Marriage always imprisons! As the whole island knows, I'm a shepherdess, their wood nymph, not anything else—not a housekeeper or cook, nor even a mother. Why don't you find someone made for that and leave me alone?"

"I haven't asked you since. We barely talk to each other, and as far as 'someone made for that,' I'm very content in current circumstances to remain single."

She knew his meaning. Her expression turned sarcastic, scoffing, but she said nothing. No concrete words could frame her thoughts.

Stepping closer, Raymond repeated, "Why are you restless? Nothing you and your mother discussed explains it. Am I wrong in assuming you feel something none of the rest of us can?"

"You suggest I'm the witch everyone suspects," Charlotte exclaimed. Again, she turned to leave, but Raymond caught her wrist. Eyes alight with bitterness, she coolly met his gaze.

"Not a witch," he whispered. "The wood nymph of Enchantress Island." Releasing her, he pleaded, "What have you seen?"

"Have none of you eyes to see for yourselves, that you must ask me the obvious?"

"The obvious, Charlotte? To you, the language of the deer is obvious, the bird, likely even the fish. What have they said?"

Finally relenting, the wood nymph whispered, "They have said nothing, but even now the trees lack buds."

"You don't think that's because the year is colder?"

"I have heard them creak and groan in their depths. First one will do it, then another. I scoff at superstition, but this is something..." She paused, then asked, "What would you think if I told you the new shoots of grass, those still under the dirt, are blackened on Castle Mound?"

Raymond shrugged. "It's evil. Only the most... obstinate of us refuse to acknowledge something sleeps beneath the castle's ruins."

"It *sleeps*," Charlotte emphasized, "but it wakes when darkness approaches. When greed or selfishness or dishonor comes near in force, it rejoices." Quietly, she added, "It is the true form of the story Arnacin told us when we were younger of the sleeping dragon, the one that ate all the islanders."

"Charlotte, how do you know this? Has it ever happened in your lifetime, or anyone else's, that you know?"

"You asked what I heard. I am telling you. Call it superstition, or call me a witch; I don't care. What I can tell you for a fact is that the grass and its shoots on Castle Mound are green, or were until this year. The rest is what I feel and suspect about the mound. At the very least, a change is coming, one that will once again shift the entire island. That, I know just by the dark delight permeating the mound. Something has woken for the first time in sixty years, and it is not small or benign."

With that, she left for the mountain, leaving Raymond to wonder if she was indeed part enchantress.

Three nights after Sir Klement's visit, moonlight danced across the ceiling from the round piece of glass softly swinging at the top of the window. Watching its pattern from where he lay in bed, Evan sighed. The council would now have word of his unofficial abdication. They would be looking at men they deemed potentially qualified for kingship. The knowledge hurt, but the idea of kingship caused his stomach to clench.

Not for the first time, he found himself hating Alexander for daring to die by the plague. It was a silly emotion. His brother never intended to contract it, but he had, and his death had left his responsibility to Evan.

Forcing that nauseating thought away once again, the prince's thoughts returned to his other problem. "Am I dreaming to think the stallion will be tamed?"

Naturally, the ceiling had no response. The prince yanked his blankets around his shoulders. Again, he closed his eyes, trying to force sleep to quiet his active mind. After several nights of restlessness, exhaustion should have won, but it had yet to do so. The chance to take responsibility was slipping away, but he had no strength to claim the throne.

Behind closed lids, he imagined the wild valley's grass waving in the cool breeze—golden wheat fields; the grains turning from yellow to brown to green and back in their swaying dance.

As the soft drumming of flying horse hooves entered his imagination, Evan saw the same breeze whipping through the stallion's dark mane as it ran toward the mountains, free. If only *free* was a word Evan himself could know...

Rolling onto his side, the prince shoved an arm under his pillow and forced his longing for freedom out of his mind. Honestly, when was he not tired of the walls surrounding him, suffocated in the prison of his world, choked on the beliefs of his only remaining family, or wilting under the disdain heaped against him?

Duty alone held him. It hardly made him accept his responsibility, but it bade him stay. The stallion knew no such duty. Was it fair to even try to force a surrender from something that had no reason to discard freedom?

Slipping out of the covers, the prince pulled on his boots and threw his cloak over his shoulders. Act of war or not, the stallion needed to be released, if only to give a horse the life Evan himself could never know. If he were to free it in such a way as to make it seem it had broken loose on its own, perhaps his uncle would not see it as an act of war.

At least, so Evan hoped.

The stallion was resting his head on top of the stall's wall when the prince arrived. Starlight sunk into the depths of his visible eye, as if the pupil were a water-filled bowl reflecting the heavens. It was astonishing how mythically beautiful the stallion was, despite appearing so twisted and evil on other occasions.

"I know there is no reason in all of Elcan for you to trust me, boy," Evan whispered, standing nine paces away for fear of ending the stallion's peace. "All the same, will you trust me tonigh—"

Approaching footsteps brought an end to the prince's question. Fire sprang into the stallion's eyes. Snorting, he dropped his head from view, and Evan could hear him thrashing about the stall.

Turning in resignation, Evan watched his cousin stride toward him.

"Look, fool," the younger prince said as he neared. "If you fail to train it by day, you will never succeed by night. You should just quit and let the master trainer handle the job."

Sighing, Evan turned up the aisle, brushing his hand over his father's horses. Andrew stomped behind him. "Ha, admit it, you lost your chance to prove yourself. Give it to men who know their skills—"

Evan whirled. "With that stallion? No one knows their skills." He stopped by a mare, considering. "But I need not tell you. You may do the honors as well as anyone. Grab a whip, open the stallion's door, run him until he is weary. Then try jumping on. If the master trainer does anything other than butcher him, that will be his method."

"I will not be tricked into killing myself, fien—" Andrew's growl turned into a yelp as the mare by which they were standing snapped her teeth at him.

Unable to hide his smile, Evan lightly slapped the mare's nose. "Mariel, you should know better. Father taught you manners."

Blowing, she dropped her head back down to the hay. But Andrew just stood there, opening and closing his mouth wordlessly. "That was a love pat!" he finally exclaimed.

Shrugging, Evan continued down the aisle.

"I waste too much time on you!" Andrew shouted. "Stay up all night! I am going to bed!"

"Poor boy," the older prince murmured patronizingly into the neck of the nearest horse—a gelding—while his cousin stormed back toward the keep. "He is too tired to follow me. Then why does he, I should ask."

As the gelding nudged him with its head, Evan sighed. "He does it just to find something he can use against me. I know their minds."

Whatever the case, Andrew had ruined any plans to release the stallion that night. If it went missing, the brat would remember Evan's presence and report without hesitation. No, Evan would now need to stay with the horses long enough to guarantee no one thought any mission had been foiled, then return to the keep himself.

For a week, Lorene had been suspicious. Now, as she crawled beneath her silk comforter, she knew. "Clare, can you tell me where the king is?"

Shutting the wardrobe, the handmaiden turned to her queen. "I believe he is working."

"On what? The bells just chimed midnight!"

An amused smile lit Clare's face. "My Lady, spring is here."

"Ah yes," Lorene sighed, her shoulders sagging. "The pass has opened again."

"Reginold waited until the last moment to send word this past fall. There is much that requires a reply."

Yes, the queen remembered that incident—and her suspicion that the lateness was purposeful, given that they could not respond until spring. "Do you know if Reginold's ambition grows?"

Clare curtsied low. "You must ask the king, my lady."

"So I must. Please tell him I need him."

"If he asks why?"

Pulling the covers higher over her stomach, Lorene replied, "Family business."

Clare knew better than to press further. Bobbing a quick curtsy, she departed. Soon thereafter, she returned with the king. Without entering herself, she quietly closed the door, leaving the couple to their privacy.

As her husband neared, Lorene sat up a bit more against her pillows. "Wilber, is there trouble in Evfel? Clare reminded me of just how much news Reginold sent at the last minute."

Sitting on the edge of the bed, the king shrugged. "No trouble. Our regent sees threats in every shadow and begs us to return."

"Well, as to our return, I agree with him. Evan is old enough, and I tire of trusting Reginold."

Cocking an eyebrow, Wilber asked, "Is Evan old enough? Right now, he is ready to slaughter all of Ansky without hesitation."

Lorene cringed. "Maybe ruling will finally teach him."

"Idealistic," Wilber muttered with a slight smile of amusement. "Is there anything you need? I must return to work. Only a fool would leave such correspondence sitting unattended for long."

"You have another child on the way, Wilber. I wanted you to know."

For a long moment, the king stared blankly at her. Then he laughed. "You certainly like waiting. We were married nine years before you became pregnant with your first child, and now another ten, almost eleven."

Smiling primly, the queen said, "My midwife tells me it was a good thing for Andrew that I waited until my body was fully mature before becoming pregnant. Miscarriages are more frequent when the mother is with child too early."

"Yes, but you waited *nine years*."

Blushing, Lorene agreed. "That probably was excessive."

"And eleven years now?"

"I promise this will be the last." With a small laugh, she added, "In another ten years, I will be too old for another."

A distant sorrow seemed to flash briefly behind Wilber's eyes, but then he smiled, kissing her. "True. I am very excited, Lorene— but I do need to finish the work I left in the great hall."

"Just come back as soon as you finish."

"I promise." Kissing her one more time, the king slipped away. With a smile, the queen sighed in contentment.

Finally pulling himself away from his father's horses as the church bell tolled midnight, Evan trudged back to the keep. The castle was dark and quiet, echoing the hiss of his dragging feet. Consequently, it surprised him as he neared the great hall to find its light flooding the corridor.

No one was present in the torchlit chamber, but upon looking inside, Evan saw many parchments filling a table set up on one side. Doubtless Evfel's business, left unattended for some urgent reason. With the pull of a deep secret, the prince felt drawn toward the papers.

After casting a quick glance down the corridor, Evan crept toward the table. Upon it lay an open letter atop a partially composed response:

Sire,

When will you return? Dissent grows in Arieh like a plague. As I detailed in the midsummer report, there was open revolt against the orphanage just this year. Although we crushed it thoroughly, whispers continue. There have been complaints of child abductions, seizure of land, and even a lack of suitable husbands due to the draft of able-bodied men for the army.

If you are as strong as you were when you left, please return soon to restore order to Evfel.

Your servant,

Duke Reginold

Trembling with anger, Evan turned to Wilber's unfinished response.

Duke Reginold,

Your attempt to discover age in me is obvious and near treasonous. I am as shrewd and dangerous as ever. My duty here is, as yet, unfinished. I expect that to change soon.

Until my business is finished, though, you must control the peasantry. If you fail, you are easily replaceable.

For now, obey this suggestion. If you hear someone complain, arrest him and remove his tongue, or publicly hang him if you feel that will quell the rebels. Above all, you must reveal Evfel's strength. Guarantee...

"Stop!"

Jumping in surprise, Evan dropped the letter and spun around. King Wilber stormed toward him, murder blazing in his eyes. "By what right do you snoop in Evfel's business? Or have I raised a quidnunc?"

Unflinching, the prince snapped, "By my right as the owner of this castle! Is this how you would rule?"

Heat rushed through the right side of his face as Wilber backhanded him across the cheek and then seized his throat. Briefly, the king's fingers tightened. Then he slid them below Evan's jaw, stroking it with his thumb.

Breathing heavily, Evan remained frozen as he stared into those gleaming green eyes.

"You are the blood of my queen, Evan Maxwell, but beware, lest I construe your interference as an act of war. You have little understanding of the way a larger kingdom needs to operate. To keep that many people in line, rulers must be harsh. So leave such matters to a king who understands strength." Releasing his nephew and stepping back, Wilber commanded, "Now go."

The prince needed no further orders. Without pause, he fled straight back outside and into the stallion's stall with its guaranteed safety from the world of humans.

Curling into a corner, he rocked swiftly back and forth as visions of Evfel's suffering filled his imagination. If he continued to avoid the throne, Ansky could turn into a province of Evfel within the year—and her people into slaves.

Angrily, he seized a handful of straw and threw it. "No! Do you understand? I hate the throne! It was Alexander's duty, not mine!"

Naturally, only the whispers of startled horses greeted the prince's outburst. Exhaling, he rested his head on his knees as his thoughts slowed. Whatever cruel tricks history had played, one fact remained: Ansky was his responsibility. He could let it slide into the Dalacorts' rule, but even so, if Wilber enslaved Ansky, it would only be by Evan's inaction. It was hopeless.

Evan stood in a long corridor filled with the nighttime fog of spring. Aided by the algae-covered walls, the smell of damp earth over- whelmed him. A massive door filled the far end, and toward this escape, he stepped.

The corridor was a gallery, lined on both sides by giant paint- ings of Anskonian kings on their thrones. Evan paused before the first portrait, then quickly looked away. His gaze landed instead on the one behind him... and the merest glance only made his blood run colder.

Each king had been painted in a cage, a miserable prisoner. One was so wrinkled, hairless and gray, he appeared better fit for a coffin. Instead, he sagged into an iron brace wrapped around his torso to keep him upright.

In another painting, the king's face had been destroyed by scars from healed boils. The grimace on his pasty face reflected his pain.

Blood trickled from the corners of another king's mouth. His blank eyes bulged, and his fingers were claws attacking his own chest.

Jerking away, Evan fled down the corridor, not daring to look left or right. Yet he felt insane eyes piercing him, mocking his health and his fear. At the far end of the passageway, he flung open the door.

Ansky's cold great hall stood before him, but in place of the throne, a giant cage awaited him. Evan tried to scream, but the sound that instead escaped his throat was a stallion's eerily familiar clarion call. And then he found he was the stallion, and that men bear- ing ropes and a war bridle were whipping him, dragging him into the cage.

Iron bars slammed around him with a deafening boom.

Evan woke with a spasm to the still darkness of morning. Dawn's dim light filtered through the stable's doorway. As his surroundings came into focus, he realized he was resting against something warm, something breathing.

With a gasp, Evan shot to his feet. The stallion lay between him and the stall door. Although its head had not moved from its sleeping position, its ears were turned back in his direction. Then, blowing a huge breath, the stallion lurched to its feet.

The prince's lungs froze in his chest as the stallion turned his massive shoulders toward him, shapely large head cocked high, as if he knew he could end the prince's life on a whim and relished that power. The nose lowered toward Evan's shoulder. He pressed against the wall, the only protection around.

"You are a fool, O Prince, to think I would stoop to killing you after sleeping beside you." The voice was deep and strong, a dragon's voice, emitting from the muzzle right beside Evan's ear.

Horrified, the prince trembled, a low gasp of fear and dismay escaping him.

Snorting, the thing backed away. "You also think me a demon?"

When Evan's only reply was the quick twitch of his head, the stallion shook his mane.

"If it is a question of the unnatural, we, the horses of my kind, speak within a few hours, whereas humans take months, years. I ask you what is more unnatural: to know how to form words intuitively or to force something alien into a tongue not born for it?"

Swallowing, the prince found his voice and made himself reason the new nightmare away. "But to speak, you would need to breathe through your mouth, and horses only breathe through their nostrils."

"There are many things you have yet to know about Elcan, O Prince. Among those secrets is the nature of my herd. Can you truly say, for instance, that you know everything about the Calmar Mountains?"

"We hardly want to know. Beyond them once lay the black skies of En… that island. But to understand what you say, you would need a human brain."

"Ha! The arrogance." The stallion half-reared with a snort. "Human brain, indeed."

"Then you understood everything I have ever said to you?" The thought was disconcerting, but it was becoming ever clearer that reason had no effect on what he was witnessing. The thing that looked like a horse was real.

"That and more, O Prince. Why else would I lie next to a moaning heap, captive to his nightmares?"

Slowly, as if his actions were running behind his thoughts, Evan shook his head. "I was not—"

"Having nightmares?" The way the stallion cocked his head was equal to the rebuke of a raised eyebrow. "Your pride can only protect you so far—particularly from me, whom you have already compared so thoroughly to your own plight."

"What?" Never once, to his knowledge, had Evan spoken of that, neither to horse or human, since he had no one in whom to confide.

"I understand more than words. I, too, know loneliness and slavery to an invisible captor. I know the yearning for freedom. That is why I deigned to warm you throughout the night."

"You are not... a dragon?" Dragons could alter humans beyond recognition. What was to stop them from changing their own appearance?

The stallion emitted a snort suspiciously like a laugh. "You would know. Have I tempted you to think or do something that sounds even slightly misguided to you?"

"No."

"Then you have your answer. I am a stallion, of a lineage about which humans know nothing. Still, some dared to enslave me."

In the ensuing silence, Evan heard the rustle of Henry bringing hay to the horses somewhere down the line. There lay his escape—a normal human being to dispel the nightmare. Still, there could be some truth to the stallion's claims.

Swiftly, before the stablehand was near enough to overhear their soft conversation, Evan asked, "Do you have a name?"

Those eyes glowed with cunning. "Darkfire." Then the stallion shook its head impatiently. "But perhaps you should tell me why you are here?"

"What do you mean?"

"Restlessness might have brought you down here the first time, but it is not why you returned."

Dropping his gaze to the floor, Evan paused. If he refused to confide in anyone, he would break soon. He had reached that point. His struggle was now too large, and there was no real reason to doubt the stallion, outside of the distrust of the unknown. But Henry was nearer than before.

"May I ride you?" Though the prince's voice quivered, he added, "There are too many ears here."

"Where would it be different?"

"The valley."

After pausing, Darkfire nodded. "But I refuse a bridle."

"You need neither bridle nor saddle."

"Then you may ride."

Sir Spencer of Arieh had just stepped outside for his daily patrol when he saw a stablehand racing for the keep. "Ho there! Why do you run?"

"Prince Maxwell has just ridden off on the stallion! It will kill him!"

"Your name?"

"Henry. But the prince!"

Sighing, the Evfelian knight asked, "Where did he go?"

"Through the outer gates. Hurry! I must tell the king before the beast throws him!"

Spencer could not hide his surprise as he grabbed the stablehand's arm. "Are you really that concerned about the prince's welfare?"

Shifting guiltily, the stablehand nevertheless replied, "Are you not? He is Ansky's future king, and your swiftest way of going home."

Spencer nodded thoughtfully. "I will tell King Wilber. Return to your work." With that, he turned back toward the keep.

As was the custom in all Elcan castles, the monarchs' chambers faced north to overlook most of the gates. He knocked at the door to the outer chamber, and Clare granted him entrance. The inner door remained closed. At the knight's questioning glance, the handmaiden shook her head. She had not been permitted into the inner room yet.

Spencer knocked all the same. "Your Majesties! Your nephew rides the stallion."

No voice answered him, but he heard hurried feet, more than one pair, moving in the direction of the window. Then came Wilber's gruff voice. "Where?"

"Across the valley."

"What?" The door flew open and Wilber stepped out. "Has he trained it by night?"

Spencer shook his head, watching Clare slip into the inner chamber and shut the door behind her. "Not to my knowledge." He looked back at his king, lowering his voice. "Do you think the stallion will throw him?"

Stepping away from the door, the king similarly whispered, "You better make sure this is the last mistake of Evan Maxwell, one way or another. Given the strange behavior of the stallion, we cannot depend upon it to complete its part, but we will never have a better story than this. Regardless, it *will* be the stallion who kills him."

"And if the sound travels?"

"You have done the training on Cyra. How far can you hear the shot?"

"The terrain is not as flat there, sire."

"If we must, we can blame it on Cyra. Only they use that weapon. Go. Make it appear you leave to rescue the prince of Ansky from his own folly."

Bowing, Spencer muttered, "I will make Ansky yours, sire."

Chapter 4

Lisya

As soon as Darkfire's hooves touched the open plains, he stretched out, continuing to head northwest from the town. Evan hunched into the stallion's whipping mane, feeling the rushing air sweep away his breath, forgetting the strangeness of the steed beneath him. Darkfire did not run; he flew.

Blinded by tears and wind, the prince saw nothing and simply rejoiced in the speed. As his lungs began to complain, he tucked his head down, wishing the wind would decrease. Then, as if in response, the stallion slowed.

After another few moments, the horse stopped, his head hanging as he coughed. "It has been too long," he gasped.

Evan collapsed atop Darkfire's powerful neck, panting in time to the heaving shoulder pressed against his cheek. Before them, the Calmar Mountains loomed large above the plains. The foothills glimmered in thawing snow and morning dew after a night of light rain.

Slowly, the stallion moved forward again, dragging his feet. First one step, then another. "Was it too much for you?" he asked when Evan remained where he lay. "I am made different. Perhaps wrap your cloak over your nose next time, so the wind will not steal away your air."

Slowing his breathing, the prince made no reply. His doubt in trusting the talking beast resurfaced, preventing him from responding.

Taking another deep breath, Darkfire lifted his head. Casting a glance at the limp form on his back, he asked, "What would you not say in the castle?"

Sighing, Evan straightened. "Why do you really want to know?"

The stallion's head bobbed to the side—a shrug, if ever a horse shrugged. "Call it curiosity. Your actions *were* out of the ordinary."

"Very well." Despite his admission, it was a moment before the prince convinced himself he needed to confide in someone—or something. Up to this point, the beast had shown nothing to indicate an evil mind. "If the heavens granted me my wishes, I would find some wild land and disappear. As it is, I would prefer to procrastinate until death... except..." He trailed off.

Softly, the stallion prompted, "Except procrastination is impossible."

There was no denying it. "Sooner or later, King Wilber would seize upon my lack of interest and, little by little, increase his authority." Wrapping the crinkled, thick mane tightly around his palm, Evan squeezed it and then shook it off. "I must confess, until last night, I would have willingly let him do so. But now I've discovered he rules only through the iron hand of oppression. He calls it ruling by strength—strength by which he would crush the independence of Ansky."

"How did you learn all this?" The stallion's voice was soft, a sigh whispering over the billowing grass about his knees.

"I..." Licking his lips, Evan forced himself to be honest. "I poked through Evfel's correspondence, which I found briefly unguarded."

"I see." For a minute, they were quiet. Then Darkfire cast a glance at his rider. "What makes the idea of kingship so terrible to you? Most humans crave power."

"I agree," the prince scoffed. "Many think they may do whatever they like as kings. Some even try, never realizing that if the people suffer from their selfishness, they too will suffer, though they may not realize it.

"Kingship is either the strain of trying to keep power or the strain of knowing you hold the responsibility for countless lives and livelihoods. It is being pushed into a box of rules and securities, just to accomplish one goal or the other—your own happiness or the people's. Gone are your freedoms, dreams, peace.

"I have heard of men who went insane under far less strain. Anyone with a shred of actual sense would detest the mere mention of a throne, whether they are to sit on it or not. For even when it is not yours, you must trust the one sitting there."

The stallion was quiet for a long moment, his head raised slightly, feeling the warm breeze that came over the mountain lift his mane and brush it against the prince's chest and arms. Finally, Darkfire commented, "I confess to never looking at it that way."

"What do you mean?"

"I am also a k—"

A sharp crack rent the peace. Both stallion and prince flinched as the turf beside them flew into the air. Another report sounded, and Evan gasped, seizing the stallion's mane in his fists. "Cyra's guns! Fly, Darkfire!"

With a powerful surge of chest and hindquarters, the stallion leaped forward. Hunching down, Evan yanked his cloak over his nose and watched the ground fly past.

No further shots came, perhaps because of their intense speed. Shadows fell across them, and the prince sensed without looking that they had reached the foothills of the mountains. His suspicion was proven when Darkfire's hooves touched wet shale.

Darkfire's gait now changed as he clambered uphill. Although the path looked treacherous, the stallion seemed to know his way, despite the occasional slip of a hoof. Evan left the decisions to him.

The trail led them behind some large rocks. Darkfire swung around one outcrop and into a small crevice, unseen until they were upon it. Yet the stallion had ducked into it without pause. It was hardly deep, but it would hide them from most angles.

Breathing heavily, they waited, not daring to move or look. Then, sometime later, Evan drew in his breath and heard a *clop, clop... clop, clop.* A horse was nearby, moving at the slow pace required by an observant, searching rider.

After every footstep, it seemed there were five minutes before the next. All the while, blood pounded in the prince's ears and his heart thumped treacherously. Their pursuer grew closer, closer, closer... then, the hooves sounded just in sight of their crack and stopped.

Evan flattened himself against Darkfire's back, not daring to look, not daring to attract attention with his movement. Even the stallion's sides stilled beneath his knees.

At last, the hooves continued up the path. As they grew distant, the prince wilted, and the flanks beneath him heaved with a long sigh. Darkfire did not remain in the crevice, however. Cautiously but quickly, he slid out and started back down to the valley.

Looking behind them, Evan saw no one. The path twisted up and then down again, but he felt watched, as if he would only turn forward and hear hooves behind them once more.

Darkfire's voice distracted him. "What are 'guns'?"

"The weapons of Cyra's assassins. It is said they project small balls as far as the eye can see and have been known to pass through five men's skulls at closer range."

"You speak of these men as a culture, a race."

"They are. Cyra's assassins are the families living on the east side of Cyra, guarding Elcan against the ocean. From the age of three, they train under their fathers as the next generation of assassins."

"Would they usually fire upon an Anskonian king or do so for profit?"

Evan shook his head. "Not to my knowledge. They are secretive, but this seems..." He paused. "Traitorous. Our first king was a Cyran farmer. His people formed Ansky to protect themselves against Evfel, making him the protectorate of Cyra. Why would they betray that protection now?"

"You had better figure it out," Darkfire growled, his pace quickening.

Reaching the valley, the stallion headed east. "If we leave the cover of the mountains, we shall make fine targets. I cannot run forever."

"But this leads to the Ice Woods!" Evan's protest went unanswered, and as he thought again of the stallion's ability to speak and think, the blood rushed from his face. "You are the creature that crawls out of them!"

"If you wish to live, you have no choice but to trust me." The statement was a grim hiss through rapid gasps. "An assassin is after you."

Ugly suspicions filled the prince's mind, but he knew, regardless, that he was helpless. Even should the assassin be a figure from the woods, sent to lure Evan in, he would shoot if his trap failed.

So Evan watched as the Ice Woods loomed before them. Seeing them for the first time, his heart froze, knowing them as the stallion's destination.

Giant trees rose from a great black pit in the ground, twisted together. They were encrusted in so much ice that many people believed no actual wood existed beneath the forest's cold, white surface. Angry wind howled between the webbed branch-icicles. One branch lay level to the earth—a pretend road enticing the foolish toward the stack of its fellows farther in, which blocked the entrance into all-consuming blackness. There lay the gate. No one had ever reached it, instead slipping on the icy path during the first few steps and falling to their deaths.

As Evan considered jumping, he heard hooves. A rider shadowed in a large cloak raced toward them down the slope they had just descended. Sunlight glinted off his weapon as he angled his steed to cut off their flight.

Heaving, the stallion increased his speed. The prince gripped his mane tighter, fearing he fled from one death only to meet another far worse.

Unsurprisingly, the stallion sprinted over the ice without slipping. Muscles bunched beneath the prince's knees as the horse prepared to jump the gate. As its hooves left the ground, screaming from both a man and a horse rang out behind them, then dropped away—their pursuer had fallen into the abyss yawning below.

Instant cold seized the prince. There was no escape. He was now inside the Ice Woods. Although the stallion had slowed to a lope, the light was rapidly shrinking behind. Only ice and the deep abyss lay beneath the hooves of the beast. Frozen particles filled the air between the gaps in the trees.

"Bury yourself in my coat." The stallion's voice was soft this time, sympathetic. "Most of it remains. Stuff your hands under your arms and lie atop my neck. I will keep you warm."

Shivering, Evan obeyed. Yet, he asked, "To what end?"

The stallion snorted. "To save your hide, of course. Also, I never *crawled* out of these woods. I foolishly went exploring too many times. If I could explore your world without biases, you can at least try to do the same." He huffed. "And save that speech about unnaturalness. Everyone's idea of what is natural is based on their environment. This is mine."

Wrapping his cloak more tightly around his face, Evan muttered, "A gloomy naturalness, at best."

"Look again, O Prince. You will see."

In the ensuing silence, striving to stay awake, blinking at the ice pelting his lashes, the prince had no choice but to look when he could. A faint light glowed through the woods, stronger above, where the sun hit the trees, then reflecting downward and paling as it descended. Although the ice was too thick to allow the sun through, except for a tiny ray here and there, the trees danced with dull colors, each bend in the ice reflecting a different hue.

Branches ran off in many directions, crisscrossing their path, some rising above and others dipping below. The trail the stallion loped along, however, appeared to head more or less straight, leading ever into the center of the woods.

More tired by the minute, Evan asked after a little while, "If you are natural, how do you not slip on the ice?"

"My hooves stick lightly to it. They are warm and release a light mist when flattened against something."

"But you are not stuck."

"I said *lightly*, did I not? If you look back, however, you will notice we leave prints, little mounds of hoarfrost. The constant fall of ice covers them after a while."

"Does it ever stop?"

"We sometimes have snow, but never a thaw. The ice level grows every month by several inches. That is why we are not likely to last long in this world. I cannot imagine the woods will be here another hundred years since the ice already threatens to swallow everything one day."

According to historians and eyewitnesses, the woods had appeared without warning only forty years ago. At that realization, Evan sat upright, yanking his cloak tightly about himself. "You can talk of being natural all you like, but unless the story that the woods appeared overnight is false, you are still unnatural."

"I did not appear overnight. I was born this way." Wrath laced the stallion's tone.

Well, there was nothing to gain by bickering with him. "Where are we going?"

Faint warmth was seeping through him, and the light around them glowed brighter, dancing more. Just visible past the trees, something protruded from the ice, sending out a soft glow.

They came to solid ground, a dry, light dirt. Before them, the trees opened to reveal a stone cottage in the middle of a suspended island. Light and warmth exuded from the building, although it had not a window. Without a fleck of ice, a massive tree rose from the opposite side of the structure. The shingles of the cottage shimmered with rainbows.

"This is our destination," Darkfire whispered, stopping before a doorway. Spiraling letters framed the wooden door. Although they were in some unknown language, the invitation in them was as clear as if a voice had spoken a welcoming word to a ragged, friendless soul.

"Knock, O Prince," the stallion advised. "You will not be turned away."

Trembling, Evan slid off. Although comfort seemed to flow from the cottage, he feared it was false, a potential trap. Drawn to the warmth, however, he stepped onto the small stoop and knocked lightly.

As if someone had only been waiting for that sound, the door instantly opened. A lean, elderly woman stood there; her white hair tied in thinning buns. Despite her age, she was far from stooped and the prince needed to look up to meet her face. She smiled down at him through sky-blue eyes twinkling under red eyebrows, piercingly shrewd. If Evan had been a clear pool, he could not have felt more transparent, and he immediately dropped his gaze.

"You are blue, Evan Maxwell," the lady said, her voice the sound of bells and birds, soft as a summer breeze over the valley.

Despite her knowledge of him, the prince felt little fear. Even so, good sense held him in place.

The lady laughed gently. "Come inside and warm yourself, Evan. If you wish an explanation, I will give it to you, but there is no need to stand here freezing."

She stepped aside, leaving the door open. Giving in, the prince slipped past her. The cottage appeared to be lit by a million pinpricks of light, yellow and bright, though the only visible source came from the fireplace carved into the tree trunk growing through the right-hand wall. Apart from a doorway in the back, it was a one-room cottage, divided into a kitchen, dining room and bedroom.

At a table before the fire, six figures—five males with closely cropped hair and one maiden—sat watching the prince, all ignoring their bowls, from which the delicious aroma of stew steamed.

Shyly, Evan remained where he was while the older lady, still at the door, called, "Darkfire, your herd awaits you." With that, the cold was shut out, and the prince felt her hand on his back. "Come, Evan, meet my children, adopted and natural."

Gently propelled toward the watching gazes, the prince felt small, but he did not fight. Most of the figures were children younger than himself. One appeared very peculiar, with flaming red hair and glinting copper eyes with the keen intensity of a bird of prey. The suspicious look he gave was matched only by the eldest there, a young man with a much more ordinary appearance.

"Well met, Prince of Ansky," the oldest growled as his gaze traveled over Evan's attire.

"Jeffrey," the older lady admonished lightly, handing the prince his own bowl of stew. "It is indeed well met. This is Evan Maxwell, a temporary refugee only."

"How fortunate."

"Oh, learn some friendliness, Jeffrey," one of the younger boys interjected, jumping up. "Leave it to me, Lisya." Bowing to the lady—Lisya—the boy turned to Evan, puffing out his chest. "Pleased to make your acquaintance. I am Thomas, of the mature age of eleven, soon to be twelve. Jeffrey there is nearly twenty."

Thomas waved his hand toward the maiden, a girl with dark curls and long lashes, bashfully lowered at the moment. "That is Carrie. She will be fifteen. Then we have Michael." Thomas nodded to the boy with flaming hair. "Carrie's natural brother and a year younger than her."

There was no similarity between the siblings, but before Evan could inquire further, Thomas had already moved on to a boy closely resembling himself. "My twin, James the Bore."

Michael snorted and James sighed as Thomas turned to the last and smallest boy. "And of course, Malachi. He might look five, but he is ten. Jeffrey will tell you that his size is Evfel's fault through their mistreatment of him."

So Malachi was Evfelian. Taking note of that fact, Evan bowed.

"Let us not skip Thomas the Theatric," Malachi added, sliding over to allow Evan a seat. "Are you really the prince of Ansky?"

Feeling Jeffrey's dark gaze on him, the prince did not answer. He was sure the young man was only waiting for a confession before attacking him.

Malachi jabbed his adopted brother in the ribs. "Jeffrey! You really need to learn some tolerance." Unlike that of the eldest male, his voice held a slight coarseness not found in the streets of Evan's home.

"I am tolerant. Do you not remember how I welcomed you when you arrived here?"

Thomas laughed. "As friendly as your clasped hands."

Jeffrey instantly stuffed his hands under the table with an unconvincingly innocent smile.

Looking around, Evan noted the different reactions, all marked by fondness. The boy, Michael, shook his tousled red head. Carrie pressed her lips together to hide her grin as she picked up a spoon. James and Thomas shared raised eyebrows while Malachi laughed outright. Lisya, meanwhile, had disappeared somewhere.

"I was terrified of you," the youngest boy remarked. "You tried to be friendly. You did. But you are a true Evfelian, hard and bitter."

"Perhaps," Jeffrey whispered, his gaze again traveling to Evan. "But you have yet to know what I was like in Evfel. Now, Prince of Ansky, what brings you here?"

"The st... Darkfire, and a pursuer that chased us. I thought..." He shook his head. "May I ask what brings all of you here?"

"This is our refuge, our home." Jeffrey's blue eyes bored into Evan's.

The prince looked away. In these woods, he had no defense. He hardly dared try the stew. Yet nothing felt like the unconquerable danger he had feared.

A small hand dropped onto his arm. Pulling away, he looked down into Malachi's sad eyes. "Carrie and Michael were born here, as Lisya's natural children. The rest of us each came here in different ways, but Lisya has proven to be a true mother to us all. James and Thomas were deserted by their parents when they were small. Lisya rescued them from the Calmar Mountains.

Jeffrey escaped Evfel..." He paused, licking his lips. "We are seen as criminals of Evfel. Jeffrey must tell his story, but mine... With your ties, you may be able to help.

"I was taken as a baby to pay for tax owed by my parents. I only remember Castle Dalacort's kitchen. Food was rare, beatings were many. I think I only survived through theft—food and water mostly—but selling information could also be useful.

"They caught me stealing bread three winters ago, branded me a thief, and sentenced me to death."

"For stealing food?" Evan exclaimed. "At your age?"

"Pray tell, why does that surprise you?" Jeffrey coolly asked. "What does Ansky do with its orphan thieves?"

"For the most part, we do not have orphan thieves. Those without parents find new ones or are raised by our churches. In the few instances when a child refuses the love of a family and resorts to stealing to survive, they will be sentenced to four months in prison. Then a new family will be found.

"They cannot be punished more aggressively until they are twelve. If an adult thief refuses to mend their ways, the punishment is the loss of a hand." Evan paused briefly before adding, "Until now, I have never heard details of Evfel's punishments. There are stories and customs that we keep to our own kingdoms."

"Then Ansky considers a twelve-year-old of mature mind, capable of taking on the responsibility and actions of a grown man?"

A trap waited in Jeffrey's tone. Meeting that piercing gaze, Evan answered, "Yes."

Jeffrey leaned forward. "Then you are nearly four years older than the age of maturity. Is it not your responsibility to do something about it? Is your inaction not a silent abdication?"

The room turned cold. Like Sir Klement, Lisya's son was pushing the prince to turn willfully away or to accept the throne—to take responsibility either way.

Again, Evan sidestepped the choice for the time being and turned back to Malachi. "At what age does Evfel consider a child responsible?"

Malachi shrugged. "Evfel has never cared. In my case, they had another drudge, so they were going to make an example of me. I was chained in a cell, waiting for the hour of my death, when Lisya appeared. I thought I was imagining things when the cell vanished and I found myself here."

He looked down, stirring his stew. "I have nightmares in which I wake up someday, back in the cell, but Lisya assures me this is reality. She says if I stop thinking of this as impossible, my nightmares will disappear, but she is... well, she is too good to be true. I am quite happy, calling her mother and friend. Maybe she will be the same for you too."

Pushing his bowl away, full though it was, Evan rubbed the bridge of his nose. The concerns of that morning—if it was that morning—were ever more pressing.

Sliding out of his seat, the prince nodded to each of the others at the table. "Thank you for your hospitality. It is time I went home, though. I would thank Lisya as well, but please, inform her of my gratitude—"

"There is no need, Evan. But thank you." Lisya stood in the open doorway, a cloak as old as herself wrapped around her arms like a shawl. The effect made her look more fragile, more aged and weary, but the dip of her chin was as regal as before. "Come, speak to me before you leave."

Evan joined her on the stoop, and she shut the door. They stood together in silence.

At last, Lisya stirred, turning to the prince. "Do you go home to claim your throne, Evan?"

"I must."

"You will need a friend, someone to rely on."

Sighing, Evan traced his fingers along the wooden doorframe's grain. "I have none."

Lisya only nodded, and they dropped again into silence. Then she spoke once more. "I would not worry about kingship, Evan." When the prince looked at her disbelievingly, she smiled. "There are joys in the struggles. Regardless, you cannot avoid those struggles even now. You are human. By birth, that makes you powerful. With a word, you can cause a heart to leap or break. With a touch, humans wound or strengthen. Is kingship another step in responsibility? Yes. But the basic rules still apply."

"What are those rules?"

"You cannot trust in your own strength. Even kings have not the power to stop the stars from falling, nor can they force a heart to forgive when they make amends for a wrong. You must trust your Creator alone."

With a wry grin, Evan shook his head. "All you say is that I should fear being human."

Lisya laughed, a golden sunrise laugh. "If you wish to be an animal instead, I can help you. But you will retain the same power. That comes from your ability to make decisions, to know right from wrong—and that I cannot take from you."

Shifting his weight, Evan looked out toward the blackness between the large icicles of the nearest tree. It was odd that he stood beside the being he did not doubt was the creator of the woods and yet felt no distrust.

Standing next to her, he recalled the strangeness of the crone who had so unnerved him. "It was you, was it not?" he asked. "You purposely stepped into my horse's path to drop all your stockings."

She smiled, almost bashfully lowering her gaze to the ground— but the laughter around her mouth was anything but bashful.

In her silence, he pressed, "The herd Darkfire says lives here; were they humans once?"

With a laugh, the lady shook her head. "Darkfire would breathe flames if he heard your question. You have heard him call humans foolish. Do you think he could have been one once?"

Evan did not reply. Lisya sighed, "Yes, I created the woods. In a night, I grew these trees, caused them to dig into the ground, eat dirt and rock until only a great pit remained. At the time, wild horses roamed the foothills of the Calmar Mountains, particularly in this area, far away from any village. I altered the herd to allow them to live here, changing their lungs and coats to withstand the intense cold, their stomachs to hold food and water for days at need, and their feet so they may never slip. And although I had no such intention, when those horses had foals, that new generation could speak, had what you might dub 'human' minds. I promise you, though, they are born naturally."

She was quiet for a moment, during which Evan said nothing. Then she turned to him. "Evan, I am not asking for your trust. I leave you to pass judgment according to your own wisdom. But so you may have some understanding, hear this: I am not human, and certainly not a witch. I need no incantations, no words. I will it, and it is. An enchanter learns, not through a book or potions, but by doing, like humans learn to walk or run.

"I am an enchantress from another world. That world is no more. I am all that remains of the place, which was not made of wood, blood and veins, but of pure magic.

"Every breath I breathe, every vein I possess, is magic. I have tried to live more like a human and nearly died. When I came here, I created this wood to keep the world of kings and wars out, a haven for those who need it—those I will protect."

She paused, but her silence demanded an answer. At last, Evan admitted, "It is a lot to ask someone to believe." Stepping off the stoop, he added, "But I will think on it."

Bowing slightly, the enchantress said, "You will find Darkfire behind the cottage."

And indeed, the prince found Darkfire standing apart from a large herd, so numerous that horses could be seen everywhere, extending back into the tree line. Beside him, however, was another stallion, smaller and honey-colored. Their heads were bent, foreheads pressed together as they blew into each other's nostrils. Perhaps it was how they communicated when alone, but it was more likely ceremonial, judging by its appearance.

Both pairs of eyes were closed. Respectfully, Evan watched the herd. Their heads were also lowered. Whatever was happening felt a private matter. The prince would not ask.

With heads kept down, the stallions took three steps back from each other. As Darkfire raised his own head, looking away, every other horse, including the second stallion, bent onto one foreleg to him.

Feeling exposed as the only one not bowing, Evan backed away toward the cottage. But Darkfire dipped his head in acknowledgment of his presence, a king granting an audience.

Nodding back, Evan shifted. "I must return, Darkfire. If you would take me to the edge of these woods, I will then go on alone."

For a minute, the stallion said nothing, snow and dark mane swirling about his head. Then his belly heaved with a sigh. "What will you say when you are charged with treason for releasing me?"

Tracing lines in the dirt with his foot, Evan shrugged. "You threw me and ran off. It was my foolishness to think you tamed. Everyone knows a horse that at first seems docile will forget once back in his homeland."

Darkfire glanced toward the other stallion. Looking around, Evan noticed all the horses' eyes were waiting, hopeful. Then Darkfire lowered his head. Stepping toward the prince, he bowed, as his herd had just done to him.

"Prince Evan Maxwell, I am no longer the stallion of this herd. I am the charger of Ansky's heir. I have named my son Brimstone Stallion of the Ice Woods."

Emphatically shaking his head, Evan protested, "But you would belong to the king of Evfel! And no one should ever own you."

Standing, Darkfire dropped his head over the prince's shoulder, a soothing horse's embrace. He whispered, "You have spoken with Lisya. You know you will never make it without a friend."

Evan jerked away. "Did she convince you to do this?"

A long sigh escaped the stallion. "We spoke, but this was my choice. I alone made it. As to Wilber... no one knows the future, but for now, I am protected by a lack of taming. For your sake... and mine, please accept."

"How is it for your sake?"

"I would hate myself if I walked away from someone who needed me, particularly someone with whom I empathize so much. If I leave you to your cell, I am a beast undeserving of my home, authority or intelligence."

Submitting, Evan wrapped his arms around that strong neck and buried his face in the stallion's mane.

Chapter 5

The Master Assassin

"Lorene..." Wilber sighed as his wife whirled to stride the five paces back to the opposite side of the tower. "Your agitation can hardly fix anything."

"Look at the sunset," the queen exclaimed, flinging her arm toward the red sky streaked with darkening purple. "Evan left at dawn! Never has he stayed away this long, and the horse is a kill—"

Sighing once more, Wilber took her in his arms, cutting off her tirade. With a small smile, he rubbed her back. "I see your dislike of him was an act."

Lorene's shoulders drooped, along with her chin. "I know I say every day that Evan's a failure to the heritage I once loved, but... Oh, Wilber, I never wanted him to die from a poor choice on my part! If he does, I will have failed his father..." She buried her face in her hands, muffling her words. "As much as I dislike the boy, I loathe the thought of breaking Phillip's trust."

"Your brother is dead, Lorene. His trust is incapable of being broken."

Huffing, the queen pushed Wilber away. "Why are you so insensitive? I failed my brother during his life. How much worse will it be to do the same in his death?"

A prick of anger ran through the king. "So, your marriage to me was a failure now?"

With a sigh, Lorene came back to embrace her husband. "No, my disregard of Phillip's concern was a failure. He feared my marriage to you. I—"

Before she could complete her thought, a call rang out from a turret below. "Prince Maxwell returns!"

King and queen both gasped. Wilber, the first to move, sprinted down the tower steps. He joined the front row of castle inhabitants in the inner bailey just as Evan trotted the giant stallion under the portcullis. Neither looked remotely injured.

Staying a safe distance from the horse, the king snapped, "Where were you? The whole castle was worried."

As the prince slid off the high back, Wilber just caught the muttered response. "Worried I might escape death, you mean."

"None of that! You are the heir. Ansky will worry regardless of their dislike for you—for which you only have yourself to blame."

Slowly, the prince turned to him.

Looking at his nephew more closely, Wilber noticed how cold and tired he appeared with his red cheeks and sagging shoulders, a cloak wrapped tightly around him. Still, his pride was clear.

"I did not choose my delay, Uncle. Some—" Abruptly stopping himself, he eventually continued, "The stallion is not as well trained as I thought."

Glancing at the beast, the king took in the fire still blazing in its eyes, but no ropes hinted at a struggle between it and the prince. Carefully, he stepped nearer. "You seem to have mastered it, though."

As he reached to touch its shoulder, the stallion's ears flattened, the lips curling back. Stepping between them, the prince glanced up to the horse's head. "We have made a breakthrough, but there is far to go as you can see."

Coolly, Wilber nodded. "You have had your chance, boy. If I cannot touch it within a week, you are out of time. Should your bid to tame it in truth be an attempt to steal it, know I will order its death before your thievery demands a war between our lands."

Bowing, Evan muttered, "I will redouble my efforts."

"See to it. As you are not dead, you may hear how foolish you were. Also, I forbid you to take it outside these gates. When next it leaves, I will be on its back. You are fortunate you managed to prevent it from escaping."

The prince made no demur.

Evan was up before dawn to practice his swordplay. Afterward, he retreated to study, glad to find breakfast awaiting him. The spiced wine and a loaf flavored with meat chunks were a great welcome after only eating the bread Lisya had handed him while Darkfire bid her goodbye the day before.

So it was that, exhausted and well fed, he fell asleep. When he woke, the sun was shining strongly through his window—a late noon sun. No one had awakened him for Andrew's sword practice. He guessed no one had even tried. Wilber would have seized the excuse to train his son alone, saying that if Evan was asleep, he wanted him to have some much needed rest.

Sighing, the prince wandered down to the stable. Darkfire was in his stall, resignedly eating hay. Apparently, no one had bothered ripping up grass for him while Evan slept.

"You know they will continue feeding you that if you submit now," the prince whispered, patting the stallion's shoulder.

Burying his nose in the straw, Darkfire blew. Hay puffed into the air. "I submitted yesterday. I might as well eat like a tamed animal."

There was nothing to say. Evan sadly patted the strong shoulder once more, this time in sympathy.

Darkfire, though, pushed his nose into the prince's chest, using the shirt's maroon velvet to muffle his whisper. "One of the Evfelian knights is missing. I heard them asking the stablehands if they had seen anything of him."

Evan snorted, stroking the stallion's forehead. "Good riddance."

"No, listen. He went out shortly after we did yesterday, supposedly to rescue you from me. He has not been seen since."

Evan's hand paused on Darkfire's forehead and remained for three heartbeats. Then the prince bent closer. "Are you suggesting he was our pursuer?"

"It would fit."

"No. My uncle had a million chances to murder me. He raised me. Why wait until now?"

"My point exactly—he raised you. Is it not possible he has manipulated your bitterness, fueled your dislike of thrones? Why kill you if he could take over legally? As of two nights ago, however, when you saw his correspondence, the likelihood of convincing you to abdicate has lessened."

The prince obstinately shook his head. "The assassin was Cyran. Only they have those weapons. Even if they had mistakenly sold one to someone outside their island, it would take years to become decent with a gun. The assassin missed, but only just, and he was firing from a very long distance. Someone could never achieve that level of skill within a day."

"No, but your Uncle Wilber strikes me as someone who plays his game well. He would always have at least one backup plan."

In the silence, Darkfire shook his head. "Either way, you should take your throne now, immediately. The sooner you drive them out of Ansky, the better."

Running his fingers along the scar across the stallion's nose, the prince sighed. "You are Wilber's property. He will take you with him, and I will not see you hauled away with a war bridle, Darkfire."

The stallion bumped his nose against the prince's chest. "For Ansky, Evan, you must claim your throne. But there are ways to ensure my freedom. Pretend to tame me, and when he rides me into the valley, that will be the last he ever touches me. I can guarantee he will believe my escape had nothing to do with you, only with the call of the wild."

"Darkfire," Evan sighed, "you would need to accept saddle, bridle and bit."

The stallion turned back to the hay, nosing its stalks aside under the pretense of eating. "For Ansky, we both must."

Evan knew the stallion did not act "for Ansky." All the same, he relented. "All right. In two days, we will pretend you are trained, at least enough for a trial. Would you do that?"

Darkfire's eyes hardened in cold submission, but Evan's stomach twisted.

"Breathe, Darkfire," Evan whispered, "or this will slip."

The day had dawned on which Wilber would sit astride the stallion, after Evan made sure his charge was ready. In the stall, the prince tacked his companion.

The stallion exhaled deeply, and Evan yanked the girth tight. Dropping the stirrup, he glanced into Darkfire's eye. Suppressed flames flickered in its depths.

Lips tightly compressed, the prince ran his fingers through the stallion's mane before turning to the bridle draped over the wall.

"Wait, Prince Maxwell!" The call came from above. Henry stood in the loft, leaning on the railing as he watched them. "The bit is wrong. King Wilber demands you use the stallion bit."

Evan froze. In his silence, the stablehand pressed further. "With him, you will be thankful for the extra control."

Angrily, the prince turned back to his miserable task. "I am conducting the training. I know what is best. That bit, which has never been used in Ansky except during Evfelian visits, puts too much pressure on the mouth. It will cause only regression."

His stance forbade argument as he inserted the normal bit—already a gag to Darkfire.

Evan's ride to demonstrate the stallion had been tamed went smoothly. For the most part, the prince sat completely still, whispering his instructions and informing Darkfire how others would ask him to take on different gaits.

He cringed when it came time for Wilber to mount. Although fire burned in the stallion's eyes, he allowed the Evfelian king onto his back. Wilber respected war horses enough to start with a walk. To be fair, he was by no means a poor rider, although he maintained firm pressure at all times, a reminder that he was master. Unfortunately, Darkfire—a king himself—responded with the patience of a coiling snake. Every step had a spring in it, every breath a huff, while the ears remained tightly back.

Watching them circle the bailey's yard between the inner and outer stable, Evan ran his lower lip beneath his teeth, waiting for the inevitable break in Darkfire's submission.

Then it happened. Wilber kicked for a gallop, and Darkfire bucked. Clinging to his steed, the Evfelian king yanked the stallion's head into his chest—but that could do nothing to stop a horse from the Ice Woods. Darkfire pushed his forelegs upward and kicked with his back ones, mouth gaping against the bit, nostrils flaring, and fire dominant.

Striding across the distance, Evan grabbed one of the reins. "Stop." Instantly, the stallion stilled, and Wilber lightened his hold.

"Uncle," the prince sighed, "this is not a plow horse. Those you may tame by firmness, but all the greatest war horses are marked by spirit. They are only tamed by gentleness and patience."

Dismounting, Wilber flung the reins at his nephew. "Rather, you are too weak. Your ideals cause rebellion and the inability to trust your steed. Until this horse yields to every command, it is not tame." He began to depart, then paused. "But you have done enough. It is time you quit the job of a stable boy and return to being a prince. Take care of it for now. Tomorrow, the master trainer will start on it."

With that, Wilber swept away. Seizing the bridle, Evan ripped it off and flung it to the ground, stomping his foot over it. Beside him, Darkfire trembled with hatred.

Looking into his companion's eyes, the prince exhaled. He ran a hand down the stallion's neck. "I doubt this is going to work, Darkfire. He will never think you tame."

Darkfire's eyes gleamed with dragon-like cunning, fueled by their hatred. "I have given him a taste of my spirit. Now, when we enter the valley, he cannot blame my escape on you. Had I wanted to toss him, he would not have remained on my back."

"To make him ride you out, though, you will need to submit fully," Evan warned.

The stallion dipped his head. "For now. But remember, the wild can call."

Sighing, the prince loosened the girth and pushed the saddle and pad to the ground. "Let them retrieve it themselves," he growled, leaving the tack where it lay and turning back to the inner barn with Darkfire.

Inside, he rubbed down the dark coat, then bent to the hooves. As he picked the first one up and turned it over, he gasped, despite Darkfire's forewarning. He ran his hand over the smooth surface. "Your hoof!"

"And what, pray tell, is the matter with it? I have perfectly shaped feet—the envy of some, in fact."

"No. Normal horses have frogs and hoof walls, dips and trenches. Yours are as smooth and flat as polished marble." Evan flinched as a light mist oozed beneath his palm.

Darkfire turned toward him, watching. After staring at the strange foot for a moment more, the prince released it, shaking his head. "I will not stop you from making your choice. My attempt to dissuade you in your home was the last. But whatever you do, Darkfire, never let them look at your feet. Thankfully, you seem to have no problem with your toes growing forward, no pressure on your hocks, no splitting. The handlers are most likely to leave your feet alone. But be careful. Your docile act must end if they ever try to touch your hooves."

For the next two days, Evan forced himself to stand aside while Wilber and the master trainer abused Darkfire's authority and his being, dissatisfied with his submission, fake though it might have been.

Once dusk arrived, the prince would slip down to the stall. There, after conversing with the stallion, he slept on both nights until Darkfire woke him just before the stablehands' morning routine began.

On the third night, the stallion greeted Evan with a soft warning. "You must announce yourself as king tomorrow or they will deem me too well trained to forget myself in the valley. They might also think of a way to force my hooves off the ground to clean them."

Evan mutely nodded, slumping against the stall wall and drawing his knees to himself. Neither said anything more.

At last, Darkfire stepped over to the prince, blowing on his hair and nuzzling his arm.

Sighing, Evan pushed his bangs back out of his face. "The stablehands sleep. You can drop your act, Darkfire."

"I act only partially, Evan," the stallion whispered. "No words can console you when your axe falls tomorrow, but I am here to support you. Take comfort in that."

With a tight-lipped smile, Evan ran his fingers along the stallion's cheek. "You already surrendered your freedom. Was it as sickening for you as it is for me?"

A low rumble of thunder filled the brief pause. Then Darkfire snorted in defeat. "For me, the axe dropped before nightfall. It felt as if my heart died as I bore you back here, but I had no time to dread the loss of my freedom. It was done. My life as I knew it was gone."

When Evan only put his arm back around his knees, the stallion again blew on the top of his head. "Dwell not on what you lose, Evan. Dwell on the reasons for losing it. Those thoughts will give you strength."

"Thank you," Evan whispered, but his heart remained heavy.

Another clap of thunder sounded; this time closer. "Go to bed, my prince," came the gentle order. "The wind is picking up, and you left your cloak behind. It will become frigid in here soon."

Pushing himself wearily to his feet, Evan shook his head. "My room will also feel cold tonight."

"It will still be warmer," Darkfire muttered.

Wrapping his arms around himself, Evan started for the keep. He had not gone far before he had to draw back into the shadows of the stable's doorway. A tall figure of medium build was striding across the humid bailey toward the knights' quarters.

In the dark, there was no way to recognize the man, but the ominousness of the late hour and the lonesomeness of the figure made the prince shiver as he remembered Darkfire's fear regarding the Evfelians' plan for Ansky. With one glance back toward the stallion, Evan slunk after the figure, using the buildings along the inner curtain to keep himself out of sight.

The figure disappeared inside the long building that housed Ansky's knights. Following him, Evan opened the main door a crack and watched the shadow knock lightly at another one near the other end.

The church bell tolled midnight as the figure slipped into the room. As the last bong sounded, the prince let himself into the hallway, praying his pounding heart was more silent than it sounded. Unlike the common soldiers' one-room bunkhouse, Ansky's knights had individual rooms off a main corridor.

Knowing a knight could be right behind each door, Evan pulled off his boots and tiptoed to the room into which his quarry had vanished. There, he pressed himself against the wall to listen.

Deep voices argued within. "Do you think that action is wise?"

Another voice replied. Evan recognized it at once as the king of Evfel. "We are out of time. You have seen his change within the past week. Obviously, he is preparing to claim his throne. He could announce himself as king in another few days, tomorrow even. Should he do so, our only path to conquest is through outright war. The Sanguinea Gorge will stand once again between us and victory as Ansky's king blocks this end, cutting off all entrance from Evfel."

Evan's heart froze as his uncle continued. "The stallion failed. For the sake of Evfel's dominion, it must be done tonight. Use a pillow. Suffocate him in his sleep. We can claim an illness took him. With how he has skipped all meals, a sickness will be plausible."

"But will Ansky be fooled?" the knight dared to question.

"They barely care for their young king themselves. With Andrew's natural claim as the next in line, I doubt they will complain immediately. Regardless, the queen is pregnant. Within less than a year, there may be other possibilities to appease them with."

His mouth dry, Evan backed away. Once at a safe distance, he fled, glad of his unshod feet. At any moment, the knight might emerge—and there was nowhere to hide.

Just as he heard the creak of hinges, he reached the exit, slipped outside and ducked around the corner of the longhouse. Moments later, the knight appeared, Evfelian tabard blowing about him. Thankfully, his pace never slackened, even though the door stood ajar. A man trained for inconspicuousness, he strode boldly across the bailey toward the keep, not a sign in his step or manner that he was out for blood.

But he would find no victim. Not inside. Would he hunt his prey down anyway?

Trembling, Evan backed away—and at that moment, Wilber followed his liege man outside. The prince dove behind the blacksmith's woodpile. Although the king glanced around, he then also strode toward the keep.

As soon as Wilber had disappeared, Evan dashed for his father's stable.

One thing he knew: unless they were foolish enough to be caught in the act, any charge of murder would be his word against Wilber's. Unfortunately, of the two, the Evfelian king held more of the people's trust. No one would stand with Evan.

The first drops of rain fell as he reached his father's stable. "Darkfire," he cried, throwing open the stall door. "You were right! We must leave!"

"Stay by me. I will protect you until morning." It was a promise, made in the voice of a deadly dragon preparing to unleash itself against the murderers. Yet Evan vehemently shook his head.

"Wilber cannot act too openly," Darkfire warned, "and if you run, Evan, you forfeit your kingdom to Evfel. Lisya cannot help you if that happens."

In despair, the prince wrapped his arms around the stallion. "I know. Please. I..." He would go insane were he to become king. Wilber would manipulate the world against him, and Evan himself had enabled that manipulation through his own bitterness. In guilt, horror and fear, he clung to his only friend, breathing in ragged gasps, unable to explain, willing the stallion to understand.

Blowing out a puff of air, Darkfire dropped his head over the prince's shoulder. "How do we escape without being seen?"

"Come," Evan whispered, creeping toward the outer bailey's entrance. "My father built a secret door out back in case of attack."

To keep it secret, no one guarded that door. Expecting a shout of alarm and running feet at any minute, Evan watched the patrol from the shadows. As soon as the guard turned his back, the stallion and prince shoved the door open and ran through.

Quickly shutting it behind them, Evan leaped on Darkfire's back, and then they were away, dashing into the driving rain. Only a few seconds passed before the deep bellow of a horn sounded from the castle. They had been seen.

Another horn followed, flying ghost-like on the wind. To Evan, it was a warning cry of approaching death, while thunder cracked through the black of night.

Climbing into bed, Wilber rubbed Lorene's shoulder. Although she mumbled incoherently, her muscles relaxed.

The call of a horn caused the king to sit upright. For a split second, there was no further sound. Then another horn sounded, and Wilber groaned.

Running feet pounded outside. The king met the guard in the corridor.

"Sire, Prince Maxwell has taken off on your stallion!" the messenger gasped.

Wilber froze. Then he raced up to the nearest tower, ignoring the pelting rain. Beside him, the guard pointed north—but at night, amid the storm, nothing was visible.

A flash of lightning rent the clouds. Briefly, he could make out a black dot in the valley, racing away from the castle.

The king pounded the parapet with his fist. "The thief! Does he so openly declare war?" Barely had the words left his mouth before his heart lightened. The Maxwell prince himself had declared war. And Evfel would happily oblige.

The guard stared in horror, as if seeing the future bloodshed looming before them. Wilber had no intention of starting the war yet, however. Turning to the guard, he ordered, "Gather a squad of knights. We will drag Prince Evan Maxwell back here and see if he truly desires war."

The guard appeared to wake. "Why would he do this in the first place?"

Compressing his lips, Wilber shook his head. "He is a very selfish young man and wanted the stallion from the beginning. Perhaps he thought nothing of the consequences, or perhaps he little cared. Either way, he deserves one more chance."

Bowing, the guard left to relay the command. Wilber followed, shivering slightly from the rain. Even the cold water, however, could not dampen his hope.

Evan's escape was downright auspicious. Now, they had a reason to attack, and no one would suspect Evan had likely taken the fastest horse merely to escape assassination.

Chapter 6

Storms, Mountains and Trains

ESPITE THE HOUR, Lisya stood in her doorway, already await-ing them as Darkfire came to a halt. Without thinking, Evan threw himself into her open arms. As her love and warmth envel-oped him, he brokenly admitted, "I tried, Lisya. I—"

"Shh," the enchantress whispered, brushing ice out of his hair. "You need dry clothes. Then you must tell me your intentions."

Yanking away, Evan protested, "At this point, I need... I need supporters who will stand up to Wilber. Someone I have not already convinced to agree with him." He again buried himself in her arms, his head only reaching her ribs. He felt very small, but protected. Not even his ice-soaked clothes, first drenched by rain then frozen by the woods, could move him. There was no point.

The enchantress nodded to Darkfire and guided the prince inside. Against the walls, her six children slept in separate beds, undisturbed as she shut the door. "So you intend to take back Ansky?" she whispered.

Evan remained hopelessly silent, though he nodded.

With an encouraging smile, Lisya added, "I know a place where you can leave your reputation for bitterness and its shadow behind, a place where you may find supporters by your true charac-ter alone."

There was only one question to ask. "Where?"

"Enchantress Island, particularly the village on the eastern side, around Alleluia Lake. The islanders living there knew me the most."

Evan yanked back, but the enchantress kept hold of his hand. "I am the enchantress for whom it is named. Does that worry you?"

The prince quivered. There was no doubt she told the truth. She was the enchantress of the place where the skies had blackened out the sun for generations, stirred the channel into constantly crashing peaks, launched dragons on the villages that once dotted the northern mountains, and pressed fear into the hearts of all. There was no denying the power in her eyes and voice.

"For what cause?" he breathed at last.

"That is a long story, which there is no time to tell. Your uncle has already sent pursuers after you. If you are to go to the island, you must arrive before them. However, I was not the only enchantress, not at first. We were an evil swarm. I was rescued."

That was all she said as she led him into the backroom, half of which was an indoor garden. Thriving plants, bathed in their own gentle light, stretched up to the roof on the half of the room taken up by the garden. That created a canopy overhead, while moss made a fern-like carpet about and through the garden's base. Aside from that odd sight, the room included a loom, a bed and a bureau.

Evan turned away from the garden as Lisya passed him clothes from the bureau. "These will both keep you warm and camouflage you. I made them in the style of the island." With that, she stepped out, shutting the door behind her.

When Evan reentered the main room after changing, Jeffrey and Lisya were at the table packing a rucksack. With a polite nod at the Evfelian, the prince wordlessly joined them.

"You want to leave your boots as well," Jeffrey muttered. "Those with less own sandals, if they own anything."

"You wear sandals in the wintertime?" It was hard to believe.

"No, before coming here, I used rags. The point is, leave them behind if you care to live."

Fondly, Lisya shook her head. "Keep them until you leave the woods, Evan, then drop them down into the abyss."

Watching them coil a length of rope, Evan shifted. "How does one travel to Enchantress Island?"

Lisya nodded to her son. "Jeffrey will show you." As the prince regarded his companion warily, the enchantress smiled. "You may trust him, Evan."

"Darkfire said you lacked the power to help," Evan commented, turning back to the enchantress and seeing again the authority in her eyes.

For a minute, Lisya said nothing, instead passing them cloaks and fastening the sack over Jeffrey's shoulders. "You ask why I refuse to help when it seems clear I can smite the ground and all Evfel will run?"

Evan shifted, clasping his cloak. "I only meant..." He meant that sending Jeffrey felt like the assistance she refused to grant, but perhaps she knew what he meant more than he did.

"You must be king, Evan. You must take the hard route and wade to clear ground under your own power. I cannot cheat for you, nor would you want me to do so. If Ansky realizes you reached the Ice Woods, you may never win the support of your people. That is why Darkfire spoke as he did. Not once did he mean I would hold back physical aid for your cause. Now, I will show you what your transport looks like."

Touching the prince's arm, Lisya turned him around, pointing to the floor. Long, moving boxes, each about a foot high, abruptly appeared on it, winding like a snake around little mountain peaks. Evan gasped in surprise, but he felt no horror in her power.

"Summos Valley calls this a 'train,' your carriage to the island," Lisya explained. "These three black boxes in the front, middle and back are the cause of its movement. See how the boxes it hauls change in the center? The first one after the front car and the last three are passenger quarters, used primarily for the train's handlers."

She glanced at Jeffrey, and Evan understood she was offering so much detail to give the Evfelian strategic information. "There may come a time when the coaches haul real passengers. Beware of any you may meet. The last type, with the double sliding doors, are the boxcars. Since you will be traveling with Darkfire, you will likely receive a place in one of them, assuming they do not fill every single one with goods to trade. I hope their greed will be enough to guarantee you room—but if it is, I pity their avarice."

After winding through mountains and over a long bridge expanding across an ocean, the train disappeared. With a half-bow to the enchantress, Jeffrey led the way outside, where the stallion waited. On the stoop, Lisya brought her son to a halt. "The pass is blocked by knights. You must go over the mountains."

"The train leaves in only three days, Lisya," Jeffrey warned. "What if—"

"You know the mountains, Jeffrey. You will know how to hide until the train returns." Turning to Darkfire, the enchantress continued, "You will insist on going. Are you willing to take Jeffrey?"

"I have submitted. I will take anyone Evan decrees."

Lisya smiled. "Do not lie to yourself, Darkfire. You will break your own spirit if you continue to submit so falsely." Turning to Evan, she touched his arm in farewell. "Providence is watching over you, Evan. Regardless, your kingship is up to you."

As the prince bowed, Jeffrey embraced the enchantress. For a moment, they held each other. Then, as Evan pulled himself onto Darkfire's back, Jeffrey stepped away. "Whatever happens, Lisya, know you did not fail. We will meet in the afterlife, if I never come back."

Sadly, the enchantress nodded in acceptance. "Just know for certain why you go. We will await your return."

No more was said. Evan helped Jeffrey up behind him, and then Darkfire set off. The warmth and safety of the cottage shrank into the distance.

They were still in the Ice Woods when the prince hesitantly asked, "Why would you not return?"

"Malachi told you, I am a criminal of Evfel. If I am caught, they will immediately hang me. I already escaped once."

Prudence prevented Evan from asking more. In silence, he watched the light play over the falling snowflakes as Darkfire ran.

This was the sort of night that caused wars to pause, and sometimes, the uncharitable to take compassion on the homeless. Shivering in his drenched cloak, Sir Klement took momentary respite beneath the shelter of the tower arch.

His watch was a joke, anyway. The black skies and pouring, icy rain blinded everyone on the walls of Fortress Tyhoronous, except when the lightning lit the sky, which was soon followed by the crack of thunder that caused even the bravest to cringe beneath its ear-splitting power.

For that matter, not only could the watch not see, they could hear nothing as well. Still, guards were required to remain on the walls. Unwilling to ask anyone to do what he would not, knight or no, Sir Klement had volunteered for this shift—and regretted it instantly.

The sky again lit, and a deafening crack caused the knight to start. Half-blinded, Klement blinked. Had he just seen a horse running toward the foothills?

Straining his eyes, the knight waited. More lightning struck, and he saw it... or them. Two riders mounted on a swift horse fled into the mountains.

Klement waited for more light, but by the time another flash had come, they were gone. Only extreme need would force someone out in this storm. The mountains would be exceptionally treacherous in the rain.

Wrapping his sopping cloak more tightly about himself, Klement turned to report the riders—and then paused. He had no reason not to report it to his cousin, Lord Tyron, but some inner voice cautioned him. Was it that no one would believe him? Was it self-comfort? He would, after all, need to expose himself again to the full onslaught of the heavens if he moved.

Convincing himself he had only imagined the riders, he continued his stationary watch. Not more than twenty minutes later, however, he heard steps behind him.

A guard stopped at his side. "Lord Tyron has called the changing of the watch early. Something has happened at Castle Ansky. There are messengers here to speak with the early watch."

"So we are not called in early out of concern for our well-being?"

Laughing, the guard slapped Klement's shoulder, causing a squelch. "His lordship ordered everyone to put on dry clothes before speaking to the messengers, but you had better hurry. The Evfelians seem impatient."

Heeding this advice, Klement hurried away, cringing as the downpour hit his head and shoulders before running down his back. After a hasty change into wonderfully dry clothes and a gulp of hot cider, he lined up with the other sentries in the main hall. Two Evfelian knights stood before them, while Lord Tyron watched from the doorway, his gaze firmly on the messengers.

"Maxwell has stolen the king's charger." A ripple of shock passed down the line, but the messenger continued. "He was last seen headed north right before the thick of the storm. Has anyone seen him?"

Silence followed. Klement glanced at those beside him. Then, someone at the other end of the line spat. "You must be insane! You were out there. If we saw anything other than our own spluttering torches, it would be a miracle. And you can be sure we heard nothing, what with this thunder ringing in our ears."

Both Evfelians regarded the line of Anskonians doubtfully. Finally, the elder of the two spoke. "Do you fail to notice your prince has just declared war on Evfel? Since our king has decided to be merciful and sent us only to bring the thief back, to ask if he truly desires war, you should fully support us."

"Bring the thief back to ask if he truly desires war?" Klement snorted. "Before the headman's block, of course."

Flushing, the elder messenger turned to him. "Do you wish to repeat that, Sir Knight?"

Carefully, but without flinching, Klement crossed his arms. "Evfel has much to gain from inventing this entire situation and quietly absconding with our prince and the horse."

Both pairs of Evfelian eyes flashed. "And the council has much to gain from allowing Maxwell his war and lying in response to our questions. Now, has anyone seen him?"

Stepping out of the doorway, Lord Tyron announced, "I *am* a member of the council. As such, I suggest you direct your accusations to me. I can answer more accurately."

The messengers dipped their chins submissively, and the lord continued. "If our prince has declared war over a horse, he has betrayed us all, and we will be glad to offer our assistance in finding him. My men know nothing, or I would have received a report of a fleeing horse before you arrived. I swear by all that is holy, I received no such report. Prince Maxwell was neither seen nor heard by this fortress."

Picking at his wool sleeve, Klement hardly heard as the lord ordered rooms prepared for the messengers, then excused them. Come the dawn and better weather, he promised they would ride out with a search squadron.

Once they departed, however, Lord Tyron sent guards out to the hallways and turned to the rest of his men. "I did not lie. I intend for you to hunt down Prince Maxwell. Find him, and find him first. Bring him here, that we may hear his response to the charges firsthand, instead of from the lips of Evfel's king."

The men bowed their agreement. As they turned to leave, however, the lord called out, "Klement! I want a word, cousin."

Freezing, the knight allowed the rest of the early watch to leave. "You know something," Lord Tyron observed. "Your accusations make it clear that you distrust their claim, but your recent report said Wilber has lied in nothing. Evan Maxwell is exactly the bitter, angry and selfish prince everyone says."

Relieved that they were not discussing the two strange riders in the storm, Klement shrugged. "To all appearances, he is, but…" He paused, trying to gather his thoughts. "He has a way with horses, a touch, a… an understanding. He can communicate with them as if he were a horse himself, or as if he knows the pain of being treated like a beast. There were also the gunshots somewhere in the valley, only a week ago."

"We never found anyone," the lord reminded him. "In any case, you cannot suspect it had anything to do with Evfel. Only Cyra's assassins carry such weapons."

"True, but the timing of the two events adds to my unease. As for Prince Maxwell himself… I lack proof, but there is a chance he was subtly trained into his anger through a lack of compassion. Certainly, I place no trust in the Dalacorts or Evfel's accusations, not even in Lorene."

Sighing, Lord Tyron laced his fingers together. "Lorene is a Maxwell by birth. She should love her nephew."

"Perhaps, but she is blind to her husband's flaws."

"Careful, Klement. Unproven accusations have caused war. Ansky's protection must come first."

Sadly, Klement whispered, "Do you perhaps mistake peace for protection?" When there was no reply, he bowed. "Evan Maxwell is our only hope. If he fails, we fall to Evfel, and there is no safety under their kings."

Evan tensed as a bolt of lightning split the rock face only a few steps away. Walking behind Jeffrey, he kept the young man's cloak grasped in hand, so as to not lose his way in the storm. In the light, he saw Darkfire's black shape, carefully leading them along the ledge while Jeffrey held onto his tail. Then darkness fell again.

Blinded, the prince felt his foot slip on the wet stone of the path. He slid, pitching into open air. A hand seized his wrist.

Undoubtedly feeling the tug on his cloak, Jeffrey had come to the rescue and was now pulling Evan to safety. They could not speak over the sound of the storm, but the Evfelian again placed the back of his cloak in the prince's hand.

Evan shook his head, shouting, "It is suicide to continue in this!" Only his release of the cloak imparted his decision to stand firm, but Jeffrey seized his wrist.

Darkfire must have had the same worry, since he nuzzled them away from the edge. Following his prompts, the two humans settled down by a rock face. There, huddled beneath their rain-repelling cloaks, Jeffrey and Evan listened to the howl of the wind and the crack of rock as lightning struck it. Light sliced through the sky, highlighting the furious raindrops.

The stallion stood above them, guarding them from the lightning with his body. Yet if part of the rock face split over their heads, they would all be dead. It was a wonder Jeffrey had agreed to this trip.

Alone, except for his companions' mostly invisible presence, Evan tensed with every clap of thunder. Most likely, they would die this night. They were too high, right in the midst of the storm.

The tempest seemed to last for days. The only passing of time was light slicing through the sky. Such were the lone occasions when his companions were visible. Though it seemed longer, the storm could not have been more than a few hours.

Finally, the lightning and thunder stopped. The rain clouds melted away, revealing blazing stars. Staring at them, Evan breathed, "Never have they looked so close."

Jeffrey settled down and shifted his cloak about himself. "We are high in the Calmar Mountains. Your valley is far below. Here, the sky reigns, stars and lightning alike."

"Is it still too dark and wet to travel?" Evan asked.

"Rest while you can," Jeffrey responded, his voice old. "I will wake you before dawn. It comes soon."

As if obeying, Darkfire curled up beside them. Huddling into his warmth, the prince hesitantly asked the Evfelian, "Lisya told you to make sure you know why you came. May I ask your reason?"

Those wary eyes opened again, black in the darkness. Jeffrey pushed himself back up, but then looked away into the night. After a minute, he rubbed his chin. Then he shrugged. "You are the true king of Ansky. That is cause enough."

Clearly, it was an evasion, a partial truth at best, but it was perhaps a compliment that he deemed the prince worthy of any answer. Accepting that response, small as it was, Evan rested against Darkfire. With all his weariness, he was soon asleep.

Despite the storm of the night a couple of days ago, Quincy dared not stop. Wilber had placed him in charge of a small force of Anskonians, including Sir Radnor, and he would not disappoint. Where other units were searching the mountains and the Sanguinea Gorge, his was to scour Elcan's northern wild, beginning with Summos Valley.

The force arrived in the valley three days after setting out, exhausted; their horses sluggish and muddy. Seeing the city for the first time, Quincy unintentionally pulled up, feeling his mouth gape slightly.

Every structure was built of stone. Not a single one was wooden. All stood two or three levels high. Gold decorated most of the lintels above the doors, and wrought-iron balconies with varied, vibrant arrays of flowers overlooked cobbled streets.

The people milling in those streets wore bright colors and quality fabrics, even the hawkers and stall merchants.

It was extravagant wealth, and the valley flaunted it without a care. True, the only entrance to that little well in the Calmar Mountains—Summos Valley—was the pass the knights had ridden through, Penelope Pass. That and the River Gold protected them from a full-scale attack, enabling their independence beneath

their elected governor. Even so, to flaunt prosperity so foolishly...
It was amazing they were still free.

Turning to two of his men, Quincy ordered them to stand guard
by Penelope Pass, in case their prince was behind them. Having
blocked that end, he led Sir Radnor and his other four men down
the cobbled streets toward the center of town, marked by the
ornate hall attached to its prized train station. Two long grooves
wound away from the station, leading to a gentle but long rise.
Those were the tracks into the mountains.

Closer to the station, the crowds increased as the knights
passed more stalls, other hawkers and stately shoppers. The
knights' arrival had not gone unnoticed. Four men in a diamond
formation awaited them on the hall's steps, the oldest on the
lowest step—no doubt the governor, judging by his dignified attire.

Pulling up his steed, Quincy hastily asked, "Have you seen or
heard of a boy on a giant black horse? Prince Maxwell has stolen
the Evfelian king's charger."

As if connected somehow, the four men folded their arms in
unison. Thankfully, only the oldest spoke. "We have seen nothing
and little do we care. What is it to us that your two kingdoms fight
and backstab? We have no connection to them, and we refuse to
be bought by whatever promises you bring."

Quincy opened his mouth to argue, but the governor cut him
off. "You may return with the news, however, that no prince will
escape you by taking refuge in our valley. We will send him back
if he tries."

"I am not much concerned about him taking refuge," the knight
protested. "If he comes with money, would you deny him passage
on your train?"

A snort sounded from one of the men, but the governor shrugged.
"I see no reason he would ask for passage. Our train goes only to
one place—Enchantress Island. It travels there to trade for valu-
ables, then returns here to unload and reload. There are no stops
along the way. The Calmar Mountains are wild beyond our borders,
and everyone fears the island—for good reason."

"Regardless," Quincy insisted, dismounting, "we must make sure. After all, he knows you go there, and what we fear might provide a shield for him. My unit was sent to travel on your next passage."

The governor's face darkened, and the knight hastily added, "We will pay, of course."

"Most importantly," the governor growled, "Enchantress Island is known for its powerful witches and its ability to turn the skies black at will. We ourselves have never dared to stay there long. We leave before dusk even falls.

"We also lack the arrangements to host you. Our passenger coaches are for the use of our staff, to enable a reasonable amount of comfort over the course of the journey. Would you expect the cook to serve you?" The governor shook his head, answering his own question. "No, you would be foolish to come."

Astride his horse, Sir Radnor spoke up. "There was a time when one of you did stay on the island overnight. The islanders returned the man who discovered them in his folly, did they not? There is no use lying. Your train speaks of that history. They will leave us alone unless they feel threatened."

At last, the governor bowed slightly. "For your money, we accept—provided you keep out of the way and board your horses at one of our local stables. After you have paid your fare, perhaps you would enjoy a tour of our train to pass the hours. It does not leave until midnight."

Quincy could not tell if the mocking tone was sarcasm, but he knew the governor would never shrink from a chance to impress the Anskonians with his valley's technological brilliance. Curious to learn what he could from that pride, the knight bowed his assent.

The Summos Valley market extended into the station itself, filling the platform beneath its frescoed roof. The train was a long, black rectangle on wheels with a horn protruding from its exact center.

"Ah!" the governor exclaimed as they approached the wooden cuboid. "Our wonderful lead engine! There are two more, in the center and back, that are mostly identical. While you waste your time on warring with your neighbors, we devote our time to the finer aspects of expansion—faster travel, reach of trade, innovation, the finer things in life."

"You can only do that because we of Ansky keep your conquerors busy," Quincy said.

Casting the knight a dirty look, the governor guided them to the rear of the lead engine. There, he stepped onto a small platform hidden by the train's two sides.

A middle-aged man stood there, wiping a long, protruding spout. "Crowther!" the governor greeted the man, slapping his shoulder. "Demonstrate our engine's voice for these men, will you, the one that keeps time for our drivers and conveys instructions to them?"

Without replying, Crowther put his mouth to the spout and blew. A deep bellow erupted above them, echoing off the ceiling. The note changed, rising and then descending, its tempo shifting with the alterations in pitch.

Glancing at Radnor, Quincy noted his slackened jaw. "Sir." He jabbed the older knight.

His warning hiss was meant to be too soft for anyone other than Radnor to hear, but the governor watched them with self-satisfaction in his eyes. Coolly, Quincy bowed to Crowther. "You are quite skilled."

"Quite." The governor nodded once. He pulled a tiny, multi-pronged wheel out of a small hatch and held it up. "This engine is commanded by its music, and driven by its multiple sizes of gears and sheer manpower. Come, I will show you the wells." He gestured to a ladder built into the back of the engine.

"I am too old to scamper about a wooden structure," Radnor complained.

"Perhaps, you may describe it to us," Quincy suggested to their guide. "What do you mean by wells?"

If the governor noticed their refusal to be further impressed, he let it slide. "The drivers' wells are where two men stand in each engine and pump the handle before them. Our controls extend into the wells. There, listening to the directions from the horn above their heads, the drivers slow down, increase their speed, or stop. With the multi-wheel system on our rail tracks, we could cross your valley in half the time it takes your steeds."

Quincy merely folded his arms.

With a smile, the governor finished. "We also have six drivers for each engine. By changing out without stopping, we can reach the island in a week. As the islanders would say in their lowborn speech, 'You can't beat that speed.'"

Cringing at the accent, a hurried, slur only fit for the street people of Evfel, Quincy refused to reply. Let Summos Valley boast. He would not believe it, at least not until he witnessed it for himself.

Chapter 7

Toward the Island

BELOW THE SHARP DROP-OFF at Evan's feet, Summos Valley shimmered under the noon sun. "So we've arrived," Jeffrey muttered next to him.

The prince had noticed over the course of their journey that his older companion had let go of his Ansky accent, his speech becoming garbled and more hurried. When Evan had commented on this, Jeffrey had shrugged. "We don't bother enunciating every syllable on the streets of Evfel. Time is too important. Besides—" His teeth had flashed. "Those highborn knights can't keep up."

Now staring into the valley, Evan asked, "Is there no way down?"

"Short of falling?" Jeffrey quipped. Nodding toward the opposite cliff face, he went on, "We could go down the tracks, but they'd see us for sure." He pointed to a place where the cliffs broke to make way for the river, and the light bounced off something shiny. "That's the glint of armor. The pass is now blocked, and we'd need to be inside to use it anyway."

Shaking his mane, Darkfire snorted from the other side of Jeffrey. "We could probably jump into the river, if it were not for the knights sitting at both ends of the pass."

Jeffrey just looked at him for a moment, annoyed sarcasm radiating from every feature. "Then drown, I suppose? I never learned to swim, and you were born in the Ice Woods."

"Horses swim by nature, without needing to learn."

Would the stallion ever forget his debate about the things altered by magic? Smiling, Evan shook his head. "Another thing you may add to your list of humans' unnatural qualities. We speak, walk and now swim unnaturally. Tomorrow, you will be telling us our hair is unnatural as well."

"Now that you mention it..." Darkfire mumbled. Jeffrey elbowed him in the stomach.

"How *are* we going to climb down, though?" the prince asked, trying to bring them back to the subject. "The guards mean swimming is not an option, even if we could, and I think we would need to know how to dive safely first."

The Evfelian shrugged. "They might lower their guard after the train departs tonight," he ventured, though his voice lacked conviction. "But we'd better leave the edge before someone looks up and sees us."

Evan took five steps back and then settled himself on the ground. Jeffrey followed. For a moment more, Darkfire remained, standing only an inch from where the mountain fell away, his head hanging as he studied the steep cliff face. Then, he joined the humans, saying, "I think I can run down."

"That drop?" Jeffrey asked. "You might be able to swim naturally, but that is an entirely different matter."

"My hooves stick—"

"To ice!"

The stallion shook his mane. "As long as you remain flat along my back, we might make it down."

After a single snort, Jeffrey fell silent.

Looking from the seriousness in the stallion's eyes to the Evfelian's furrowed brow, Evan bit his lower lip. "If you are sure, Darkfire, then I trust you," he finally sighed. "We should wait until the sun is low enough to blind anyone looking upward and then try."

Exhaling, Jeffrey jerked Lisya's sack off his shoulder. "Fine. I've taken many risks, but this seems suicidal to me." He passed out dried fruit and nuts before asking, "Darkfire, will you agree to a rope bridle? There are knights down there. The more humble and pathetic you appear, the better."

The stallion's large stomach filled with air before he released it. "I consent. You might as well cut my mane and tail too. Keep enough mane to hold on to and remove the rest."

He was looking at Evan, but the prince glanced away. No one needed to tell him a horse's mane was his crown, and Darkfire owned an astounding one. Cutting it off would be another mark of slavery—to say nothing of how mane and tail protected a horse from flies.

Naturally, Jeffrey was the one who dismissively said, "Easy enough." Pulling a white knife from his belt, he stepped behind the stallion.

"Just watch out for my bone," the stallion muttered, head dropping slightly.

"Trust me, will you? I want to avoid the hacked-off look. If it's hastily done, they might have cause to be suspicious."

Snorting, Darkfire grumbled, "With a blade, it will look hacked off, no matter what."

"I said, trust me. Have patience. This is going to require some pulling." Craning his head around the stallion's haunches, Jeffrey stared at the prince for a moment. "You can start on the mane."

"With what? Is there an extra knife, or did Lisya pack scissors?"

"Never mind," came the response. "I just hope I can finish before the sun starts to set."

With a glance at the yellowing sky, Evan pushed himself to his feet and thinned the stallion's mane, a few strands at a time. Darkfire's gaze remained distant, his head lowered as they worked.

Lovingly, the prince ran his fingers along his friend's neck. "Thank you, Darkfire," he whispered. It was all he could say, though it helped little.

After a moment, the stallion shook his head. "I refuse to be sorry. Would I not be a hypocrite if I dwelled on my losses?"

"No, you only said it helps not to. You never pretended you were immune to that pain."

The sun was low when Jeffrey decided their work on Darkfire's mane and tail was good enough. While Evan twisted their rope into a passable bridle, the Evfelian removed two last inches of mane from right behind the stallion's ears to make a bridle path. Although this was never done in Ansky, Evfel had long removed that portion of mane on their warhorses. In any case, it added to the humble appearance of the steed.

"We have no time now, but at the bottom, Evan, you should pull your hair back and hide it."

Nodding, the prince slipped the rope bridle through Darkfire's teeth and over his ears. "I promise not to pull," he whispered as he hauled himself onto the stallion's strong back.

As Jeffrey followed him, Darkfire ordered, "Flatten yourself back as much as possible. Jeffrey, I give you permission to grab my tailbone." Lowering his voice, he added, "Evan, keep your knees and legs tight like never before. I swear, you will hear no complaints if they dig into my shoulder blades."

As the Evfelian sat down behind him, the prince nodded minutely. In a surge of muscle, Darkfire ran to the edge and pushed off.

Evan scrunched his eyes closed while wind snapped about them. They were plunging, faster and faster. His knees trembled due to how tightly he clung. The only other thing he was aware of was the glaring sun, burning green spots behind his closed lids and heating his face.

Then, Darkfire lurched so abruptly that the prince slipped. With a small cry, he dropped relatively lightly onto wet grass. Jeffrey had landed on his feet and was leaning against Darkfire's haunches. They had made it.

For a moment, Evan lay there, listening to the heavy breathing of his companions.

Slight pricks in his fingers roused him. Raising his hands to his face, he noticed the long black strands wrapped tightly around his fingers, jerked out of the stallion's mane. Laughing, he removed hair and rubbed his hands together to restore their circulation.

"Evan," Jeffrey said, while binding their sack around Darkfire's girth to give the impression of a pack horse, "take care of your bangs, and wear this." He flung something toward the prince, who caught it instinctively.

It was a small cloth cap, the type worn by peasants in the fields. From inside, a piece of string fell into Evan's lap. Obediently, the prince attempted to pull his bangs to the top of his head—without success.

Sighing, Jeffrey approached. "We should have cut it before leaving home." Deftly, he yanked all the wayward hairs back, tied them together, then jammed the hat over the whole thing.

Stepping back in front, he nodded. "Hopefully, this will fool everyone."

"For Ansky, we had better succeed," Evan muttered, pushing himself to his feet and brushing grass off.

Jeffrey picked up the pretend reins trailing on the ground, then led the way toward the dusky city. "This better succeed, for our sakes."

With a smile, Evan took up the rear.

The trio wandered down the roads, past open shops, and up the station steps. As they did so, everyone's eyes fixed on them except for the two men scampering over the black box leading the procession of train cars.

Ignoring the attention, Jeffrey strode toward the man barking orders next to the engine. "We would like passage to the island."

Whirling toward the group, the trainmaster appraised the Evfelian. "Oh, would you?" His glance passed over Evan, and then he called out behind him, "Is this your prince?"

"Prince!" Jeffrey's tone conveyed both scorn and shock. As he spoke, two men stepped out from the train's coaches. Anskonian knights—Quincy and Radnor.

Paling, Evan dropped his gaze and stood immobile. If he so much as twitched, the knights would likely notice him. It was hard to believe they had not done so already, considering the loud hammering of his heart.

Jeffrey, however, hardly paused. "I'm Jeffrey Gombe, a far better name than that of any prince."

Quincy suspiciously flicked his gaze over the Evfelian. "What is your business on the island, Jeffrey Gombe?"

Eyes glimmering with craftiness, the Evfelian replied, "Trade was good here, but I'm done. I walked the tracks when I had no need for a packhorse. Now we, myself, Matthew here"—he nodded toward Evan—"and our animal, wish to go back."

"How good was your trade?"

"You thieving Anskonians would like to know, wouldn't you?"

Evan expected Quincy to demand an answer, but the knight made no reply. It was the stationmaster who spoke. "Your trade must be prosperous if you can afford passage for two people and a horse."

Smirking, Jeffrey twitched his fingers and turned his hand over. Three lumps of gold rested in his palm. Although seemingly unimpressed with the sleight of hand, the stationmaster stared at the gleaming rocks.

Enticingly, the Evfelian promised, "This is raw gold, friend. I can pay for your greed. You may have these three now, and three more when we arrive."

His eyes twice their usual size, the stationmaster sighed. "Done. Take your passage." He pointed toward a boxcar, that stood five cars down from the lead engine.

Without a word, Jeffrey dropped the rocks into the outstretched hand.

At once, the gold vanished into a pocket. "Load up!" the stationmaster called. "We leave in five minutes!"

Surprisingly, the Anskonian knights boarded with only one last glance at the threesome. Evan's heart, however, continued to race.

As Jeffrey lightly tugged on Darkfire's makeshift bridle, the station master briefly grabbed his shoulder. "While you are on the island, boy, you should think about planting your rocks. They might grow into gold trees there." Lowering his voice more, he whispered, "Their wool is like no other. Their dyes are made from grasses and flowers." His eyebrows rose pointedly. "They make crimson red fabric from roses, purple from dogweed and violets. With that magical ability, gold should sprout like a seed."

Laughing, Jeffrey brushed past the man. "No one'll stop you throwing all your money into a hole near the island's station. If gold-colored trees grow, you'll know first."

With that, he led his companions up a plank into a straw-filled car with one post to which to tie a beast. The sliding door was hauled shut and latched from without.

Only once the rumble of the train had started did Evan breathe evenly. Two small doors, too tiny for Darkfire, led fore and aft from either side of the car. Their only escape was the main door, now sealed from the outside, but at least they had a little more time to plan.

As soon as the train began to sway beneath them, Jeffrey examined both little doors. "No locks. The knights could come in at any moment."

Darkfire nodded wearily.

Studying the Evfelian, Evan wondered, "Is 'Gombe' actually your last name?"

"To the best of anyone's knowledge."

Unable to control the mistrust he felt, the prince spoke. "Then why did you give it?"

Jeffrey's guarded eyes fixed on him. "They're Anskonian knights." Evan continued to stare holes through him, and the Evfelian sighed. "Will they have heard my name? Most likely. Evfel knows I escaped their kingdom. They also sent troops to search the Calmar Mountains while I hid there. But Ansky will be less concerned about an Evfelian criminal. They maintain loyalty only to a degree, seeking ever the independence of their own home. Some might even *congratulate* a rogue—as long as he's Evfelian.

"Besides, their knowledge of me would give our story credibility like nothing else. Only a criminal would risk the dangers of the island."

"You were gambling, then."

With a wry smile, the criminal reminded him, "I said I took many risks before jumping off the cliff face. I was known as 'The Fox,' Evan. Risks are natural to me."

Sighing, Evan pulled out the string holding his bangs back. The tension was giving him a headache. He could feel the Evfelian watching him as he shook his hair out and freed Darkfire from the camouflage of his sack and rope bridle. He ran his fingers sadly along the stallion's cropped mane.

"You may wish to remain as disguised as possible until we reach the island," Jeffrey muttered.

Evan paid him little attention. A light had gone out in Darkfire's gaze, and his head was hanging. He had subjected himself to torture. Although his expression and silence were in part due to sheer exhaustion, there would be no rest for his wild heart while he wore ropes.

Jeffrey did not push his argument. "Evan," he asked instead, "when you're king, what'll you do if Evfel marches to war?"

Slowly, the prince turned to face his human companion. "What are you asking?"

Instead of answering directly, Jeffrey lowered his gaze, uncharacteristically playing with the hem of his tunic. "My parents died in a fire when I was an infant. Afterward, our neighbors sent me to the orphanage in Evfel—meaning the king's workhouse. The orphans live, sleep and eat there, but they're worked hard, whether boy or girl, young or old. They sew, carve, weave or do any number of worse jobs. Even the three-year-olds can write in excellent hands, though they may not understand a word of it. All the orphans' work is taken to the castle, along with any money they earn.

"When I was five, they forced me to sweep chimneys. At six, I was too broad-shouldered, so I started weaving. I spent only a year doing that before running away, ready to take any job offered to me as long as I was treated fairly. Well, I found a job, working with cows alongside an older boy—until he burned down the barn, killing the cows."

Anger lit the Evfelian's face. "And somehow, I was blamed for it. The town complained to the king, and he had me arrested. Wilber condemned me to death without one shred of proof."

Jeffrey grew silent for a while. His anger seemed to dissipate as his gaze lowered. "The real culprit came to help me escape my holding in Tier Castle, although the coward never admitted his wrongdoing. I guess I ought to be grateful, but I had to hide and run for two years because of him—two years I wish I could burn from my memory. I became a thief and a double-dealer. I cheated families out of their food, led my pursuers to their deaths."

Jeffrey fell silent once more, then his eyes finally focused on the prince. "Wilber cannot stay king, Evan. Remember that. Should you leave him his throne in Evfel, he will destroy Ansky."

"No!"

"Evan," Jeffrey persisted, stepping closer and lowering his voice, "why do you think Lisya wouldn't shelter you under her roof?"

"I chose not to shelter there."

"Think, Evan. Her first question was if you intended to allow the Evfelian king to take Ansky."

Not meeting that burning gaze, Evan replied, "I have something I must do, and it cannot be done if I just go into hiding. We both know that. But that has nothing to do with Evfel's throne."

Sighing, Jeffrey backed away slightly. "Is that so, think you?" His highborn speech patterns had returned, a sure sign he had put a wall between them. "I asked Lisya why you would not stay in the Ice Woods. I asked her if you were fated to deliver the oppressed."

Despite the slow, constant shaking of the prince's head, the Evfelian pushed forward. "She refused to tell me anything she knows, but she said you alone can collapse Evfel's foundations beneath its feet. It has been a sewer of filth and putrescence for too long now. Will you stand aside when you alone can help?"

"How would acting like my uncle help anyone? That is why he wants me dead—because he is a thief, not because he foresees some terrible, absurd fate you wish to be a reality. Is this the real reason you agreed to come? For revenge?"

Evan's last angry words echoed within the wooden boxcar.

When the reverberations died away, Jeffrey sighed. "No. I would do anything for Lisya. She rescued me in more ways than one, and she asked if I would volunteer for this. But it is true. I do crave the destruction of Evfel. I crave the liberation of the persecuted, now that I have learned to care. Can you honestly, guiltlessly, withhold from them the chance you have been granted? Lisya painted a different picture of you."

The prince released his breath. "I would become a thief, Jeffrey. Moreover, the bloodshed and pain would liberate no one."

"I know ways to do it without your presence—"

"Jeffrey!" Evan interrupted. "While you might come from a background that makes this almost impossible to understand, you must trust me when I say, my becoming a thief will liberate no one. They might have no idea I acted through skulduggery. They might not realize I did anything but pull them out of oppression. But the secret would slip. Anyway, the fear of discovery in itself creates death."

"Very well," the Evfelian whispered. "We will find a way to open an exit large enough for Darkfire in the morning. For now, rest. We all need it."

As the train lurched forward, Radnor grabbed for the nearest handhold.

Quincy laughed, drawing a glare from the older knight. "This thing does not move naturally. But of course. One can hardly expect anything natural to travel to that island."

"Except for us." Pressing his fingers into his forehead, Radnor settled on the coach's right-hand bench, which doubled as a bed. "Notice Wilber only sent Anskonian knights on this cursed journey.

If he thought no one would think twice about endangering Ansky's knights over Evfel's, he guessed wrong."

Quincy rubbed his mustache, absently listening to the murmur of the knights' voices from the other side of the coach's divider. Radnor was right, of course. Wilber obviously preferred to risk Ansky's forces rather than his own. But considering they were sharing a voyage with an Evfelian criminal, perhaps that was providence itself. Jeffrey Gombe might be more willing to work with them than with his own kind—and when chasing a thief, a criminal could be very handy.

"What did you think of Jeffrey Gombe's companions?" he asked at last.

It took a second for Radnor to respond. Running his thumbs together, he shrugged. "That depends on when you ask me. The horse drew my gaze immediately. Its fine lines were bred for a noble, its strength for a charger, not a pack animal. Indeed, it looked like the one our prince ran away with. Yet the more I examined it, the less I thought so. The beast Wilber hopes to make his own has a..."

In the ensuing silence, Quincy nodded in understanding. "If ever a horse could think, it would be that one—but with thoughts of the darkest kind. Murder and hatred, power... revenge, even. Then Prince Maxwell runs his fingers along its nose and a different horse emerges. The power never leaves, though."

"Right. Gombe's horse was as dull and unengaged as any pack animal. No horse could act out such a change, no matter how intelligent."

"That is an interesting thought. Unnerving, actually." Lowering himself onto the opposite bench, the younger knight rubbed his thighs in agitated contemplation. "I was struck more by the boy, uh, William, was it?"

"I believe it was Matthew."

"Matthew, then. He appeared no older than twelve, shy, inexperienced, soft-spoken. His eyes looked so round and big for his face. Never could our prince appear so naturally innocent, with none of his arrogant authority, and yet... the eye color, the build..."

Quincy flicked his fingers upward dismissively. "Oh, what logic is there in thinking a criminal aligned with a prince? For goodness' sake, such a pact could sign a warrant for Gombe's hanging within a year. The Fox of Evfel is surely too clever not to know that."

He was quiet in contemplation only for a moment. "Logic aside, I think we should arrest Jeffrey Gombe tonight, when we might catch him least prepared before he decides to escape somehow. Logic suggests our prince ran into the mountains. Therefore, since the Evfelian is familiar with that region, he is our best guide."

Radnor's eyebrows rose. "I think he will be more willing to aid us if we refrain from immediately arresting him. We can use that as extra pressure, but we want to appear understanding of his plight. He strikes me as too stubborn a man to bow to a request from an outright enemy. However, we will be able to scrutinize his companions more thoroughly while they sleep."

"What if they are awake?"

Radnor shrugged. "Maybe that will help all the more, as long as we are not heard or spotted. If they are talking together and the boy is indeed Evan Maxwell, we will recognize his voice. If not, then that is not our prince, and we can wait for sunrise to press our request on Gombe. Either way, they have no escape until we reach the island."

Evan did not sleep long before a hand pressing over his mouth caused him to jerk awake. Jeffrey crouched next to him, a finger on his lips. A few paces away stood Darkfire, ears pricked and head erect.

The prince did not need to ask what they feared. The small door leading fore was inching open. Instantly, Jeffrey shifted. "Matthew," he moaned, as if just waking. The door halted. "What're you doing? Stop creaking and sleep."

Instead of waiting for Evan to speak, Jeffrey immediately replied to his own complaint—but in a voice abruptly changed. "I have not budged." This new voice, this protest coming from Jeffrey's throat, was younger, higher than a mature male's. Perhaps a little too young. It sounded like Malachi's voice, a sound the Evfelian should not have been capable of producing. And yet, he was. "Jeffrey," the youthful, shy voice continued. "Most people are afraid of the island. Does anyone know the real story behind it?"

Opposite them, the door closed. Jeffrey, once more in his natural voice, exhaled in exasperation. "Are you not going to sleep?" He paused. Presumably his imaginary companion shook his head.

Then Jeffrey nodded. "Lisya told me it was once the northern tip of Elcan, the peak of Mount Jade. There was a valley that separated it from the Calmar Mountains. At some point, the valley disappeared beneath the ocean. Now it is a channel between the island and Elcan. Lisya is the only one alive who could tell you the details, although there is much she never says. Still, I asked her..."

Trailing off, Jeffrey glanced over at Darkfire. "They left," the stallion said, in response to the silent question, "when you first mentioned Mount Jade."

Evan's attempt to speak came out as a shocked wheeze.

"How much of that was invented?" Darkfire wondered in the prince's silence.

"Nothing about the island." A wicked smile highlighted the Evfelian's even teeth. "He, or they, might have learned something if they stayed."

"What trick is that?" Evan managed at last to ask.

For a long moment, Jeffrey remained silent, lying back in the hay to stare up at the roof. Then, he answered, "It is a trick we orphans used back in Evfel, both for fun and to escape trouble by using another's voice to blame whomever we pleased. It came to be extremely handy while on the run."

Challengingly, the Evfelian turned to Evan.

Perhaps he was waiting for a rebuke of his use of scapegoats. Instead, the prince pushed himself to his knees and placed a hand briefly on the former criminal's arm. As odd as his gesture felt, he knew it was the right one. Jeffrey's shoulders relaxed with a soundless exhale.

"Rest some more, Evan. Darkfire and I can keep watch."

"I think we need to open the sliding doors now instead of waiting for tomorrow," the prince countered. "If they do come in, we need an exit."

"Indeed, but it might take more strength than any of us currently possess. Once we rest and eat some breakfast, we can attack that door. Somehow."

"I may be able to open it with a good solid kick," Darkfire commented. "I doubt your blade will fit through the crack. Even if it could, you will undoubtedly lack the leverage needed to shift or cut through the crossbeam they slid into place to secure the door."

Evan slid his bottom lip through his teeth. "Will a good solid kick cause the train to sway?"

"Tomorrow!" Jeffrey ordered. "We will keep watch. You can't listen while sleeping, so leave it to those of us who rest lightly."

Curling up against Darkfire, Evan relented with a sigh. In all likelihood, the Evfelian was right. The prince was mostly asleep by the time he felt the stallion's soft nose brush across the top of his head.

Morning light streamed through the thin strips between the boxcar's slats when Evan woke to the swaying bounce of the floor beneath him. Stretching, he looked about. Only Darkfire was there, just uncurling from his position of rest. "Where's Jeffrey?" the prince asked.

"He went to discover what he can of the other passengers. Once he returns, we will work on the door. In the meantime, have some breakfast."

The stallion prodded Lisya's sack toward him, and Evan resignedly accepted it. "I can care for myself, you know."

Darkfire smiled as only he could, remaining silent. In companionable quiet, they ate a small breakfast. After a while, Evan asked, "Do you think it would be better if we opened the door and jumped? We could follow the train tracks ourselves, without the need for them to take us there."

The stallion shook his head in defeat. "It would take forever to reach the island on foot, during which time, the people of Summos Valley would travel there and back several times. Someone on the train would spot us and possibly take word back to your uncle. Soon, a force would follow. If Wilber had the help of the valley, we could never outrun them."

Ripping his bread into shreds, the prince nodded. "I guess so. Our sudden absence alone will probably be all the proof the knights need, anyway. With our hunters so close, though, and with nowhere to disappear..." He shook his head.

"Ah, how the hunted animal quakes," Darkfire muttered. Snorting, Evan chucked a handful of hay at him.

"So, our escaped convict and murderer has shown up where escape is well-nigh impossible." Quincy and three of his knights had surrounded Jeffrey Gombe, whom they'd found leaning on a railing between two coaches. "Not only that, but he has the audacity to tell us his name from the start. What say you to that, my young cockerel?"

Looking heavenward, the criminal said, "So even Ansky has heard of me."

"You likely knew that beforehand," Quincy growled. "We have every reason to hang you as soon as we reach the island."

Turning around with a cocky smile and leaning the back of his elbows on the rail, the criminal replied, "We are both enemies of the Evfelian king. Why would you kill an ally?"

"For sure, you are a rogue," Radnor whistled. "We are not currently enemies of King Wilber."

"Oh, so you yield to him as your liege lord?"

The oldest knight huffed. "Absolutely not. Currently, however, we have a prince to catch. Is it your arrogance that caused you to flaunt your name?"

Jeffrey Gombe shrugged. "You owe no allegiance to Wilber."

Laughing, Quincy shook his head. "Your confidence is something else, young man." Receiving in response only the twitch of a cocky smile, he pressed on. "What makes you so sure we will leave you and your companion to disappear on the island?"

"You've more important matters on your minds," the criminal remarked carelessly, studying his travel-dirty fingernails.

At a nod from Quincy, one of the knights seized the criminal, shoved him around, and yanked his arms behind his back.

"Can you be certain of that?" Quincy asked, resting against the railing over which their victim was now pressed. There was no answer, though Gombe's face had paled somewhat under its smirk. "At the moment, I am very interested in you. We are all Anskonians here—aside from you. If there is one thing we all appreciate, it is a cocky, smart outlaw. Perhaps it would be beneath us to hang you for your crimes. After all, we are born by descent to be cocky, smart outlaws against the might of Evfel."

He leaned closer to his captive's face, lowering his voice. "However, hang you, I will. Unless... I understand that you spent some time living in the mountains. Help us search them to find Prince Maxwell, and I will let you live."

Chapter 8

Over the Cliff

JEFFREY'S PALE BLUE EYES flickered in delight, but he made no reply. As the knight holding him shoved him harder into the rail, however, he winced.

"What say you, Jeffrey Gombe?" Quincy pressed. "The prince has likely hidden in one of the mountain villages. You are an outlaw—more importantly, an outlaw who lived in the mountains for some time. You know the land, perhaps even the people living in the mountain villages of Ansky, such as Woodell. Certainly, you could be a massive aid in locating our prince. In exchange for your assistance, we offer you your life and Ansky's protection."

"What a tempting offer," the captive breathlessly mocked.

"Refuse, and we will bind you now for execution later. You will, of course, have meager comfort in our coach, with good food and actual beds for the rest of the journey. Although you will probably enjoy it little, since it will be the last few days of your life. Do not think there will be any escape from Ansky. We are not going to let you out of our sight from here on."

The criminal laughed, pushing himself upright. "I might be more willing to agree if not for a large flaw in your plan." At Quincy's blank stare, he continued, "You choose to hunt down Ansky's future king, if I have heard right. By closest blood, that will make the Evfel prince rightful heir to the throne. What Ansky shall there then be in the future to protect me, or even you?"

Quincy's face darkened. "Evan Maxwell has shown all the disdain of Evfelian royalty. If the Maxwells and Dalacorts wish to fall out, let them. If neither of them prove our type of ruler, there will be time to dethrone whoever survives the battle later. Meanwhile, if some of us gain favor for our services to the more virtuous, all the better. We must appear faithful until that time. So what say you?"

"I have an alternate deal for you... if you will allow me to turn around and speak to you as a gentleman."

Quincy hesitated for a moment. Then he nodded. As the others formed a tighter circle around the knight holding the captive, he released his hold.

Turning, with head held high and a smug smile on his face, the criminal made his offer. "After you reach the island, send word that the last you saw him, Prince Maxwell was on this train, but that he took flight and could be anywhere in this part of the Calmar Mountains. Press upon the king how much organization and skill you need to find him. Then, when the king turns up on the shores of the island, ambush him—with the aid of the islanders, if you must. They will gladly murder any king, it is said.

"When Wilber lies dead, you can support the crowning of your prince and assist him in his certain attack against Evfel. Once Queen Lorene and her son are disposed of, you may do what you like with your monarchy. Entirely overthrow it. Set up a new line for all I care. I will back you and work with you for as long as it takes to ensure the ruination of Evfel if you follow my suggestion. In fact, you may even use me as a scapegoat for all the treachery, so long as you make sure I'm never found. Now, what say you?"

Shutting his gaping mouth, Quincy exclaimed, "That is out of the question. We intend an open attack against Evfel only when the time comes." He stopped, noticing Radnor's up-flung palm.

"You seem to misunderstand our intentions when it comes to Prince Maxwell," Radnor said. "We are not here to betray him, only to force him to act with some sort of justice. Should he refuse to carry out any honorable action, we realize Wilber will finish him off, using the claims of war as a pretext. That appears likely as things stand now.

"When and if Andrew then becomes our king, should it be necessary for Ansky to revolt, we will. But that is not what you offer. You would ask us to throw away all honor for our cause of freedom."

"Oh, is that so?" the criminal asked indifferently. "You can justify mutiny against Andrew Dalacort through a long war with Evfel, and you can justify standing back and allowing your king's murder through faithful service to Ansky, but you cannot twist honor just a little more to justify my offer for your country's freedom? I see. Evfel is a den of thieves, sirs. Attempt to deal with it, and you shall find no honor. But play your game. Perhaps it shall take you far."

"Then you accept our offer?"

"If you give me until the last day of this trip, I will think about it. Currently, I have nowhere to go, but you forget I am from Arieh, the capital of Evfel. There, we crave the downfall of the kingdom's ruling class. Give me a concrete plan that achieves our greatest wish, and I shall very quickly apply myself to it. Good day." With a mocking nod, he shoved his way through the knights, who allowed his departure after another signal from their leader.

"Very well then, Jeffrey Gombe," Quincy muttered. "We shall give you a few more days, but we will be watching." He turned to the knights. "We did make sure to bring the crossbows, did we not?"

At their nod, he ordered, "Good. If ever anything jumps over the side of the train, shoot it. Wound it, if you can. And signal to those near the back engine to do the same. I want to give him one more chance to change his answer before the rope tightens around his neck."

"Evan," Jeffrey gasped as he slammed the door shut.

Noting the lines of concern across the Evfelian's face, the prince stood. "Let me guess," he growled. "Your gamble turned into a dagger sliding between your ribs?"

For a second, Jeffrey stared at him. "How do you know?"

Throwing his hands in the air, Evan turned back to his breakfast. "Would calm, collected Jeffrey Gombe flinch if there were *fifty* knights from Ansky? I think not. Yet here you stand, pale and trembling. Something must have gone wrong."

The older male sighed. "I have until the dawn of our arrival on the island to agree to help them hunt for you. If I still refuse, then…"

Raising his eyebrows, the prince glanced over his shoulder at the Evfelian. "What would prevent The Fox from lying?"

Jeffrey deflated like a punched ball of risen dough. "At one time, I would have been foolish enough to do so, but I know they will hold me to my word. They will chain me to them while I lead them around the mountains and slit my throat when they have finished with me. And if I lied… You may not think much of my honor, but I do have some."

Closing his eyes, Evan took a slow breath before turning back. "Even if you have sunk us, Jeffrey, I will continue to protect you in any way I am able. If I thought revealing myself at the last minute would spare you, I would. But I suspect it would instead mean certain death for you."

Oddly, the Evfelian only stared at the floor. "I know you would… That is why I must confess trying to force Ansky's hand against Evfel."

It was hardly amusing, but it was so like Jeffrey. Burying his face in his hand, Evan felt his shoulders shaking in silent laughter as he shook his head.

"Evan." A note of exasperation entered the Evfelian's voice. "We should try opening that door now. There appears to be no other action we can take at the moment. There are only six or seven knights, but I have no desire to see more of them."

"How do you suggest we do it?" the prince asked.

Stepping forward, the stallion spoke. "I still think I ought to kick it."

Jeffrey nodded. "I also think that is best. Evan, come stand on the far side with me. If Darkfire's kick unbalances the train, maybe our weight will prevent it from derailing. The cars are not linked tightly enough to cause one car's shaking to affect the others."

As the stallion approached the large sliding doors, the humans hurried to the opposite side, resting their backs against the wall. After two powerful kicks, they heard a sharp crack and the car lurched.

Then its motion smoothed again. With a determined yank, they pulled the doors apart and the broken crossbeam fell away, welcoming them with the wonderful sight of open sky shining off the bare, flat-topped peaks over which the train ran.

"The plateaus of the Calmar Mountains," Jeffrey whispered. "If we must jump in the end, we will be running far away from the grassy valley of Ansky."

His *far away* was doubly meant, though he might not have known it. They had entered places completely alien to Ansky, wild to all. For hundreds of years before the tracks were built, no human had touched the plateaus. Yet that unknown was hardly the worst they would face. They were headed toward the origin of all Ansky's darkest fears—willingly so. The island and its forces had caused the plateaus' desertion so long ago.

Over the next four days, the journey was smooth. Jeffrey spied on the knights while Evan stayed with Darkfire, watching the landscape roll by through the crack they had left between the sliding doors: tan plateaus, green valleys and shimmering waterways.

"I doubt Summos Valley cares about this beauty," the prince commented as he and the stallion sat next to the doors, looking out through the crack, evening light bathing everything in purples and golds. The train now traveled along a steep cliff. Far below, the ocean waves crashed against the mountain. "This view is a treasure."

Lifting his nose to the cold breeze, Darkfire said, "If they did care, you can be sure they would build towns in the valleys." He paused. "Considering their fear of the island and its dragons, however, the wildness of this place may have nothing to do with whether they appreciate the view."

Grimacing, Evan said nothing more.

They resumed their silent study of the sky and terrain until Darkfire huffed, "What happened with your family, anyway?"

The prince looked up in question. "They died of the plague. Have I not told you?"

Darkfire shook his head, his short mane rippling in the movement. "I mean how is it that Wilber was ever allowed to marry into your family? Why is Lorene so blind to his true nature and... what happened during the plague? How did it kill your parents and brother at the same time?"

Evan took a slow breath, and the stallion turned away. "You have no obligation to answer if it is too painful. I just wondered."

"Only parts are painful," the prince whispered. For a minute, he pushed the hay around with his feet without further comment. Then he relented. "My grandparents thought that the marriage between their daughter, Lorene, and the young king of Evfel would strengthen the goodwill enforced through the Sanguinea Peace Treaty. That part is written in our history. But then, there is the rest."

"What is that, if I may ask?"

"From what I gather, my father never liked Wilber. He tried to convince his sister to refuse the political arrangement, but she had already become smitten with her intended somehow. She disregarded her brother's concerns and willfully married. In return, he disowned her, a choice made easy by the distance between Evfel and Ansky.

"I think he eventually sent an apology, but it was too late. The plague came too fast for them to ever meet again. Sometimes, I think my aunt feels guilty for not acting sooner instead of waiting for him to forgive her, but if so, she never allows that guilt to tint her adoration for her husband."

He fell silent, in bitter thought. Beside him, Darkfire lowered himself to the floor. After a moment, the stallion asked, "May I inquire about the plague? Do you remember any of it?"

Staring into those wide-set eyes, so horse-like and also so unlike any eyes known to man, Evan remained silent. The honest question, even without his answer, brought flashes of colors, laughter and deep fear up from behind sealed doors. The last thing he wanted was to speak of those fading memories. But in truth, they were only fading in clarity of recall, not in the pain they left behind.

Sighing, the prince submitted. "I was only four. Alexander would have remembered more since he was twice my age, but I will tell the facts instead of my fragments of memory.

"My mother was the only child of Ansky's physician. He had taught her secrets to medicine no one else had ever known. In the crisis, she felt duty-bound to teach others her secrets since her father was no longer living. Although she could not be away from her three-month-old twins for long, she left to do so.

"Unintentionally, she brought the sickness back to the castle. Alexander and I went to see her the morning we heard she had returned. She was...."

Evan stopped himself, unable to put words to the hazy memory of the ashen, sweaty, murmuring woman that had resembled his mother as a ghost might their living counterparts. Instead, he said, "I had stopped in the doorway at the sight of her, but Alexander tried to wake her. Father returned that minute. I guess he had woken to her fever and gone to find a physician, but he paled at sight of us and shouted at us to leave."

For a minute, the prince stumbled. "That was the last I saw of either of them. And Alexander... No one thought anything of his fever on the day of his coronation. He had been so nervous about becoming king at eight years of age, but then he collapsed...."

That part was as far as Evan's self-control could take him. He could go no further. "Why could I have not caught it, Darkfire? Why was it everyone else?"

In response to his misery, Darkfire nuzzled his shoulder, but Evan knew there was nothing to say anyway. There was no answer any mortal could give.

"But what about the twins?" the stallion finally asked.

"They never made it through the winter... They just refused another mother." Evan shrugged. "Other milk—"

The soft click of a door caused them to look up as Jeffrey wearily joined them. With each passing day, he appeared paler. Noting his new lines of concern, Evan placed a hand on his shoulder, shutting his own pains deep inside again.

Smiling slightly, the Evfelian removed the prince's comforting hand. "The knights are becoming restless. There is more talk about you."

"Naturally," Evan muttered.

"No, I mean, they doubt that you two are Matthew and a pack-horse. The voice I gave you soothed them for a while, but we may have to leap tonight, despite the risks. If we wait, I fear they will catch us for certain."

As Jeffrey rubbed his forehead, the prince asked, "What means of escape do you think is best?"

The Evfelian's gaze shifted from Evan to Darkfire and back. "Do you trust me?"

"No," the stallion answered, even as the prince nodded.

Meeting Darkfire's expression, Jeffrey laughed. "With Evan's life or yours, Darkfire? I lived in the woods before you were born. In fact, you have no choice but to trust me with *your* life. I helped Lisya rescue you from your mother's womb."

The stallion raised his head in mock challenge, impishness dancing in his eyes.

Shaking his own head, the Evfelian gravely replied, "The knights need to be preoccupied when we jump. If they catch us spying outside their door and recognize you, they will chase us when we leave. That will only give us a few moments respite from their readiness, but God willing, that will be enough for us to escape in the chaos. It's the best distraction I can think of."

Both Evan and Darkfire were momentarily silent. Then, the stallion puffed as the prince asked, "Would it not be wiser to hold them off at the door?" He nodded at the small entrance facing fore. "Only one can come through there at a time. If your skills with a blade are not sufficient, mine will hold them."

"Their shouts will alert the knights in the back," the Evfelian warned. "We would be attacked from both sides, and we only have my knife between us." He inhaled like someone preparing for a jump, then said, "I think the only way to beat them back here is by going over the coach roofs."

"What?" stallion and prince asked as one.

"We are going to race them over the roofs?" Evan added. "On a speeding, swaying train?"

Smiling, Jeffrey asked, "How do you think I have been watching and listening to them without their knowledge?"

Faced with their continued protest, Jeffrey held up his hands. "I asked if you trusted me. This is why. There is no time when they *all* sleep. Their crossbows are always pointed at us. Should we jump, no matter when, they will be ready.

"We must lower their ability to aim well, if not trick them into leaving their crossbows behind. That means I need you. With you standing before them, they may grow excited and sloppy. No doubt they will grab us, but we can wrest ourselves free. I have done so many times before. But in the brief struggle, they will already have cut off our exit. The only escape will be over the roofs. And while they will need to pause to open each door, we will not have to stop as we run toward the rear of the train."

When Evan continued to stare in shock, Jeffrey added, "I was willing to trust you and to jump off a cliff face. Will you not give me at least that much?"

Yielding, the prince nodded. "Very well, Fox, I accept your gamble. God be with me if I fall."

"He'll prevent you from falling."

Evan's sole response was a long look of doubt.

"There were many reasons I decided the boy was not Prince Maxwell," Quincy's voice carried to them through the closed door of the coach. Outside it, Evan and Jeffrey were crouching in the night's darkness, wind whipping over them. "Most importantly, the voice was completely wrong. And yet, our criminal's reluctance is peculiar.

"What does it all mean?" Quincy continued. "No one has tried to jump, but it seems our Evfelian is just stalling."

"Of course," another voice spoke up. "*He* has no intention of aiding Ansky unless it suits his personal goal."

"I think we should just arrest him now," Radnor huffed.

"And break our word?" It was Quincy's voice again. "No, he is as good as a captive. I will give him the extra day. He can waste his time trying to think of an escape. We have cut off every avenue."

The train shifted around a curve, allowing moonlight to stream into the space between the two coaches. Jeffrey's face followed the moon, waiting as if he knew the light signaled something. Not daring to ask questions, Evan shivered.

Inside, the knights' voices paused, causing the prince to stiffen. After a moment, though, they resumed, soon joined by the soft pad of purposely light feet approaching the door against which the eavesdroppers were leaning.

Shifting, Jeffrey put himself between the door and his companion. Seconds later, it flew open to reveal one of Quincy's men.

The knight's gaze fixed on Evan. "I saw a shadow beneath the door—and, lo, it is our prince!"

"Run!" Jeffrey ordered as the knight caught him.

Obediently, the prince leaped up the ladder that led to the roof of the car. Below him followed a ripping sound, a scuffle and then a scream. Someone had fallen from the train.

Evan dared not look, instead hauling himself onto the sickeningly swaying roof. Footsteps and shouts echoed below.

Just as he gained his feet, Jeffrey joined him. "Jump!" Without even reaching the first roof, the Evfelian leapt from the top of the ladder to that of the following car. Below, the feet of their pursuers clanked against the rungs they'd climbed up a moment before. Evan took five preparatory steps back. Just as Radnor's head poked up above the roof, the prince ran and leapt over the knight.

A hand seized his ankle, even as Jeffrey grabbed his elbow. Thankfully, the grasp on his ankle slipped. The prince banged onto the edge of the new roof with a wince.

"Keep running," Jeffrey gasped, hauling his charge to his feet and giving him a light shove. "Four more! The train helps the jump!"

Shouts followed from below. A door had already slammed. Taking another breath, Evan nodded and raced forward. The train's movement nearly slid the new roof into the space below him. Meanwhile, feet pounded under them. Doors banged.

At the last car, Jeffrey grabbed the ladder and slid down, landing with a thud. Evan did the same. He dashed through the door into the boxcar, where the stallion waited.

"Darkfire! Jump!"

Slamming the door and bracing it with his shoulder, the prince ordered, "Toss me your knife! I will hold the door for now."

Jeffrey shook his head, striding back toward the fore-facing opening as the stallion bounded out the boarding doors. "You're going first."

There was no time to argue. The door of the boxcar before theirs thudded. Running to the opening, Evan checked for Darkfire and found him miraculously keeping pace with the train. The prince jumped. With a painful thump, he landed on the stallion's spine. Scooting forward, he made room and called, "Jeffrey! Now!"

As the Evfelian landed behind him, Darkfire broke from beside the rails. Unfortunately, they were now facing the steep drop where the mountain descended toward the ocean. The boxcars temporarily blocked their escape onto the open plateaus.

Muscles bunching, the stallion pivoted to run in the opposite direction of the train. His riders leaned deeply forward.

Though the stallion flew, a dark feathered arrow landed at his feet. Clearly, the archers in the back were ready. Over the salty wind lashing their faces, the twang of their arrows was inaudible. Abruptly, Jeffrey gasped in pain. His grip around the prince's middle loosened.

The prince grabbed the Evfelian's arm with one hand. Glancing over his shoulder, he saw the feathers of an arrow shaft jutting at an odd angle from his companion's back.

The last engine passed, clearing their escape—but as it did, Darkfire reared in torment. Evan's fingers slipped. And all three plunged off the cliff.

Chapter 9

The Enchantress

WATER CLOSED OVERHEAD. Thrashing, Evan tried to surface. Hooves churned the current above him. He began to rise, then something grabbed his collar, hauling him closer to shore.

As soon as his feet touched the sand beneath the waves, he tried to use his own strength. A burning pain in his arm weakened him. His head spun. The undertow pulled at him, and he was grateful for the force that tugged him farther ashore. There, Darkfire—for it was the stallion that had hauled him to land—released him and turned back to the depths.

Crawling to the safety of the damp shoreline, the prince choked and coughed up more saltwater. After a moment, Darkfire returned with Jeffrey. A shaft protruded from the stallion's shoulder, but Jeffrey looked closer to death, and Evan dragged himself over to him.

His weak, futile probing caused Jeffrey to stir slightly with a frail, raspy moan. "Leave it. There's nothing you can do."

The garbled words gradually penetrated the prince through the gathering darkness inside him. "No, Jeff—"

"Evan..." The hoarse whisper cut off his protest. Struggling with the words, the Evfelian finally mumbled, "Become king. Finish Wilber for m..."

Evan heard no more, if more was said. He had lost the battle for consciousness. As darkness took him, he thought he saw a large glowing bird circle and swoop toward them.

After weeks of shearing, washing and detangling, four large baskets stood ready for Matalaide. "Charlotte," Talliaha said as the maiden bent to pick up one of them, "will you leave half of one here? It's nice to have some for my own use."

Without reply, Charlotte found a smaller basket to fill. Barely had she turned around before Raymond entered through the open doorway. Gritting her teeth, she continued with her task, wishing that a door left standing open could mean something on the island other than "the homeowners are admitting visitors." Not that it would change anything in this case.

As he bent to heft one of the baskets, however, she snapped, "Most of the work is done. You may return to your butchery."

Ignoring the slur on his occupation as the local hunter, Raymond lifted the basket. "I'm helping."

Meeting her mother's sad gaze, Charlotte sighed. "You've been helping for days. Matalaide's home is only two minutes away. If I must take several trips, that's nothing."

With a small smile and a nod, he walked out the door with two full baskets.

"Charlotte," her mother whispered.

Seizing the remaining basket and a half, the maiden fled. "I don't need his help!" And yet, following ten feet behind the man, she bitterly admitted to herself it was much easier carrying two apiece than all four.

Matalaide lived in what was considered the nicer section of the village, the last rise before the shore. The first line of huts provided a clear view of the ocean and Alleluia Lake. Not only that... Far from both bodies of water, the homes on the rise had wooden floors, unlike those right on the lake, which were even now mucked with water.

A happy bleat rose from the pasture beside Matalaide's home. The fencing around this half-acre field had been built by their friend Lazarus for the sheep when Bozzic and Talliaha first moved their flock off the mountain. After the recent shearing, the enclosure was filled with the animals.

"Don't worry," Raymond said as he passed by. "Your shepherdess will bring you back to the mountain soon enough."

Charlotte's heart beat faster at his words—words of freedom.

"Oh, you're here." The weaver sighed in relief as the shepherdess entered her home. "Can you do me a small favor?"

Placing the baskets next to the others, Charlotte nodded. "Whatever you need."

"Humph," Matalaide muttered, crossing her arms. "Obviously not whatever I need. I need the shepherd family line to continue." Leveling a finger toward the maiden, she lowered her voice. "Now, I was watching you and Raymond in Larry's pasture as you sheared all—"

"What do you need done, Matalaide?"

Sighing, the weaver crooked a finger, beckoning Charlotte closer. "The train will be in shortly. Will you take one of the baskets up there and trade it for..." She paused before lowering her voice further. "I need a bolt of blue silk. Or any silk. I will dye it if I must."

"A whole bolt? Of silk? What's wrong with our wool? It's the softest in all Elcan. Don't tell me someone's put on airs and asked for a silk wedding gown."

"Believe me, girl. I would say the same thing as you if someone asked for such extravagance." Again, the weaver paused. Then she admitted, "I had a dream, a very real dream. I've never had its equal, and now I need silk. It has something to do with Lisya."

For a long moment, Charlotte stared at the elderly lady. "To my knowledge, Lisya doesn't send people messages in their dreams."

"No, no. The *silk* has something to do with the enchantress, not the dream."

"Alright," the maiden sighed. "I'll find some for you. If I didn't know better, though, I'd think you'd had a bit too much to drink."

"I'll go with you," Raymond quickly volunteered. Although Charlotte cast him a scornful glance, she kept quiet. If this was a trick of the weaver's to force them together, this would be the last favor she ever granted.

The train was just pulling in when Raymond and Charlotte arrived at the large track loop, in the middle of which Summos Valley regularly assembled their market. Islanders from other villages were also arriving or milling about with baskets, waiting.

One of the boxcar doors was already yawning wide. As a shudder journeyed along Charlotte's spine, she whispered, "Something is wrong."

Raymond leaned closer. "Is the grass still black on Castle Mound?"

"Yes. It has begun to look like there are regular campfires up there."

Raymond touched her arm, but she flinched away. "Don't think too much of that door. Perhaps something really heavy fell out when they rounded a corn—" He broke off as six men with swords jumped out one of the coaches. Another man, similarly dressed, could be still seen standing on the rear platform.

While all the other islanders retreated and dispersed, Raymond stepped protectively in front of Charlotte. "Why are you here?" he asked the men, clearly paying no heed to the low snarl at his back.

No one answered, but Charlotte heard the oldest of the men speaking to the engineer in the clear, occasionally sharp diction of Elcan. "You cannot wait a day for market. One of our knights must return immediately to Ansky."

"You have no authority over us," the engineer retorted. "We need to make this trip profitable. A trip here just for your benefit is hardly a profit. You already cost us pay thanks to that devilry two nights ago."

"We can make it profitable if you fulfill our request." The man pulled something from a pouch at his waist. As his fingers touched it, warmth seeped up Charlotte's back. She gasped as the armed man whispered, "Here is all the gold that young man had. Grant us this boon, and it belongs to the valley."

At the maiden's sharp inhale, Raymond turned to her, a question in his furrowed brow. "That gold isn't real," she answered, nodding toward the exchange.

"You mean they're cheating Summos Valley?"

"No. I mean..." Pausing, Charlotte tried sorting through the warm sensations. "It's not from this world. It might be real somewhere else, but it's not our gold."

"What?"

Charlotte had no answer. Shaking her head, she approached, knowing by the greed on the engineer's face that anything these men asked would be given. "Pardon! Before you leave, do you have a bolt of blue silk?" Behind her, she sensed Raymond following closely.

Jumping, the engineer answered, "What do you have in exchange? Hurry, we must leave."

Several of the armed men studied her. One of them muttered, "There is a definite witch," but she ignored them, holding out the basket of wool. She was too familiar with the comments on her demeanor, thin lips, pale skin and deep black hair to give them any notice.

"Crowther!" the engineer called out, grabbing the basket from her. "Toss out the bolt of blue silk and start up!"

"That much?"

"Hurry!"

In moments, the train blew its horn and began clacking away. Standing by the overturned bolt, Charlotte and Raymond, the only islanders still present, watched the train leave.

"What is happening?" the latter whispered.

The maiden only shook her head.

The armed men who had remained were also watching the train. Raymond turned to them. "I ask again, what do you want with our island?"

Most of the men eyed the two islanders warily, but one of them approached with a slight bow. "We beg your pardon. We want our prince."

"Your prince?" Raymond's tone dripped with cynicism. "On our island?"

The man sighed. "It is doubtful he is here, although considering he was on the train before he jumped, he is likely on his way." He paused and his gaze briefly turned toward Charlotte, still standing by Matalaide's purchase. Licking his lips, he repeated, "You must pardon me. Are you practitioners of magic?"

Unable to stop the upward tilt of her lips, Charlotte remained silent. To her amusement, Raymond also avoided answering directly. "We'll be honest with you, sirs, when and if the time comes. Shall we start with why a prince of Elcan was traveling here and why you are searching for him? Your honesty may protect you."

"He stole the king's horse. We seek to bring him back, hopefully with an apology. If you see a big black horse and a brown-haired boy with brilliant blue eyes, around fifteen, will you inform us? His name is Evan Maxwell, although who knows what alias he may choose. He *was* recently going by the name of Matthew."

For a long moment, Raymond simply stood there. Charlotte left the answer to him. Finally, he bowed slightly. "We shall see if you speak truth."

"We do," the man assured him. "I am Sir Quincy."

With another nod, Raymond turned back toward Charlotte. Each taking an end of the bolt, they started down the root-eaten trails of the mountain. Halfway back to the village, he asked, "Do you believe them, Charlotte?"

"That a king's son stole his father's horse? Completely. They also believe what they said. Beyond that, I know nothing."

She refused to speak the rest of her thoughts, but Raymond finished for her. "Something is at work, something far beyond the works of man. I just hope we'll know which side is in the right."

"If any," Charlotte breathed. Her skin crawled as she remembered the glow of the gold, a glow only the last of the enchanters could generate. The mound's evil might come sooner than she expected, but perhaps they would meet the light as well.

For quite some time, Evan shifted out of feverish dreams into strange ones filled with thrones, dragons, witches, prisons and thieves. He woke slowly, becoming aware of the tang of salt, the wind, the wash of waves on shore, the sound of bird calls, and the sunlight behind closed lids.

Turning away from the intense light, the prince opened his eyes. Lisya stood next to Darkfire, lathering a paste over his arrow wound. Though the stallion twitched, as if a fly had landed on it, he did not complain or otherwise move.

Without turning from her task, the enchantress asked, "Do you feel better?"

Evan's left arm was in a sling, but he felt healthy—at least while he was lying down. He pushed himself up to a sitting position and was relieved to feel no dizziness as he scanned the nearby spit of land jutting into the ocean.

Jeffrey was nowhere to be seen. The prince did not need to ask why. Lisya turned to him, fresh tears glistening in her lashes, the tracks of slightly older ones streaking her cheeks. Now that Evan was facing her, he realized this was not the Lisya he had seen before, though it doubtless was her.

Her loose hair sparkled like dew under the sun as it waved in the breeze—gold and red, brown and silver. This time, she was robed in summer green—perhaps the main reason, aside from her all-seeing eyes, that she looked the very essence of an enchantress.

But Evan was drawn to her tears and horrified by their meaning.

In the silence, Lisya whispered, "We will meet again. For some, it will be sooner than others, but I know we will meet again." Despite her assurances, her voice wavered with pain.

Evan's memory spun over the short time he was part of Jeffrey's life. One thought drew his attention. "Why did you send him?"

There was an appalled accusation in his question. "You knew! You had to have known!"

"He chose—"

"No! You asked! You sent him to his death!"

Lisya's gaze was dead. Not a muscle twitched. Only her hair and gown blew in the breeze. At last, she drew a breath, dropping her eyes to the shore as her lips compressed in torment. "Jeffrey was my son, Evan. I loved him, and I always will. But love cannot be love without allowing someone to make their own choices, to walk their own path.

"I asked him to guide you in the same way I asked you if you intended to leave Ansky to your uncle. I confess, many would say I told him to lead you... but I would never force anyone, Evan. The choice was always his."

Pausing, the enchantress met the prince's gaze with earnest eyes. "I know nothing for certain, except that we each have a path to travel. This was Jeffrey's. No one else could do it. I cannot say he was born for this, but it *was* his choice, and he made it. Of one thing only we can be certain. If we can trust our God, we can trust our end. It will not come too soon."

With a trembling nod, Evan accepted her words. He heaved a ragged sigh, then wrapped his good arm about her. Resting her cheek against the top of his head, the enchantress sang in another language, likely her own. Power flowed through her words. The visions her voice and tune stirred within him were all echoes of her grieving but hopeful heart. Jeffrey had been her son.

Understanding that, the prince accepted her explanation.

Lisya had hidden Jeffrey's grave beneath the ocean. At low tide, she brought Evan out to a medium-sized rock on a firm part of the beach at the very edge of the waves. Though Darkfire had been there for the burial earlier, he limped beside the enchantress and prince to accompany them. Saltwater washing over the rock made it a beautifully speckled strawberry color. The same script that adorned Lisya's doorway swirled over it.

Wrapping his cloak tightly around himself, Evan stared down at the stone. The anger and despair he had felt this afternoon had disappeared. Instead, a hollowness filled his chest as he studied the rock. "I have few friends," he finally whispered. "Despite your frustrating quirks, Jeffrey, you were one—a very good one, as a matter of fact. I will miss you."

To complete his farewell, he bowed in homage. As Darkfire bumped his arm, he stroked the stallion's nose and then turned to Lisya.

In the setting sun, a light appeared to shine from her, although it might have been a trick of the sky. Despite the glow, she stared down at the reddish rock in such a distant way that Evan knew she was staring through it.

Knowing that expression and the emptiness behind it, the prince lightly rubbed her arm. With a sad smile, she looked up, pressing his hand once in return before leading them back to high ground. "If anyone searches the shores, there will be no sign we were here, as long as we leave as soon as possible," she whispered.

There was no need to respond.

For a week more, Evan and Darkfire stayed with the enchantress on a spit of land at the northeastern foot of the Calmar Mountains, washed daily by ocean waves, while the stallion healed enough to walk naturally. Thankfully, they were far enough away from the full war of waves crashing against the rock face. As they waited, they ate what Lisya provided.

Only once did the enchantress leave them for a night, to check on her home. When she vanished before their eyes, the stallion told Evan, "The Ice Woods exist on her breath and presence. Most of us fear they will evaporate if she remains absent too long. What she fears, she keeps to herself. But she never travels for long, either."

At the end of the week, Evan awoke to find Lisya again checking Darkfire's wound.

The enchantress glanced at him. "The days grow longer. Spring is nearly over. If we walk the rest of the way to the bridge to the island, it will take us another twelve days. Darkfire cannot yet bear anyone, but we dare not wait anymore."

As Evan dusted sand off himself, the enchantress paused, appraising him. Warily, he met her thoughtful gaze. "I can go as fast as Darkfire," she mused, then smiled slightly. "Indeed, I can go much faster, although that is far too unnatural."

Looking at Evan, she asked, "In your imagination, you believe you know my capabilities. Would you ride me if I changed into a horse? That would cut your travel to the northern coast almost by half if Darkfire is up to it."

For a moment, the prince considered his response, trying to imagine riding a beast that was not a beast at all. Then he laughed. "Lisya, I have trusted your food, allowed you to wrap your arms around me, and sing words of which I lack all understanding, except in feel. If you turned *me* into a beast as a disguise, I would trust you, though I would hope it would be very temporary."

Beside him, Darkfire snorted, but made no comment.

The enchantress turned to the stallion. "You are in charge of setting the pace, Darkfire. Listen to your body. It still needs rest, even if it is mostly recovered. Evan will need your strength."

Tucking his injured leg beneath himself, the stallion bowed low in submission.

With a smile, the enchantress transformed. To the prince's shock, there was no slow change. Instead, Lisya appeared to fade for a moment, and then a bright white mare tossed her mane before him—taller than Darkfire, lither, but without the draconic appearance. She seemed more like a marble statue, glowing with magic and sudden life.

She folded her front legs to allow Evan to climb on her back. Tentatively, the prince reached out to touch her shoulder, watching his palm shine as it neared her white hide, literally aglow with light.

For a second, he nearly pulled away. But looking into the eye fixed on him, an eye that was every inch Lisya's, he gathered his courage and slipped onto her back. With Darkfire in the lead, they set off at a lope.

After Evan Maxwell's disappearance from the castle, the great hall was again a safe place to read the reports on Evfel. Tax revenues were down in Fuego, supposedly due to hardships. The Lord of Comsta wanted more men after a bout of the flu had left half his army dead and the other half weakened. He was now struggling to keep rebellion at bay. Duke Reginold had refused to grant him more, claiming that the flu appeared to be a major problem in Comsta and that more men would mean more deaths. However, Reginold warned the lord, retreat would only send a message to all rebels in Evfel.

Rubbing his eyes, Wilber drew in a long breath. He sometimes wondered if he actually *wanted* to return to Evfel. But his abdication, subtle or not, would cause an uproar—and he had to think of Andrew. The boy deserved his throne, if he would just find some self-discipline. Judging by the way he was acting, slinking around the castle to watch everyone he distrusted, he apparently wanted to be Evfel's spy instead of its king.

If Andrew continued as he was going, a sibling could be a potential threat to his right to reign. In Evfel, his new child had more of a claim to the throne, regardless of age, if he learned faster or seemed stronger. Perhaps making Andrew's sibling a steward of Ansky would prevent any unpleasantness, but Andrew needed to start applying himself, regardless.

A polite cough made Wilber straighten. An Anskonian knight stood in the open doorway, holding out a roll of paper. "Sir Quincy sent this, sire."

Springing up, the king impatiently gestured the knight forward and hurriedly snatched the scroll out of the man's hand. Tossing the knotted ribbon onto the table, the king unrolled the message.

Sire,

We found your nephew on the Summos Valley train,
heading toward Enchantress Island with the Evfelian
criminal Jeffrey Gombe. In our attempt to catch him, he
took the stolen beast and jumped from the train with it
and his aforementioned companion. All three went off the
cliffside on the northeastern coast of the Calmar Mountains.

We continued to the island, where we await your word and
watch for the prince's potential arrival. Sadly, I lack the
men to search the coast where we last saw the prince, but I
sent word to you immediately, so you may decide the best
course of action.

We await your orders.

May Evfel's king never grow old.

Sir Quincy

Crumpling up the message, Wilber snapped at the knight standing there, "Prepare the men. Send some to find the troops still searching the northern parts of Ansky and Cyra. Tell them to make a thorough hunt of the northeastern coastline, fanning out from there for any signs of habitation. In one month, they are to join us on the island. I will take a force directly there."

As the messenger withdrew, the king drummed his fingers on the table. He would first have to inform Lorene of his departure.

Eight days after leaving Jeffrey's burial site, Evan stood at the northern tip of Elcan, at the base of the mountains, the sea waves licking his feet. Tracks ran above their heads into the cloud-covered night. Not even the northern star, Resplandecer, shone through the black mass of sky.

Staring up at the thick wooden bridge used by the train, Evan commented, "Even if we could climb up there, they are bound to keep a watch."

"You are right." Lisya nodded. "We must make a raft. The island is only two leagues away now. When you see it, row away from the tracks, but use it as a guide at first. Should the waves toss you from the raft, they will also serve as safety. Storms come quickly to this channel."

Evan looked nervously at the black sky overhead, but during the night, it was impossible to tell if there were storm clouds.

Turning away from the tracks, the enchantress shooed them off. "We must gather driftwood and seaweed. Hurry."

The prince glanced skeptically at Darkfire, but nevertheless obeyed. "Fear not," the stallion whispered. "She will transform anything we find into something useful."

When they returned with their pitiful collection, Lisya shook her head slightly and sighed. Before their eyes, the twigs of fallen tree branches and strands of seaweed grew into strong ropes and tree-width logs, each the breadth of outspread arms.

"That is all the cheating I am willing to do for now," the enchantress huffed. "Let us turn this into a raft."

Bending to the task of tying knots, Evan found the courage to ask, "Why do you not dare to do more? Surely, you did the hardest part already? Is it so much harder to make a raft itself than to make the resources needed for one?"

Lisya paused with a small smile. "It is purely a matter of judgment. I am trapped, Evan, in a psychological game. My every act must be weighed. Am I manipulating events to my will or just using my abilities to help? With that question in mind, I try to make things progress as they would normally. I will heal, but only to start the process. I then let blood, skin and muscle do what they should. I will make the resources for a raft, but then labor to lash it together.

"All the same, I am rarely certain. Had I been able, I would have lived as one of you, but as I said, I am magic itself. To stop being myself was to shrivel away, to prevent my blood from pumping. I tried it all the same, even at the risk of killing myself. Then Yulcer, my friend, ordered me to use what I am. The knowledge of when and how to do so would come from falling and standing back up, he said. So, I fall and stand, but am still never certain."

For the next two hours, the enchantress and the prince bound the logs fast. "I hope this stays together," Evan muttered, yanking on one knot to tighten it. "I had no need to learn to swim—or so I thought."

Forced merely to stand by and watch, Darkfire shook his mane. "Well, you know one thing. If I helped out, it most certainly would fall apart."

Smiling slightly, the prince looked up at his friend's dark outline. "I guess humans *are* natural at something. We have hands."

Darkfire's only response was an indignant sniff. Even that was a begrudging surrender.

"All right," Lisya spoke up as she finished checking each knot one last time. Straightening up, she spread her hands, palms upward. Something flickered into shape—a long sword, sheathed in black and silver.

"Unfortunately, you will need this, Evan. I made this at home and only called it here. I had no time to finish it before you were forced to flee Ansky."

Accepting the weapon, the prince gasped at its lightness. "Will it not shatter?"

"I craft all my blades from a white ore, hard as rock and light as air."

Cautiously, Evan drew the blade from its silver-swirled scabbard. At once, a soft glow pierced the night. The blade brightened like a firefly underneath glass. Through its depths ran Lisya's flowing script.

"The light will only shine by night. Without it, the words will fade," Lisya explained, watching him. Even Darkfire had stepped near to peer into the sword's depths.

"What does it say?" the prince asked.

"In your tongue? There is no direct translation, but if I were to simplify, it warns against the first failing of mortals—self-glorification. Remember to serve, Evan, at all times. But the light of the sword... I thought it appropriate for a king who deeply desires to make a better world—though I fear I gave you a weapon that could incriminate you as an islander. Yet it is for that reason that I give it. With Wilber ahead of you, the islanders will never trust a prince of Ansky. But they might trust a friend of mine."

Sheathing the light, Evan asked, "Is anyone else able to draw it?"

"Normally, yes. If you are apprehended, it will disappear from sight, though remain at your side. To certain hands, it will also not stay solid under such circumstances." For a moment, she was silent as the prince buckled the blade about his waist and pulled the folds of his cloak over it. Then, she said, "I must go home, but take care, Evan. Many await their king."

The prince briefly embraced her in gratitude. Then, turning, he helped Darkfire shove the raft into the water and jumped on before it could float away. A single paddle lay there, which he drove into the shore to hold the raft in place while the stallion joined him. Then he pushed off.

For quite some time, he could look back and still see the faint glow of the enchantress watching them from shore. Then, at last, the darkness swallowed her from view.

Chapter 10

Strong as a Bear, Loving as a Puppy

DARKFIRE AND EVAN made slow progress, as the prince fought the westward current with every stroke of the paddle. At least they were on the east side of the tracks, so the current helped them stay next to the wooden structure ascending from the waves.

"The wind is rising," Darkfire warned. Evan only shook his head, not daring to stop. Regardless, the stallion spoke rightly. The waves had grown and turned choppy.

Darkfire's sharp whinny floated above the storm. The prince whirled around just as a great swell rose over them. Below their feet, the raft lifted—and overturned.

Thrown into the ocean, Evan thrashed wildly. He broke the surface for a moment, but was sinking too fast to draw air. Water poured into his lungs. As new waves swept him along, he grazed one of Darkfire's kicking legs. Then his head slammed into something hard. Darkness fell, relieving the discomfort of his panicking lungs.

Standing in the rain, the knight trembled as Charlotte watched him from the trees. Lights were approaching through the night's darkness, the twin lanterns hanging from the train. It slowed to stop, and ten armed men jumped off before it had even come to a halt.

"Sire!" the knight exclaimed. "I was expecting orders—"

"Quincy, has there been any sight of my nephew?" the king demanded.

"None, sire. Sir Radnor is in charge of the group watching the southern tip. There has been nothing, although he sickened in this terrible weather. Unfortunately, we have been exposed to just about every condition. To be fair, though, he is the oldest among us."

"Do you have a camp?" the king asked.

"A small one. Come, I will show you."

The king turned back toward the train. "Unload!"

He had not brought only ten men. At least fifty more erupted from the train, scurrying back and forth. Ramps were lowered from boxcars, then wagons and horses were hauled out.

Eyes wide, the knight—Quincy—shook his head. "You made good time, sire."

"Quite," the king agreed. He turned to the engineer. "You may return to pick up your goods."

The horn blew. As the train departed, the newcomers followed Quincy into the woods.

The silence of the rainy night fell once more on the market clearing, and Charlotte let out a soft breath. After a moment's contemplation, she slipped soundlessly away.

Cold wind blew across Evan, waking him with a violent shiver. As something lightly thumped on his back, he jerked over. Darkfire was standing over him, his frame blocking the sunlight as he nosed sand and shell splinters into the air like a regular horse—not one from the Ice Woods.

"What are you doing?" the prince asked, pressure pounding behind his brow.

Pausing, the stallion tipped his head in his unique expression of sarcasm. "Protecting you, as much as I am able. You are soaked, and the wind alone could kill you." When Evan only continued to stare at him uncomprehendingly, the stallion huffed. "You are not fully conscious, are you?" He paused for a response. None came, so he nudged the prince with his nose. "If you are able, remove your clothes and roll all over in the sand. There is a slight rise before the village, which might hide you from view if you keep to the ground."

It slowly penetrated Evan's thoughts that Darkfire himself was covered in sand. Only afterward did the young man jerk to his feet in realization, heart hammering in fear. "We are near a village?"

On the horizon, beyond the shore, a green mountain soared. At its foot stretched a pine forest, its tangy aroma borne on the breeze. Between Evan and the trees, afternoon sunlight glinted on a pond in the village center, fed by a stream that disappeared into the woods farther on. Figures flickered between the thatched cottages. Every play of light on the scene before him seemed somehow sharpened.

"I think I will avoid stripping," the prince muttered. "Is this... the island?"

"The eastern side, yes. I believe this is the village Lisya stayed in when she lived here."

Another cold blast whisked in from the ocean. Evan's body quaked from head to toe at the sensation, and he hugged himself for warmth. The movement brought another pang to his temples, and he lowered himself back to the ground. "I guess I can try rolling."

"Hold," Darkfire warned, stepping over the prince. Approaching from the village, a large man sauntered along the shore, a pole slung carelessly across his shoulder. He was staring up at the sky, whistling, seemingly unaware of the twosome almost in his way.

Looking over his shoulder, Evan scanned the shore for the man's destination. It was not hard to find. A small boat was pulled up on the beach, nets draped over its sides.

Darkfire's angry snort jerked the prince back around. The stallion had reared. Beneath those thrashing hooves, the man stared upward, frozen, before gasping, "Easy, mate! I just want my usual catch of fish!"

Stepping between them, Evan quietly warned, "Darkfire!" A slight tremor passed through the ground as two hooves slammed down behind the prince, but he dared not turn away from the fisherman.

Something flickered behind the man's round, green-eyed gaze. Taking his hat off, however, he merely bowed, revealing brown tufts of hair that stuck out in almost every direction. "My thanks, mate. I thought I was dead for a moment there."

"I know. I—" In the midst of his sentence, Evan sneezed. Rubbing his nose, he finished, "I was beneath his hooves once."

Concern filled the man's face. "Come." He beckoned for the prince to follow him. "You need warm clothes and the rest of my tea."

When Evan hung back, the man repeated his gesture. "You look half-dead already. Come, bring your murderous stallion as protection. I mean no harm."

His life seemed a small price to pay for dry clothes and a hot drink. Yet, even as he sneezed again, Evan shook his head. His weakness was temporary, and lives depended on him. Without knowing what the knights of Ansky had told the villagers, the entire island could be searching for him.

True, it was for just such an eventuality that Lisya had given him the sword—to prove his connection to her. But he questioned how the islanders would react. Forty years later, did they continue to love and trust the enchantress? If so, how many?

Darkfire's nose bumped his arm, silently encouraging him to take the offer. He could hardly ask why, not with the fisherman there, but trusting the stallion, Evan nodded at last.

"Good," the man said, flopping his hat back on his head and turning around. Just as jauntily as he had come, he led them to a small hut on the first rise. A long green pasture stretched away from the building, separating it from the nearby structures. "Your steed should like it here. He needs to stay closer to the eaves, though. People are searching for some other horse, and I don't want him mistook."

Evan exchanged a pointed look with Darkfire. Despite having fallen off the cliff, it appeared too much to hope that they were presumed dead. "Take care of yourself, before you become sick," the stallion muttered into the prince's shoulder blades, pushing him toward the door through which the fisherman had disappeared.

The warmth of the fireplace immediately drew Evan as he stepped inside. The man was on his knees, stoking the fire. His fishing pole rested against the doorway, hat on top. Only a bed built into the wall and a small table accompanied by one lonely stool broke the pattern of the logs underfoot. Despite its blandness, the square hut was a welcoming place.

"That's right," the man sighed, brushing his hands off before standing. As he stood beside the fire, his thick, undisciplined brown hair and wide shoulders made him resemble a bear, yet his soft green eyes belied that image, sparking with good nature and compassion. "I'll fetch you my spare clothes." He walked across the room to his bed and pulled a long shirt and a pair of pants from below the mattress.

As he handed the clothing to the prince, the man laughed. "You remind me of some of the sheep we just sheared a few weeks ago—little scared things, ready to fly at the slightest movement. I'm only Lazarus, son of the late Meckeer, Larry to some, and certainly not a dragon. Now, your horse, on the other hand... You two must be of the fairy folk who some say dwell on this island."

Evan laughed nervously at the joke. "I am Max... Matth—" Stumbling on his lie, he looked away. Though Jeffrey had used Matthew, if the knights had beaten them here, it was just as likely that the islanders would have heard the name.

"Well, Max, you can stop shivering and change while I warm my Chondrus Crispus tea."

As soon as Lazarus turned his back, the prince peeled off his cloak—and froze. Lisya's sword still hung at his waist. He had forgotten it. For just a second, he looked at the man's back, uncertainly. Hopefully, it was invisible to him, but Evan had no way of knowing.

Hastily, he unbuckled the sword, bundled it inside his cloak, and dumped his other layers of clothing over it, as fast as he could strip. Only then, shivering, did he yank on Lazarus's clothes. He sighed at the feel of dry, fleecy wool on his skin. Unfortunately, the shirt fell down to his calves. He rolled up the pant legs and then started on the sleeves.

He was still rolling them when Lazarus turned around with a clay tankard of steaming tea. "Well, look at you," the fisherman chuckled. "A fish in pajamas, swimming as you might expect."

Making no comment, Evan gratefully accepted the tea. Steam touched his face, and he held the cup there, briefly closing his eyes.

If Wilber sought to maintain the pretense of innocence, he would not have asked the islanders to do anything more than bring Evan to him alive. The worst the drink could be was drugged. And with Darkfire outside, no one would carry him away.

He took a sip. It had a strange flavor, but deliciously heated his throat all the way down.

For a moment more, the fisherman continued to stand there, studying the prince as if looking for something. Then, with his usual smile, he said, "You don't need to stand on ceremony. You can sit by the fire without being burned, if you want." He bent down, hands reaching for Evan's clothes. "I'll just wash off this sand for you."

"No!"

But it was too late. The fisherman's fingers had closed on the hard lump of the sword. Eyes widening in surprise, he flung back the folds and gasped at the sight they revealed. "Lisya!" His green eyes pierced the prince. "Who are you? Not Evan Maxwell! You know the enchantress! That's her name down this scabbard!"

Evan stilled, caught. Without a good excuse or lie, he was at the fisherman's mercy, but through that paralyzing awareness he looked at where Lazarus still pointed. It was indeed the writings of the enchantress swirled in silver, now that Evan looked at it in the light. That the fisherman could read it was another surprise. "Evan Maxwell knows Lisya," the prince confessed.

Looking over his shoulder, Lazarus threw his arm in the direction of the door, finger pointing. "The king's horse, out there, you stole him?"

"Darkfire is his own master! He is hardly a horse. He is…" There were no words to describe Darkfire. "He is one of the herd from Lisya's home, capable of speech and intelligent thought. He was Stallion of the Ice Woods before he… appointed his son as successor to grant me his life service."

Lazarus shook his head, brow furrowed in confusion. "Then what's with this accusation everyone's spreading around?"

With a sigh, Evan set his tankard on the table and stooped to fold his cloak back over the sword. "It is a matter of convenience. No one knows who or what he is. They would kill him for being a demon if they did. Darkfire was captured in our valley and given to the king. I was to tame him. That was before we knew anything about each other."

"So…" The fisherman paused. "Were you spotted trying to help him escape?"

"No," Evan breathed. "I am the heir of Ansky, and I decided to accept my responsibility. My uncle found out, and he tried to make sure I died before I informed the council. When I escaped with Darkfire, he must have claimed I had declared war by stealing his charger."

In the silence that followed, Lazarus turned away, gazing out the open door.

Heart pounding, the prince waited. After a moment, he whispered, "So, you know my story."

At last, the fisherman turned back to him. "Why are you here?"

"Lisya sent me. If you ask why I did not stay to raise an army against my uncle…" Guiltily, he dropped his gaze. "No one would believe me. I have been too selfish and bitter for my people to think anything other than what Wilber tells them. Anyway, I have what they see as the king's charger. There is no explanation I could give them that would not make it seem as though I had sold my heart to the evil in the Ice Woods in exchange for their assistance."

"Is that what they think of Lisya?"

"They have never met Lisya, only her woods. But the rumors from this island mean they would never give her a chance to prove herself even if they did meet her."

"You are Elcan born, and yet you trust her."

"At first, I only trusted her some."

With a sigh, the fisherman uncovered the sword and slipped it beneath his mattress. Then he hefted Evan's sodden clothes. "Warm up, Max. I'll think of what we can do while I wash these."

"I promise," Evan hastened to add, "I never intended to be followed. I will leave if I put you in too much danger."

"Max, a prince your age, without a single human friend to support and teach you... I doubt you know even one thing you need to know to survive. Why else would Lisya send you here? We'll figure this out. Stay inside, but don't worry."

Lazarus returned sometime later with a pheasant for dinner. A grin filled his face. "I begged it off Raymond, with the promise of fish for him tomorrow. We bachelors must stick together."

"Is that usual?"

"Of course. Every once in a while, we need a change. The only trouble is, Raymond hunts for the Lady Talliaha and her daughter, Charlotte, as well. So if I promise him fish, I have to catch more than just one. He tells me not to bother, but I do."

Evan was silent a moment, wondering if he had the courage to ask about the apparent "lady" of the island.

The fisherman said no more, pulling out a bucket to pluck feathers.

"You have nobility on the island?" Evan finally asked.

Lazarus snorted. "That family, yes." Then he laughed. "No, but Talliaha is the oldest in this village. She is well respected, and her line has long had a certain... air to them. When the dragons enslaved the islanders, forcing them to mine treasure for their heaps, everyone lived trapped on the mountain. Then the enchanters came, as my parents always told the tale, to take vengeance on the dragons for making off with some magical treasures of their world. That war began the enchanters' warring among themselves for power, and while they fought up on Castle Mound—our mountain's peak where the ruins of the old castle now stand—everyone fled to the shores of the island, as far away from them as possible. Everyone except her family. They stubbornly refused to raise their sheep anywhere but on the mountain, with enchantments filling the air around them—and, we suspect, permeating them. They don't seem quite human anymore.

"Be that as it may, they live here now. The older generations are deceased, all the males in the family have died off, and Raymond has chosen to provide for the two remaining ladies—when Charlotte allows him to do so."

"Why would she refuse help?"

Lazarus shook his head. "Long bitterness, Evan. She's immensely independent, and to heighten matters, he dared *insult* her by asking her to marry him. She refuses to, as she says, 'become any man's slave.' The gossip is that she threw him out of the house by threatening to kill him the night he asked. She's a deadly shot with an arrow. It seems she can anticipate your actions before you think of them. As I said, they're not quite human, if you understand me."

After a second's hesitation, Evan probed, "When you speak of the warring sorcerers, do you include Lisya? Was she evil?"

Pausing in his task for the first time, the fisherman looked up, gathering his thoughts. "I was a baby when the sky reappeared... but yes, with natural pride in her heart, she fought the others of her kind for a place as sole ruler. I don't know how they all warred for seven hundred years."

A distant look came into his eyes. "Seven hundred years of your only thought, your only purpose, being murder. I'd have thought they would all go insane and kill themselves.

"Anyway..." Lazarus returned to his bird. "Lisya came with them over the sea but lost in the end. She knew she had death before her, so she escaped, straight to the only home in the mountains—the home of Talliaha's father. She demanded he hide her. And somehow, that aged shepherd had the patience and love to not only obey, but to teach her compassion and selflessness. Thus changed, she returned to persuade her own. Perhaps that was why only she survived when the mountain heaved in the earthquake that belched blue fire from the earth. Afterward, nothing remained of their castle or the other enchanters."

"What did they all want so badly from this island?"

"For one thing, a crown. Powerful beings were too numerous where they came from to have one, but here, there were only a handful. Second, and perhaps more importantly..." Lazarus hesitated. "You must wonder why we allow ourselves to appear so evil to Elcan."

Evan waited patiently.

After a while, the fisherman shrugged. "Well, you're backed by Lisya, so I will tell you. The mountain is said to be a treasure trove of precious stones, not only the natural ones but all the things gathered by the dragons, including those stolen from the enchanters' world. We have never dared discover the truth of the rumor, but we fear someone might stumble upon it. Summos Valley is greedy enough without knowing our legends."

"Yet I think you knew who I was the moment you saw me and still helped me."

"Ah, yes. 'Larry's weakness,' some call it. I wouldn't turn in a dog in the condition I found you. That's where the weakness comes. After allowing it to lap water from my hand, I won't turn it in either, even if it rips out my throat afterward."

Lazarus was quiet for a moment, a distant smile on his face. Then he looked up. "Which brings us back to your problem. I think you can hide here, in the open. Tonight, under cover of darkness, we'll take your horse—Darkfire, you said?—to the woods. There is water there, and trees to hide him. I imagine he's cunning enough to stay out of sight. Our one concern, I think, is Charlotte. She's often out and about by night. If she sees us, I don't know what will happen. She would never turn you in, but… well, I'm not sure what she *would* do.

"Aside from that, we'll cut your hair and burn the evidence. It will make a stench. I'll have to invent some story, but it's the only way to ensure it doesn't turn up later to betray us. Meanwhile, you'll be seen helping me fish, scavenge, clean, carve. Whatever you don't know, I'll teach you. Just keep your mouth closed around others. Their suspicions will disappear."

Evan shook his head. "I cannot hide forever."

"No. Once you become a part of everyday village life, I will ask to have our summer festival early. Usually, it's in midsummer, but I'll talk to people, see if they're interested in holding it sooner. A party would help relieve the tension everyone's been feeling, what with those prowling knights.

"With everyone scurrying about at a festival, large groups carrying on quiet conversations will go unnoticed. Once you are ready to meet those face to face who I think can help you the most, we'll pull them in here and shut the door. No one will notice the numbers, what with the regular comings and goings. Does that sound like a plan?"

After a moment, Evan shrugged and spread out his palms. "I lack a better one."

"Good. Darkfire needs to stay in the woods until all the knights are gone, though. We are being watched. The word came this morning that the king himself is here."

"Wilber is here!" the prince exclaimed, shooting to his feet. "Has he asked the islanders for assistance?"

"We give none, Max. Not to kings."

"Yet you intend to ask this village to support me?"

"Lisya sent you. That makes all the difference in the world. There might be some islanders who wouldn't understand that, but not in this village. To those of us who are forty or older, the enchantress is practically our queen. She was our doctor, our children's playmate, our counselor, our protector, and our friend. If she supports you, so do we. I love Lisya, Max, and I wish she'd return. I was ten when she left, so long ago. You might think that a long time to feel great loyalty. For some of us islanders, it is. But I have never forgotten. She was that special."

Lazarus paused, his gaze distant. Then he shook his head. "How could I describe it? She has the power to easily make everyone her slaves, yet she chose to serve us. I'm sure you've felt it. Once you look upon her and hear the depth in her voice, you'll trust her in everything. I would do anything for her."

Lazarus waited until the very middle of the night, when even the insects slept, to help Evan slip out with Darkfire. Stallion and prince were silent as the fisherman led them into the woods and the sound of their footfalls changed to the crunch of dead leaves. It gave Evan some peace to think they would hear if anyone else were out, but Lazarus, seemingly guessing his thoughts, laughed grimly. "Oh, all the knights are farther up the mountain, and you would never hear *her*. Even the deer don't startle at her presence."

His heart beating faster, the prince strained his ears despite the fear that it was futile. Each squeak of an insect—more numerous in the woods—startled him. "Why are we going so far in?"

"I want to show you Whistler's Falls. The river carved out a long tunnel where it will be safer for Darkfire when he wants to drink, and the sound of the falls will cover any snorts, puffs and so forth." The fisherman glanced at the stallion. "Honestly, I don't even hear your hooves, mate, but when you want to make some noise, the falls can be your retreat."

So Evan and Darkfire followed the fisherman in relative silence. Something about the trees was reminiscent of the Ice Woods. Green sparkled like emerald under the shimmer of moonlight lancing through the leaves. As if complaining about the human presence, the trunks groaned.

After a moment, Lazarus whispered, "That's the first time I've heard them. Raymond says Charlotte's been hearing them for a while. Strange."

"Does it mean the forest is dying from age?"

"No, we make sure to take care of it, at least down here." Another creaking groan filled the woods above their heads. "Raymond said no more. Of course, it meant nothing particular to me. I asked him what Charlotte thought. That's when he grew quiet, the over-protective..."

The fisherman fell silent, then muttered, "You know, I don't think she deserves him. But that's okay, I guess. I doubt they'll ever marry, and I enjoy having my companion bachelor. Makes us a team."

Smiling, Evan faintly shook his head. He stiffened in anticipation as the low whisper of moving water reached his ears. Not long after, it turned into a roar. The trees above thinned. They came to a high arch, the height of at least twenty men standing on each other's shoulders. A river rushed out through the center of the arch, and the threesome trailed along the barren rock beside the rippling water.

Lazarus took them to the foot of the falls, where a small pool collected beneath a large circular opening in the archway above. Through it, stars blazed downward. They all stood there as the cold water flecked their faces.

At last, the fisherman led them back the way they'd come until they could once more hear themselves speak. "Darkfire, there is also a small alcove behind the waterfall where you may sleep safely in hiding. The rest, I leave to your wisdom. Perhaps, being Lisya's, you are more native to this island than I." With that, he turned back toward the village.

Before following, Evan briefly threw his arms about the stallion. "Enjoy yourself. It is beautiful out here."

Nuzzling him, Darkfire breathed, "I will remain close to the village most of the time. Be careful."

Sorrowfully leaving his companion behind, the prince caught up with Lazarus.

Afternoon light spread over the villagers working in their local garden. In three new rows, Raymond and two other young men, Bounen and Tevin, were planting more lettuce seeds.

"So we have Elcan snobs here?" the latter sniffed, irritably poking the seeds into a hole. "We better work on our diction, making sure each letter is pronounced." Holding his nose in the air, he lifted his pinkie. "Those islanders," he mimicked their accent, but raised the pitch of his voice to a near squeak. "They know nothing about proper speech, or anything else, for that matter."

"They don't do that," Bounen quipped with a smile. "You're thinking of the valley. To my understanding, only those living in Summos Valley hold out their pinkie like it's diseased all the time."

"What do you know? Anyway, it's 'do not' and 'you are.'"

"Oh, oh," Raymond had to tease. "You, the proper man from Elcan, just said 'it's.'"

Tevin glared at him. Bounen flapped his hand in dismissal. "We don't want to sound like them anyway."

"If we try, they might leave faster out of irritation."

"They'll just have your head faster, you mean," Raymond muttered.

"Not at all. I'm an islander. I can transform them into toads if they displease me."

Turning to hide his smile, Raymond patted dirt down. "You could have fooled me."

"You know what?" Tevin exclaimed. "Why are you even helping? If there are two people who don't use this garden, it's you and Larry, so you could be doing something else."

Charlotte's frequent retort that his help was never needed rang in his ears. Raymond tried to shrug it away. "Ah, but I'm the village pest, apparently. I'm always helping when people don't want it." He paused, slightly bitter, then laughed. "*Only* when they don't want it, of course."

"Well, in that case, scram! Shoo," Tevin ordered, throwing seeds at his friend. Then, abruptly, he straightened, puffing his chest out, coughing and smoothing out his shirt. With an air of nonchalance, he returned to work.

The other two young men looked up to see Gwenre watching from where she had been gathering kale. Bounen and Raymond shared a long glance, then started coughing to cover their laughter.

Tevin was turning redder by the moment. "Some friends you are," he muttered, only to renew their outburst. "Raymond, as the oldest, you should be the wise one who tells her what a fine young man I am and that she shouldn't let me go. That's what a friend would do."

Shaking his head, Raymond rubbed the bridge of his nose with his knuckles. His laughter grew. "Tevin…" he squeaked. "Tevin…" he tried again. On the fifth try, he finally managed to gasp, "I swear you need to be examined for insanity."

He and Bounen broke out in laughter once again. Tevin cast them a sideways glance and pointedly continued working.

Then Bounen jerked upright, his merriment stopping. "Hold it." He pointed down the shore. "Who's that with Larry?"

Halting, the other two turned in the indicated direction. The fisherman was scavenging in the distance as usual, but beside him was a boy, whose short dark hair was parting in unusual ways in the strong wind.

"I don't know." Tevin shook his head. Then, as if to underline how little he knew, he shrugged.

"Oh, that's Max!" Gwenre had joined them, shading her eyes with her hand.

Scrunching his nose, Tevin repeated, "Max?"

"He's from the southern part of the island, I think. Very cute." As Tevin glared at her, she shrugged shamelessly. "Yes, cute, young, shy. A boy of misfortune, Larry said. Poor thing burned something this morning in his nervousness. It was the smell that brought me over. It was terrible. Anyway, he hasn't said a word, but it's obvious he's a hard worker. You know how Larry is about the misfortunate."

"Yes," Raymond muttered thoughtfully. "Strong as a bear and loving as a puppy."

Folding his arms, Tevin scoffed. "That boy's anything but cute."

Gwenre laughed, "You're cute too when you're jealous." As Tevin turned the color of a bright pink rose, she touched his arm. "In all seriousness, have you ever heard me call a handsome young man cute? Boys are cute. Men are handsome, except when they're not. Max just seems so young and guileless. I hope Lazarus can do him some good."

As she turned to go back to work, Raymond asked, "Gwenre, who's his father?"

Gwenre shrugged. "Larry didn't say." With that, she picked up her basket and headed off.

"You're thinking something, Raymond," Bounen muttered at the hunter's shoulder. "What is it?"

"I'm not sure." Maybe he was being overly suspicious, but the boy had appeared like magic. And there could be other reasons than shyness or nervousness for clumsiness and a refusal to speak... On the other hand, Lazarus was hardly stupid, and there had been no signs of a horse. Either way, the newcomer would merit watching.

Chapter 11

The Witch of Enchantress Island

"**W**ow, Max,**"** Lazarus commented once they were sitting safely on the wide ocean, their fishing net hung over the side of the boat in the early evening. Beyond them, the village was a darker spot along the shore. "I thought you appeared older when I first cut your hair, but when you don't speak or look people in the eye, you actually seem younger."

"What was I supposed to do after you told the lady I had burned something in my nervousness? Of course I turned red. There was nothing I could say at that point, even if I did sound like you."

Chuckling, the fisherman shook his head. "Oh, if I hadn't thought to burn some sauce over the fireplace, I don't doubt she would've inquired further. As it is, we can count ourselves blessed."

Evan gave him a long-suffering look. Lazarus reached over to pat his knee. "I won't take it back—blessed. Gwenre, sweet as she is, is a tongue wagger. Through her, the whole village will know who you are, who she took you to be. Most won't even ask for further details, nor think twice about the name 'Max.' Not yet. Tomorrow, when I raise the question of an earlier summer feast, they will all be for it. They will be starving for a day off—not the usual day of rest and family, but a day when they can all indulge their curiosity and meet you.

"No," the fisherman added, shaking his head, "now that Gwenre has swallowed a few fables and jumped nicely to the assumption that 'south' means the island's south, I cheer—"

"Darkfire!" Evan suddenly exclaimed, rocking the boat as he lurched to the opposite side. A dark head was swimming toward them.

"I came from a distance outside the village," the stallion said. "And I stayed low while in the shallows."

"All the same..." Evan's voice trailed off helplessly. Nothing could articulate his concern and frustration.

After a moment, as he thought of the horse's legs churning below the waves, he exclaimed, "Darkfire, you must be scaring all the fish!"

Darkfire snorted, his nostrils briefly growing larger. Clearly, it was difficult for him to hold his head high enough to speak. "Swimming right here, I will chase them into your net. It is on the opposite side."

"Max," Lazarus said, shifting, "help me pull in this net, and we'll all go across from that rocky bit of shore, where people will be less likely to see us. Who knows, we might have more fortune there with the fish."

Assisting the fisherman, the prince asked, "Is it hard to catch anything?"

"I usually catch something, sooner or later, but sometimes I'm out here all day. Occasionally, I find nothing at all. That better not happen today, or I'll be starving two lovely ladies."

Gathering the empty net in beside them, they picked up oars and followed the stallion's head toward the rockier shoreline outside the village. "Are they really that dependent on your promise to your friend?" Evan asked, pushing deeply on his oar. "You did say he told you not to worry about it."

"He did, but I'm giving them something tonight, and that's final."

Evan smiled at the emphatic response.

Upon reaching the new location, they cast their net once more into the ocean and sat back. As Lazarus watched Darkfire swimming a little distance away, he pointed toward the horse. "Why don't you join him? A swim might be nice, and I can watch the net. It will give you something to do."

Wrapping his arms around his knees, Evan exhaled. "I never learned how to swim."

"What? How did you reach our shore then?"

"Darkfire carried me… I think. I rammed into the bridge supports, and that was the last thing I remember until I woke up here."

"I see." Shrugging, the fisherman threw his hands into the air. "There's no time like the present to learn, and the sea's fairly calm today. You have this boat and Darkfire nearby. Just take off your shirt and slip over the edge, on the opposite side from the net."

Evan shook his head, shrinking back. "At best, my thrashing will scare all the fish."

"Max," Lazarus sighed. "This knowledge might be a matter of life and death someday. If you hadn't been protected, it already would have been. You don't thrash in the water. You let it carry you."

"But do the waves not pull you under?"

"Hold on." Looking out into the ocean, Lazarus called, "Darkfire, how's the undertow?"

The stallion changed direction and swam toward them. Once he reached the boat, he answered, "It is currently out farther."

The fisherman nodded in satisfaction. "There you go. Darkfire, your service today is to teach this prince how to swim."

Looking at Evan, the stallion's eyes glinted. The prince sighed, yanking off his shirt.

"That's the spirit," Lazarus exclaimed, patting him on the back. "When you first jump in, grab onto Darkfire's mane. He'll help you stay up."

As soon as Evan was submerged, the stallion took him closer to shore. "Just kick your feet with strength, but not frantically," he whispered. "Fish, I have found, glide through the waves. Never do they struggle."

With Darkfire beside him, staying afloat was not as difficult as Evan feared. Eventually, as darkness set around them and Lazarus landed three fish, the prince swam onto the stallion's back. They returned to the boat, where the fisherman was just pulling up the last of his net.

After whispering in Darkfire's ear, Evan impishly called, "Race you to shore!"

"Hey!" In Lazarus's haste to pick up the oars, the boat almost tipped over. By the time the fisherman had balanced its swaying, the stallion had already reached the shallows, triumphantly racing amid the waves.

As Lazarus had predicted, he returned to his home the next evening with word that the village had agreed to an earlier festival date. Unfortunately, the consensus was for three weeks away—three weeks during which Evan had to keep his secrets. The two exchanged a long look, sharing their fears, then Lazarus dipped his chin.

"We'll keep busy, Max. If anyone stops by, we'll always have something to do. I need to carve a new stool for you, anyway. I can teach you how to carve, so you can keep up your shy act by burying your nose in the task. As for the other villagers, they will be preparing for the festival in their spare time. I think we'll be all right."

Mutely, Evan nodded, unrolling his blanket next to the fireplace. They had no other choice.

For a minute, the fisherman sat on the edge of his bed, watching the prince with concern. "You'll be all right?" he asked at last.

With a sigh, Evan whispered, "Three weeks is a long time to keep up a lie, to say nothing of the chance that the knights shall wander through. If someone has so much as a suspicion and no reason to swallow our story, we are both dead."

"I know... but I'll keep trusting my God. It's the only thing I can do."

The villagers were exceptionally busy over the next few weeks. Girls wanted new dresses, or at least redecorated ones. Any food that could be made in advance was prepared. Someone with an instrument began practicing in earnest, filling the village with fun, springy music every evening. All the while, normal life continued.

Evan helped Lazarus carve a new stool, make seaweed cakes for the festival, and catch or dig up meals for the day. Raymond stopped by a few times, but no one else did. At those times, the prince silently worked on the stool, knowing the young village bachelor was watching him now and then with shrewd gray eyes. Rarely did he probe, but the day before the festival, he stopped by again.

"Raymond!" Lazarus said, wiping his floury hands on his pants. "All ready for the festival tomorrow?"

"Larry." The hunter's tone was serious, a soft warning. "Our island is being scoured by Elcan knights. Some of them stop by the flock frequently to watch Charlotte."

Sighing, the fisherman leaned against the table and folded his arms. "If we try to force them off, they'll only attack. What else can we do? We certainly haven't seen anything of what they say they're searching for. For all we know, it's just an excuse to lay a claim here."

There followed a silence, and Evan looked up. Anger and sadness mixed in Raymond's cold gaze which flicked briefly to the prince before returning to the fisherman. "I think you're lying, Larry, and I don't understand why. If there's a good reason for us to keep silent, tell us. If not, why are you playing games?"

The fisherman shifted and sighed. "You might as well say you think Max is the prince, though there's no horse to back up your suspicion."

Glancing at Evan, Raymond's chin rose slightly. "All right. Beyond the description we were given, I lack proof, but I *do* think you're hiding their backstabbing thief."

Swiftly, Evan ducked back to work. His heart clenched as he felt both pairs of eyes on him.

At last, Lazarus exhaled. "If there's no horse, then they lied. Why would I give away information about an innocent boy?"

"You're sidestepping. Larry! I want to know what I'm endangering people for. Some of the knights are disrespectfully feasting their eyes on Charlotte. They look on her as a witch, and her pride and bitterness just fuel that. I was up there with her yesterday, and we were asked about their prince. I said we had seen absolutely nothing and suggested they ask the other side of the mountain. So now I want to know. Why are we lying?"

Lazarus lowered his eyes. "The festival is to cover our planning. We must decide how best to remove the Elcan camp on Castle Mound, but we must not seem as if we're holding a large meeting. As for Max..."

As the fisherman paused, Evan again looked up. If Talliaha's family had a certain air, so did Raymond—an air of authority, wisdom and ability. It was clear he was ready and able to defend his homeland.

At last, Lazarus continued, "Lisya sent the boy. When I explain everything to a large group, all at once, I will reveal the rest."

"Lisya?"

"I'm sorry, Raymond. For one more day, your ignorance may still protect you. Wait. But when it comes time for Max to tell his story, I hope you'll be one of those in the darkness of this hut."

Throwing a last challenging glare at Evan, the hunter bowed in submission. "Tomorrow, then."

The festival was held in Lazarus's long field. By midmorning, it was filled with tables heaped with food and drink. Fish, pork, pies, soups and potatoes steeped in cream filled the air with a delicious aroma. Someone had even brought a barrel of their best for the occasion.

The fisherman placed himself by the gate to greet everyone and direct the festivities. Right behind him, Evan registered names, nodding shyly to each visitor. When Raymond appeared, helping a majestic-looking woman carry a square basket, Lazarus called, "Talliaha, did you bring food for everybody, all by yourself?"

"Hardly," the lady laughed. "But I made several types of pudding, and of course, the mutton."

"Where's Charlotte?"

"She skipped the greeting and is in your field already," came the cheerful response.

Lazarus shook his head.

A tall man with bright, straw-colored hair walked up next, a stringed instrument shaped like a double gourd slung over his shoulder; its lute-like neck pointing upward.

"Vilo, you play that instrument very well. We've all enjoyed your music these last evenings."

"Thank you," the man said with a theatrical bow. "If only our dog were such an admirer. He chewed up my last one like it was a bone, and that one came from Summos Valley."

"I'm sorry to hear that."

"Well, this one I recently finished making myself. I decided on a double hollow for an extra echo. It truly has a masterful sound." Smiling, Vilo looked over at the prince. "Do you dance, boy? My two children dance together, but my wife's looking for a partner; I can't do it, obviously."

Evan retreated a step, shaking his head. The minstrel laughed. "Good! I'll tell her you would love to." He stepped away as Gwenre approached with another young man.

She had swept her hair up like the older village women, but it remained uncovered, and her simple-cut dress was of rich violet. She beamed at the prince, and he nodded shyly.

Greeting the young man, Lazarus warned, "Watch out for your friend's feet in the first dance, Tevin, or she'll likely not speak to you again."

Laughing, Tevin said, "You worry about that. I'm as light on my feet as a bird." Perhaps inevitably, he stepped on Gwenre's skirt, tripping. They broke out in laughter.

"Ah, we heckle him just to hear things like that," Lazarus sighed. "Of course, he can return it twice over."

Music sprung up from the other end of the field. Partners were lining up together. As a middle-aged woman approached Evan, Lazarus excused himself with a cheery, "Have fun, Max."

"My husband asked me to teach you to dance," the woman said with a soft voice that could have charmed the birds into landing on her finger. She held out her hand, and Evan accepted it.

Before the boy knew it, the lively music had swept him along. Fast and merry, the jig continued as partners changed rapidly and then reunited. Following everyone else, Evan found himself panting. Thankfully, it did not seem too long before everyone was called to the tables for the feast.

Not all of them ate at once or together. The prince spotted Lazarus by a lone tree, speaking with ten other men. Although they maintained the general lightness of a social gathering, Evan noted the furrowed brows that hinted at their real conversation.

Not far beyond the tree, a black-haired maiden was also watching the group of men. She was wrapped in dark green, her loose hair waving about her face. Despite the distance, her gaze seemed to fall on Evan. Inhaling, he spun away. She had certainly not come through the gate while he was there. He could well believe the accusations about her—Charlotte, the witch of Alleluia Lake, deadly and beautiful.

When Lazarus came for the prince half an hour later, he whispered, "I gathered thirty who I think will be able to help us. Come."

Evan's heart stopped. With a glance toward the mountain, he followed the fisherman. They had to rid themselves of Wilber's threat somehow before a great many people died. That thought renewed his resolve.

Despite the absence of the table, which was on loan for the festival, the inside of the hut was packed. Every fifth occupant held a candle, which seemed strange until Lazarus shut the door behind them, plunging the hut into darkness.

"Here is Prince Evan Maxwell," Lazarus introduced, a comforting hand on the prince's arm. To Evan, he whispered, "I already told them all I know of your relationship with Wilber, your right to Ansky's throne, and the truth about Darkfire. Those that are here have volunteered to help you remove your uncle from the island. Do you have any plans?"

Taking a preparatory breath, Evan nodded to the group. He recognized Vilo, Bounen, Tevin and, of course, Raymond, whose brown hair appeared black in the sharp candlelight. "Thank you for at least trusting Lazarus, if not Lisya."

"You speak of Lisya," Raymond spoke up, challenge in his eyes. "I think some of us would like to see her mark for ourselves first."

Many of the young men nodded their agreement. Submitting to the request, the prince pushed through the group to the bed and brought forth the sword. Instead of passing it around immediately, he first drew it slightly out of its scabbard. Light burst from the visible part of the white blade.

With loud gasps of pain, the gathered men hurriedly shut their eyes and turned away. Even Lazarus inhaled sharply.

Letting the sword slide back into place, Evan waited for his eyes to readjust to the dim candlelight. Then, he passed it to the closest man.

After it made its rounds of the room, it was silently returned to him. "If you still doubt my claim, you may leave. I trust this village's wisdom to choose the best course of action." He smiled slightly. "I *have* been living here for the past three weeks."

"Is there anywhere else for you to go?" Bounen whispered in defeat.

Evan fell silent for a moment. Then, running his fingers down his scabbard, he breathed, "No. I know this is not your fight. But I spent too much time making enemies when I should have been more open. When I told Lisya that there was no one to support my claim, she sent me here."

"Forgive us for seeming self-absorbed," Vilo said, "but we have families to protect, a home we love… and your battle has just entered our island. What I mean to say is…" He coughed. "Lisya is part of our heritage, our legends and our culture, but we're not about to sacrifice all we love for her, not most of us. What we want to know is how we can kick your uncle off our island without bloodshed."

"I wish I had an answer for that. I heard yesterday that Wilber is making his knights scour the island. You know your home. Where are his troops? How many does he have? Is there a spot on the mountain where they can be trapped until necessity drives them to accept banishment?"

"You want to besiege them?" Tevin gasped. "Starve them off?"

"If possible. Do you have the information we need?"

Raymond shook his head. "No. Most of us stay off the mountain."

"Then we need a spy. Is anyone willing? I know the risk involved, but I lack all skill in that art, and the territory is unfamiliar."

No one answered, and the silence stretched on.

"I will be your spy." The soft statement came from the corner of the room, between the bed and wall. Evan whirled toward the sound, dropping his hand to his sword hilt as Tevin raised his candle. The cloaked figure standing there pulled back its hood: Charlotte. Evan shivered. The shadows accentuated her darkness as a self-satisfied smile played about her lips, and her ebony eyes glimmered with cunning.

"You know of my skill, I presume." She stepped forward, repeating, "I will be your spy."

For a minute, Evan stared. Then he shook his head. "No!"

Charlotte tossed her head defiantly. "Why not? I am the daughter of Bozzic and the Lady Talliaha, shepherdess of the mountain, and granddaughter of the enchantress's first friend."

Oh, was she ever royalty! Despite that, the prince shook his head. "I am sure you are skilled. I have heard quite a bit on the subject. However, I know a little of the men on the mountain. Those of Evfel covet their honor, but have lost all true commitment to its Maker.

"You are a maiden..." Evan paused before adding, "an extremely beautiful and mysterious one at that. If they catch you spying, they will regard you as unworthy of respect. Under the circumstances, you would be an invitation for them to give in to their animal ways."

Anger burned in Charlotte's gaze, but she said nothing. Then she straightened until Evan became acutely aware that she stood a head taller than him. "I refuse to demean myself by describing my talents to you, a king"—cocking her head, she raised her eyebrows—"of fifteen. Know this: I would never be caught."

With that, she stormed out through the path that opened for her as if by magic. Evan did not have time to respond even if he had had anything to say.

Glancing around, Evan noticed the closed expression in Raymond's eyes. Some emotion lurked there, but it was not anger, nor wariness. Those gray eyes met his glance, and the hunter spoke. "No one else will be able to perform your task for you. Charlotte alone can remain undetected. But go ahead, ask again for volunteers."

All eyes were suddenly wary, as if scared he would simply select one of them. With a sigh, Evan bowed. "Thank you, everyone. I will consider what you have told me."

With that dismissal, everyone blew out their candles and left the prince alone with Lazarus. Silence followed, and the fisherman appeared to be waiting. Finally, Evan snapped, "What?"

Lazarus shrugged. "Are you going to ask Charlotte?"

"No! It is pride to think there is no way possible for them to catch her! What would we do if she was?"

Sighing, the fisherman sat down on the edge of his bed. "This is Enchantress Island, Max. Her family was closer to the enchantress than anyone else. How the magic that seeped into the mountain—or even Lisya herself—changed them, we don't know. But we do know they were changed. Talliaha had three healthy children after she was fifty, the last one in her sixties. Her hair is still predominantly black, despite her losses and trials. There is an unnatural youth and energy in that family. And like a personality flaw, it grows stronger in the children.

"Charlotte is called a witch by those who only know her bitterness and skill, and a nymph by her family, for good reason. She will *never* be seen or heard. She is no more than wind over the grass. She can walk beside wild deer without alerting them. She can sense danger in the breeze, better even than the animals.

"None of us consider her natural, but we do know she will be perfectly safe—the only islander who could go with such certainty. No one else will go. They would be risking their necks and their families for someone they don't know. Your plan makes sense, but you need Charlotte."

With a moan of defeat, Evan joined the fisherman on the edge of the bed. After a moment, he shook his head. "There must be another way. Maybe I should go by myself. If I were caught, it would just be my life, not any islander's."

With a sad sigh, Lazarus clapped the prince's knee. "You know you can't. You don't even sound like an islander. If they so much as passed you, they would know, even if you didn't blunder around up there."

When Evan remained silent, the fisherman shrugged. "Or you could try doing nothing. Perhaps they'll just go away."

Raising his eyebrows, the prince asked, "Are you willing to risk your life on that? If Wilber decides to make a final search before he leaves, he *will* find me. He will then proceed to execute anyone he can even slightly pass off as a conspirator. As independent citizens, you lack a king to protect you."

Lazarus nodded. "But we do have a king. That is the only way we function, though those who deny Him hardly realize that."

The fisherman was quiet a moment, staring at the opposite wall. When he spoke again, it was in a whisper. "That is our other fear, Evan. We all know where we can starve them out, if we could but find the openings. If the legends are true, the mountain once had hundreds of passages into the mines underneath it. The dragons closed all but one, which they left open, then forced islanders into them to gather more stones to heap onto the monsters' troves. It sits somewhere on Castle Mound. No one knows if the enchanters closed that off or if it was buried in the quake. What we do know is that something besides treasure was left beneath the earth up there. A trace of their magic or something. It thrums in the air, for those who can feel it, and scares most of the animals away.

"My point is, mines are deadly places to be besieged in, as much for whatever magical harm it could do to a person as for the chance of collapse. But if we secretly opened one and somehow lured Wilber's army into it... if they found anything down there... I doubt they would ever leave for good. We would be forced to let them all die."

Evan shifted, guessing at what the fisherman had not said. Still, he asked, "Tell me honestly, Lazarus, what do you think they might find down there to keep them?"

Lazarus shrugged with a grimace. "Treasures enough to fund any ruler for life, obviously. But worse... There might be a dark magic deep below our mountain that could grant any man an immortal power in exchange for a soul. It is that magic which Charlotte thinks the scent of bloodshed awakens like a living thing, waiting only for someone to call it. I dread even trying to find those mines."

Placing a hand on the fisherman's back, Evan sighed. "I'll find Charlotte."

Barely had he stepped out of Lazarus's door before Matalaide met him. "Max," she whispered. "May I show you something?"

Warily, he nodded, and she led the way past the field to the hut next door. Stepping inside, she beckoned him to follow. Recognizing that no one knew where he was, he wished he had not stuffed his sword back under Lazarus's bed. Yet he obeyed.

There was no denying she was the village weaver. Wool carpeted the floor, spilling from baskets. Two spinning wheels and one large loom filled most of the house. Squeezed around them were various chairs and a small table. A long chest rested against the back wall, and the weaver went over to it.

"I enjoy taking as much of my work outside as possible," she said, dusting off the chest. "Oh, every year it becomes harder to keep up with everything."

Unlocking the chest, she rummaged her way to the bottom and then pulled out a pile of blue silk. Shaking it out, she held up a hood and an elegant blanket for a horse. "These are yours, O prince. Your steed may not need them for years, but there will come a time in your reign when he will have to look like a king's royal charger. There are moments when appearance alone can deflect a war."

"But how did you...?" Evan gasped.

"I was told to make them in a vision. Now, there is one thing I must ask. What is your kingdom's emblem?" She held up a long triangle of blue silk, lovingly hemmed on all sides but completely blank.

"Ansky has no need of a new standard. Our castle holds all of them."

"It's not for Ansky. It's for you. You may not be able to retrieve your native crest for years. But you should have one to rise above your army in the coming war, to give them heart and courage. Also, Evan Maxwell, Ansky's standard will mean nothing to us islanders. We need something that has meaning to all of us."

"Why would it need to have meaning to the islanders?"

"Tut. Until you recapture your throne, we are your army. I think you should realize that. True, none of us are yet willing, but stay here. Remain honest with us. Share our hardships and joys. You will almost become an islander yourself, and when the day comes that you are forced to raise your standard, the island will roar for you."

Trembling, Evan shook his head. "I never want to hear the island roar for me."

"I know," she sighed. "Only fools think it glorious. But you'll want us by your side. Now, I need a place to start in designing a new standard. If you don't have any other ideas, tell me... What is Ansky's emblem?"

"The horse."

"Perfect! That's something I can work with." The weaver began folding the silk. Then she paused. "The herd stallion, your stallion... What's his name?"

"Darkfire?"

"Oh, very good. Thank you. You may do whatever it was you were doing."

With that dismissal, Evan left Matalaide's home, turning to the woods. Darkfire waited for him in the shadow of the trees. Together, they searched for Charlotte.

Whether by scent or hunch, they trailed upstream along the watercourse that ran down the mountain, through the forest at its feet and into Alleluia Lake. An hour later, Darkfire and Evan found her near the broadening of the stream in the cover of the woods.

She sat against a thick tree, her arms wrapped around her legs, her gaze downward. While the trees shone reddish gold in the setting sun about her, she appeared an entirely different creature from the witch of before. Now, she was the wood nymph, almost hidden in the foliage and just as likely to disappear once the prince dismounted from Darkfire's back.

Fearing that disturbing her might resurrect her prior character, Evan swallowed as he slid to the ground. A soft nicker from the stallion emboldened him, however, and the prince stepped forward. The nymph hardly stirred, although her lashes rose as she looked up.

Wordlessly, the prince settled beside her. There was nothing he could think to say that would preserve the peace.

Oddly, Charlotte herself broke the silence. "There is so much calm out here, I can actually contemplate everything."

"Then you feel it also?" At her surprised glance, the prince blushed. "Back home, I was forever hostile and bitter toward every person I passed. There was always something that annoyed me. When I could no longer take it, I retreated to the wild valley, the stables or to the tower by night. There is a presence in the wind and the skies, the voice of power and love. First, I would feel comforted, then guilty about my disgust with humankind... until I returned to its bustle."

He looked back up to see Charlotte studying him, but he kept as quiet as he would with a wild horse and met her gaze unflinchingly. After a long moment, she turned away, shaking her head. "You are the last person from whom I would expect to hear my life so eloquently expressed."

"It is the reason I am on your island," Evan said, shifting. "Believe me, though. I had no desire to bring danger to your home. I just needed... some form of companion. But danger has followed and..."

"I know," Charlotte whispered. "I'm also sorry. You have no reason to trust my skills."

"I apparently have no choice." As Charlotte turned to him in surprise, he explained, "It is up to you to defend your island, and honestly, I have no authority to stop you. I will not refuse to listen if you bring word." He took in her fine features, her black hair and her ebony eyes, and whispered, "Please, just be as good as you say."

A small smile transformed her face. "Then you permit me to do so?"

"If you want me purposely to send you, to trust your skill completely, you ask the wrong person. I have never seen it. In good conscience, I cannot ask you to do anything. But what I said is true. You may choose on your own." He smiled slightly. "If there is one thing I know about you, it is that you are quite capable of that."

Charlotte laughed. Then she glanced down and nodded. "Will you tell Mother I won't be home tonight? If you follow the stream, we live in the sixth house facing it." When Evan inclined his head, she stood. "Then I will go. Perhaps, Evan, you are not the only one who can start anew."

Then she was gone into the twilight. The prince turned questioningly to Darkfire, who shook his head, snorting.

With a smile, Evan pushed himself off the ground. "Shall we find this nymph's mother, the Lady Talliaha? She must be an interesting character if she raised such a maiden."

"Perhaps," was all Darkfire said as he bowed to allow Evan to mount him.

Chapter 12

The Quiet Before the Storm

RAIN FELL. Mist was gliding up from the ocean as Darkfire returned Evan to the village. Finding the house Charlotte had directed him to, the prince dismounted, whispering an assurance to Darkfire that was as much for himself as for the stallion, and knocked. Warm light spilled out as the door opened.

"Prince Evan," Talliaha greeted him. Smiling as he paused at the salutation, she stepped aside to allow him entry. "Raymond told me." A sad note rang in her tone.

"Is Raymond related to you?" Evan asked.

"No... and yes. He's lived in the house next to us all his life, and he's been nearly living in ours since he was five. When his parents died years later, he was too independent and hurt to accept us in their stead. But we're around each other so often, it worked out regardless."

Sympathetically, the prince wondered, "Was he young?"

"Eleven." Twisting her hands in her skirt, the lady dropped her gaze. Then, releasing her hands, she asked, "You let Charlotte be your spy, didn't you?"

His heart stopping at her distress, Evan nodded. "Lazarus said I should. Do you know something you have not revealed to him?"

"Good old Larry," the lady sighed. "I would trust his wisdom, Evan, not mine."

"But you are her mother."

"Aye, and Charlotte is all I have left."

Hearing the pain in her voice, Evan placed his hand on her arm and lightly squeezed it.

With a sob, Talliaha put her hand over his. "As an island, we trust the enchantress. I know her better than all the rest. But I'm unwilling to..." Pulling away, she stoked the fire.

"Is there anything I may do for you?" the prince asked.

With a sad smile, the lady gestured at a chair. "Tell me of Lisya. It's been forty years since anyone here saw her. Is she well?"

Obeying the request, Evan launched into all he could tell her of the enchantress of the Ice Woods.

For the next two days, Raymond watched the sheep on the mountain. Once, a knight passed by, asking about the shepherdess. Coolly, the hunter said, "I told her to stay home until you clear the island."

"You keep your eyes out for the prince, and we will leave. Remember that." So saying, the knight departed.

On the second day, a happy yip followed by an equally delighted bleat made Raymond turn. Charlotte stood in the flock's midst, pulling leaves out of one lamb's wool.

With some relief, the hunter approached her, coding his question carefully. "Does this mean you are finished with your chores?"

"There are no ears nearby," Charlotte answered without glancing up. "I'm more concerned that we make sure not to *look* like we've anything important to discuss. And no, I'm not finished with my chores, but I saw you. This evening, when you go home, tell Max there are men scattered all over the woods."

"Max," Raymond scoffed. Then, swallowing his disgust at the easy way the name tripped off her tongue, he asked, "How many are there, do you think?

"In total, perhaps fifty. I never see more than five at a time, and they move from camp to camp constantly. The Evfelian king stays atop the mound in a big tent with fifteen men. They watch everywhere and comb the woods. Darkfire needs to stay covered. Tell Evan to have him retreat to Whistler's Falls."

And with that, she was gone.

"You know, Evan," Bounen quipped, "we think you were insane to agree to Rihannon's request." The man paused to wipe his brow as he applied clay to the holes in the side of his family's house. Earlier, he had asked Lazarus if the prince could help him.

"Who is Rihannon?" Evan inquired, looking up from his clay-caked hands. "This stuff washes off, right?"

Laughing, Bounen slyly replied, "Only if you wash it off fast enough."

"Liar," someone called. They turned to see Tevin stop nearby.

"Tevin, shh! You don't have a right to call *me* a liar, anyway. How many lies have you told in your days?"

Tevin instantly turned scarlet. "Bounen, if you said that anywhere near a lady, I would have to kill you..."

"Particularly Gwenre?" Bounen grinned devilishly.

Tevin jabbed him in the ribs. "You were talking about Rihannon." Turning to Evan, he explained, "It's what we call that witch, Charlotte. She would never do a thing for a male. She hates them. No one knows for certain, but it is said she attempted to murder Raymond just because he—"

"I heard," Evan cut him off, "but there is no reason for it. Is there not a sensible—?"

"*She* doesn't make sense," Bounen interjected. "Her very birth didn't make sense. Everyone deemed Lady Talliaha barren. When she had her first, it was already long past the time when she should have been capable of it. And then, miraculously, she had two more—one ten years younger than the last.

"If you don't think that odd enough," he continued, disregarding the puzzled furrow of the prince's brow, "only three years after Charlotte's birth, Raymond's parents died mysteriously.

And it didn't stop there. One by one, all the males in her family have perished, until only she and her mother remain. No, she just wanted to satisfy herself when she agreed to spy for you."

"So you call her a witch just because most of her family died?" Never had Evan heard anything so pathetic.

Shifting uncomfortably, Tevin explained, "You've seen her yourself, Evan. I wouldn't believe the rumors about her using magic to murder men, but she is peculiar, and—" He halted abruptly.

Turning to follow Tevin's gaze, Evan spotted Raymond approaching them. "Good evening." Tevin smiled innocently as the newcomer stopped beside them. "We thought you were up with the sheep."

"Did you?" Raymond replied coolly. "I just returned." Pointedly turning away from Tevin and Bounen toward the prince, he said, "I have word. There are around fifty men, all in various camps. They are making thorough searches of the woods. Your spy thought it would be best for your stallion to stay in Whistler's Falls more permanently. Would you like to tell him yourself?" Without waiting for an answer, he continued, "If so, we should go now. Pull up your hood."

Grabbing Evan's arm, Tevin warned, "That's not a good idea with all the outsiders roaming about." When Evan silently drew his hood around his face, Tevin turned to the hunter. "Don't ask him to go with you just because of our conversation. We weren't talking about you, Raymond, honest."

"I know," followed Raymond's curt response. Then he and Evan walked away, stopping by the stream briefly to allow the prince to clean his hands.

When they were again heading toward the woods, Raymond at last sighed, "Please don't listen to what they say."

A quiet moment followed while the shadows of the many trees flickered over their hair and faces. At length, Evan inquired, "Why do the villagers call her Rihannon?"

Looking askance at the younger man, Raymond sighed. "The name 'Charlotte' means noble and free. To them, it doesn't match anything they think of when they speak of her, which you can imagine is often. At first, they would say, 'That witch,' 'That spirit,' or 'That amazing beauty,' and everyone would know about whom they spoke. But then someone put it all together into a different name: Rihannon, the name of one of the enchantresses of old." With a sad smile, he added, "Don't ask me about the enchantress who bore the original name. I only know she was as thoroughly wicked as most of her kind."

Shuddering, Evan pressed further. "Did Charlotte ever hate men?"

No answer came. When the silence had lasted long enough, the prince's thoughts turned back to their search. To himself, he muttered, "Darkfire might even be at Whistler's Falls now."

Raymond nodded. They continued to follow the stream, watching for the stallion, before Raymond answered Evan's question at last. "No. She's just searching. Perhaps you helped her find meaning.

"As for her family and mine, the younger generation likes a thrilling story. I don't know why my parents grew sick and died, but there is nothing to indicate Charlotte was behind it. As for her family, excluding her father, I'm more responsible for their deaths than she is.

"Bozzic was just old. Energetic, but old. His age finally caught up with him during his last two years, and there is nothing strange in that. In fact, there is nothing strange in any of her family's deaths. The young men just don't like her."

"Why are you different?"

Staring at the ground, Raymond recalled, "I believe Lady Talliaha told you I adopted them at five. They haven't always been the easiest family to embrace, but they gave me the siblings I'd always desired and later the wisdom and comfort I could flee to when I needed it. In many ways, they are my family. I admit life would be much less burdensome without them, but I don't know what I would have done if they weren't there for me, or even who I would be now."

His gaze flicking to the ground, the prince muttered, "I wish I could say that."

Raymond grinned. "Everyone can say that. Not a soul enters our lives who doesn't change us. Whether that change is good or bad is up to you and the Creator, but others will help shape it."

The prince returned a sad, tight-lipped smile. How he hoped Wilber had not helped make Evan Maxwell! The very thought was nightmarish.

Evan and Raymond found Darkfire at the falls, drinking and then shaking water from his mane. A soft blow was the stallion's only response to Charlotte's declaration that he should stay at the falls. "I have already noticed. That will not prevent my occasional checks on the village, Evan."

Running his hand along the horse's damp neck, the prince muttered, "I am protected."

"But if something does happen, I want to be there." When Evan said nothing but only stared at the ground, Darkfire arched his neck, placing his forehead against his chosen master's.

Stepping back, Evan rubbed the stallion between his ears. "The choice is yours, Darkfire, as it always has been. But be extra careful."

Five more days passed. Evan spent most of them honing the island-ers' individual battle skills. Some were very good with quarter-staves, but the majority were not—so everyone worked on pole defense. Most, Lazarus explained, were already superb archers. Vilo even spent a few hours outside his home trying to sharpen the prince's skills with a bow.

"It's the aiming skills you lack, m'boy," the minstrel said after one of the prince's arrows bounced off the nose of the wooden bear they were using for target practice. "You seem comfortable enough holding it and all that, but you haven't spent half as much time as you need training your eye."

Sighing, Evan pulled another arrow from where they protruded out of the ground by his feet. "We prefer the sword back home.

Archers are defenseless as soon as an enemy stands before them, so we practiced with the bow only a little."

As Evan drew back the bowstring, Vilo stepped behind and placed his hand over the prince's right fist. "Here. I'll show you what it looks like when it's lined up properly." Taking both Evan's hands, he adjusted the bow, aiming at the target ten paces away. "See where the arrow now lines up with the bear's eye? That's what it should always look like. Study it for a moment."

Then Vilo lowered the bow and stepped back. "Now, find the spot on your own."

With a preparatory breath, Evan brought the bow back up—just as a small boy bounded up behind them.

"Papa!" Vilo's little son Anka exclaimed. "May I challenge him? Please? I'm learning too."

Again lowering the bow without firing, Evan glanced at the beaming five-year-old. Vilo laughed. "Why not? That is, if our Max doesn't mind."

Round brown eyes with long lashes shone upward at the prince. After a moment, he shrugged. "Why not, indeed? For all I know, you are a master at hitting the bear's eye already."

"Yay," the boy hollered. "I'll bring my bow!"

"Thank you, Max," Vilo sighed fondly. "His sister is nine already, and she's rather good at her archery, so he doesn't really have anyone to challenge without feeling miserable at the end."

Shaking his head, Evan laughed. "Thanks for making me feel so skilled myself."

"Ah, did I hear some of our accent slipping in there?" Vilo asked, patting the prince on the back. "I know you'll limit yourself against him, that's all."

The boy now rushed outside with a much smaller bow, and Evan asked, "Are you ready?"

"Yes! Um... Papa says you're a beginner too. Do you want to share my bow? It's not as hard to hold."

Had that question come from an older person, the prince would have reddened, if not grown angry. As it was, he shook his head with a small snort. "I think I can manage."

"Split his arrows, Anka," Vilo whispered.

Somehow, Evan took the blatant bias in stride. Instead, he pulled back, trying to recapture the alignment from before, and released the arrow. To his surprise, it landed on the bear's eyelid.

Vilo clapped. "Good shot! You learn fast."

Then Anka let fly. His arrow thudded directly into the bear's neck. For a boy his age, his skill was deadly. The prince shuddered as Vilo clapped again.

"The next shot, you'll have it!" the minstrel encouraged his son.

After five more shots each, Evan had missed the bear almost as many times as he'd hit it, and little Anka had landed a bullseye. The boy jumped into his father's arms for a victory embrace, and the prince watched sadly.

After a moment, he asked, "So why does Charlotte say Mother and Father when almost everyone else here says Mama and Papa?"

Rolling his eyes, Vilo lifted his son onto his shoulders. "It's the pride in that family. You always recognize their line, right until it's so diluted it's nonexistent. Even Raymond called his parents Mother and Father, and he's distant enough. Of course, I don't remember if things were different before he started all but living with that family."

"What made him insert himself into their family?"

"Arnacin."

"Who?"

"Arnacin—Talliaha's first child." For a moment, Vilo was quiet. Then he sighed. "Honestly, he was a beautiful boy, full of wonder and love." The minstrel laughed distantly. "Daring as a baby dragon—pardon the expression—and proud as an eagle."

"What happened to him?"

Vilo's eyes focused. His stare pierced the prince's face in earnestness. "Either Charlotte or Lady Talliaha must tell you that, or Raymond if he feels like it. It's their story to tell. Honestly, though, he's been gone so long..." He paused, then sighed. "I don't know what your belief is there on the mainland, but here we know we'll meet our loved ones again in the afterlife. Not that the knowledge makes it any easier. I take that back. It does make it *easier* for them than if they thought they'd never meet again, but who knows how many long years it will be before then. And to add to their pain, there are quite a few gossips who will recite all sorts of exaggerated or downright untrue tales. All I will say is that Arnacin was never quite the normal islander. But then, in his family, what's different about that? Talliaha herself grew up a defender of her sheep and her father against the creeping blackness of the enchanters' war."

On the fifth day, rain came again, this time a drizzle rather than a downpour. Turning away from his view of it through Lazarus's open doorway, Evan leaned against the table. Sitting on his stool, the fisherman was whittling away. Each shaving curled and drifted to the floor.

"Can you do everything, Lazarus?" the prince asked after a moment.

"As in, would I need any help to survive if I lived outside a village?" When Evan nodded, the fisherman shook his head. "I can't card, weave or sew to save my life. I would have to take Matalaide with me."

At the image of the woman and Lazarus living alone together, Evan laughed.

The fisherman blushed. "No, it would never work. She'd wind up knifing me.

"Besides that, you're right, there isn't too much I don't know how to do, except perhaps hunt. Raymond's a killer with a bow and knife." He paused, looking up. "I should rephrase that. He's not heartless, simply skilled. If he was defending someone..." The fisherman shook his head. "I wouldn't want to be the aggressor. You know the people in Elcan think we're pushovers because we live simply? Tut! Raymond could scare them to death with his abilities."

"I can imagine—"

A light knock interrupted them. Turning around, Evan saw Charlotte at the door, her hair, cloak and dress stuck to her. Pale, soaked and dripping, she shivered. "I have word."

Lazarus jumped up. "Not right now, you don't." Taking her arm, he pulled her inside. "First, you're going to dry off and have something hot. Then you can tell us."

Retrieving his spare articles of clothing, he passed them to the maiden and then nodded toward the door. "Come on, Max. We'll let the lady change. Let us know when you're finished."

Pulling their cloaks on and their hoods up, the two males slipped outside, shutting the door behind them. It was not long before it reopened and they could return to the warm interior.

Charlotte was taller than the prince, but more slender, and the fisherman's shirt covered as much on her as it had on Evan. The biggest difference was that she had tied a rope around Lazarus's shirt, shortening it by letting it fold over the makeshift belt.

Barely had they stepped back inside before Charlotte said, "They're planning to attack us, Evan. The king has ordered all his men onto the mound tonight. As they were packing up, one said, 'Finally, we shall see some action.' We have to stop them."

Taking a slow breath, Evan asked, "Are you positive they plan to attack? Is he not perhaps calling them to prepare for departure?"

"It's in the air, Evan. No, there's no proof other than that, but if he even attempts a thorough search of our villages, there will be consequences. Many islanders will refuse to allow him to paw through their homes, and he will retaliate, even if he never finds you."

Evan said nothing. "At the very least," she persisted, "I think we need to hear their plans. We must witness this meeting of theirs, with a group large enough to stop them immediately, should the need arise."

Nodding in thought, the prince replied, "So it is war either way, you mean?"

Neither Charlotte nor Lazarus offered anything more.

Evan nodded with a sigh. "Alright, we will go. Hopefully, we will have time to make our own plans afterward. Are they already in conference up there?"

"No, they are breaking camp. The king has called the meeting for midnight."

"How long does it take to reach the mound?"

"They watch the paths, but I can lead you up in three hours by taking lesser known trails."

Turning toward the fisherman, Evan asked, "Lazarus, would you be willing to alert as many single young men as possible? I want to leave those with families alone for now. Tell them we will gather at the stream as soon as it is dark."

Lazarus bowed and turned to go, but then halted before departing. "Max, make sure Charlotte has some tea and food. Hang up her wet things for her."

"Honestly," the maiden muttered—but the fisherman was already gone. "As if I'm incapable of taking care of myself!"

With a smile, Evan grabbed the rope Lazarus strung between two hooks on his wall whenever he needed a clothesline. "He just cares. Was it raining harder this morning?"

Charlotte flung her wet garments over the line. "It slowed as dawn broke." Her gaze met the prince's, and she looked down. "I want to thank you again for trusting me. You didn't even doubt I would find food." She smiled impishly.

With a puff of amusement, Evan shrugged. "That was one area I had no doubts about. I am sure you know how to find sustenance up there. Also, I figured you would go home from time to time if you needed anything. I see you refused to do so."

"I had to stay up there to make sure I didn't miss any news," she said.

The prince turned to the fireplace and the pots there, while Charlotte settled herself by the fire, pulling her long hair over her shoulder. She had apparently found Lazarus's comb, which appeared in her hand as she began ripping the wet tangles out.

"It's funny," she thoughtfully commented after a moment. "All those things they say you did, the way they say you acted... All their gossip, all the years they lived with you, and they can't see why. They can't see through it. But I do." She looked up at the prince, and he quickly turned away.

"You have met me in different times, Charlotte. I have tried to change."

For a moment, there was silence. Then Charlotte whispered, "You've done well. If only I had the will to do the same."

When the tea had steeped and the seaweed cakes warmed, Evan poured her a cup and placed a piece beside her. She nodded her thanks, but continued tugging on her hair.

After a moment, the prince asked, "Would you like some help before the tea grows cold?"

Dark eyes stared at him, and her hands froze in her hair. Then, without a word, she passed him the comb, almost as if under a spell.

Timidly, Evan sat down behind her, pulling her long black tresses to her back. Trembling slightly as he touched the locks of someone many deemed a witch, he started combing at the bottom. She remained unmoving.

After a moment, the prince asked, "Is this all right?"

A shudder passed through her. "Will—my younger brother—would help me with my hair when he felt sad. Somehow, it comforted him."

"What happened to your brothers, Charlotte?"

There was a long pause, then the maiden twitched. "Arnacin went to sea four years ago..." She turned to the fire, staring into it, as if she could see the past. Evan just continued combing her hair. "He had to go," she finally said, more to herself than to him. "For his health, he needed to go. I so wanted to go with him. I should have. He might've returned if I had. It's been too long, though. He's gone."

For a moment, the only sounds were the swish of the comb and the pop of the fire. Then Charlotte shook her head. "Or so logic says, but I can't accept it. As for little Will? He died last year of... sickness. I also grew sick, though I survived it, but he was only five."

Looking over her shoulder, she whispered, "To tell you the truth, I don't even know how long I'll have Mother. She's healthy in many ways, but her heart is burdened, and at her age…"

"Are you scared?"

"No, just… tired." The maiden's tone darkened. "Matalaide keeps suggesting I should marry soon, but that I'll never do. She can go to another village for her wool, for all I care. We'll need a new weaver before she'll need a new shepherdess, and the hypocrite isn't even married herself."

"There may be other reasons she wants to see you marry," Evan suggested.

"She's still a hypocrite."

Smiling, the prince remained quiet.

"The train arrives tomorrow," Wilber announced to the assembly gathered around the maps on the table that each camp had drawn over the past month. "Twelve thousand Evfelians have joined the search units in the mountains. If they hear no more word of Evan Maxwell, we will force the islanders to a confession."

"What if they truly have seen nothing?" Radnor asked.

Piercing the knight with a dark look, the king growled, "If there has been no sign of the prince on the mainland, Radnor, then what is your conclusion? He was headed here."

"He might have been swept out to sea. They did fall—"

Something outside snapped loudly. "Find out what that was!" Wilber barked. "If there are spies out there, let none escape! I want them alive!"

"Gag all prisoners!" someone else ordered, as all but the king and two Evfelian knights rushed out of the tent. "We do not want them alerting others. Who knows how far a scream will echo on this mount?"

Stepping around the table, Wilber placed his hand on his sword. "The proof of their guilt might lie before us in one of these prisoners."

Chapter 13

Raymond's Hour

"**W**E'RE DISCOVERED," an islander whispered beside Charlotte. She, Evan and twenty others were fanned out in the trees surrounding the mound. Although she had volunteered to creep into the camp to listen at the tent flap during Wilber's meeting, Raymond had held her back. "If one of us makes a mistake," he'd said, "you will be the first found."

Instead, Tevin was sent to approach the tent. But it seemed either he or someone else had erred.

From the darkness around three of the islanders, Charlotte breathed, "Drop to earth. If you make no noise, you may be able to escape."

"You're leaving before we are," Raymond commanded, grabbing her arm. She jerked away, but approaching feet discouraged debate. They flattened themselves against a tree.

"Raymond," Tevin's frantic voice hissed. "There are more forces coming on tomorrow's train!"

In response, Raymond shoved Charlotte backward. "Go. Warn the others."

Even in the dark, he could tell her eyes sparked with flames, but then she was gone. Empty air filled the place where she had stood.

Rushing feet were coming down the mount toward them. "Stay low as you retreat," Raymond ordered those around him. "Quietly."

Over the hurried sound of the knights, he winced at the soft swish of the retreating islanders. Stringing his bow, he drew closer to the tree's base. A dark form shifted nearby, accompanied by the heavy thump of booted feet.

Raymond released his arrow, and the knight dropped to the ground with a cry. "Over there!" someone shouted. "Bring a light!"

No other shadows appeared, but Raymond heard many feet circling his area. He loosed another shaft toward one rustle. An ensuing grunt rewarded him. Then he heard the twang of a heavier bow and dropped to the ground.

The surrounding trees were lit by the flare of torches. Not ten paces away, he faced a crossbowman. "Toss your bow aside, Islander," his opponent growled, training the weapon on him.

As more knights approached, Raymond surrendered. Forceful hands seized his arms, binding them behind his back as another knight rammed a wad of cloth in his mouth.

Hardly able to breathe, he was dragged up the hill and thrown to the ground beside a blazing fire. There, his captors bound his ankles together. Struggling to rise even slightly, he looked around. Several other captured islanders caught his eye, sharing his worry. A few lay senseless.

Then his gaze landed on Evan. Unconscious, unmoving and bound as tightly as the rest, the prince lay in plain sight of the knights. Feeling himself pale, Raymond quickly glanced away. They were all dead if someone should recognize the prince. His hair may have been cut in the islanders' style, and his clothes would easily pass inspection, but if the knights scrutinized their captives, it was unlikely they would overlook him.

The crackle of branches and crunch of leaves in the distance indicated the search was still in progress, but more captured islanders were gradually joining them.

One knight dumped Bounen by Raymond's feet. His expression changed to recognition, even as the hunter's memory stirred. It was Quincy.

"Sire!" the knight called, seizing the islander's curls and jerking his head back. Raymond closed his eyes. "I think this one is their leader. He has that quality about him."

"Bring him here."

More knights approached. Without unbinding their captive's ankles, they dragged him before the Evfelian king and set him on his feet. Mercilessly gagged, Raymond panted, staring into green eyes nothing like those of Lazarus's emerald ones.

Wilber studied him a moment, then coolly pulled out the gag. "You must have put up a good fight, Islander. Someone tried to strangle you."

Gulping in air, Raymond said nothing.

The king briefly allowed him his silence, then asked, "So, you are the leader?" When he received no answer, he viciously back-handed his captive.

With his ankles bound, Raymond tripped and landed on his backside.

"Answer!"

"Careful, sire!" A knight spoke up. "Remember their magic."

Wilber stepped closer to his fallen captive. "I have no fear of that." Crouching down, he stared into Raymond's eyes. "Do you know how many witches Evfel has hanged and burned without anything happening? Some were caught speaking to spirits of the dead."

The captive looked away, expressionless. Even meeting the expectant gazes of the knights standing guard around them was preferable to allowing the Evfelian king to read whatever might reveal itself by looking into his face.

Wilber shrugged. "You are courageous. I will give you that. I can start with your companions if you continue to defy me."

Raymond's breath caught. He searched the king's eyes for a bluff, knowing there was none. At last, he nodded. "I led, some-what. Actually, I just took charge for the moment. We don't have leaders on this island."

One of the knights snorted, but their king did not echo that sentiment. Instead he asked, "What were you trying to do?"

"We were keeping watch on your movements, as we have been since you stepped foot on our home." There was not a tremble in Raymond's voice. It was simply a fact.

Wilber nodded. "Calculated. I would almost believe you, except that you forgot a few things. Your marksmanship exceeds most who live simple lives, and your movements tonight have the ungainly discipline of a hastily trained unit. For what are you training, if not for the fact you have joined with my nephew?"

"I'm a hunter by trade."

"That answers nothing." Wilber's smile was unnerving.

Raymond shrugged, refusing to quiver. "It's the truth, though you may choose to disbelieve it."

A knight hurried forward. "Sire, I think we have all of them."

His breath catching, Raymond gazed at the heap of islanders. It did indeed look like they were all there. Only Charlotte was missing. Breathing a silent thanks for that, if nothing else, he looked back to see Wilber studying him with a smirk.

"Do we have all of them, Islander?"

"If I said yes, you wouldn't believe me. And why would I say no?"

"Do you think torture would loosen his tongue?" the knight whispered.

Wilber's fingers pressed under Raymond's chin, pushing his head up, forcing their gazes to lock. The captive clamped his jaws together, and the king laughed darkly. "It might, although I think he cares about his friends too much to make it necessary."

Releasing his grip, Wilber stood. "Ten of you, stay here. The rest, continue the search."

Grinning conspiratorially, the knight asked, "You mean ten of us Evfelians?"

"You know exactly what I mean. Ansky is not seasoned enough for what might happen here."

With a bow, the knight turned to bark out orders.

Wilber, meanwhile, glanced down at the captive at his feet. "Are you too proud to beg for your companions' lives?"

Raymond snorted slightly. "For certain."

"Then you will tell the truth."

Raymond glared back. "I have been telling you the truth."

"But not all. Perhaps some islanders have certain innate skills for strategy and archery, but that many?"

"We're not mere islanders. We are the islanders of Enchantress Island, steeped in magic for hundreds of years." He dropped his gaze to the ground. It was blackened, as Charlotte had said, but as it had served as Wilber's campsite for the past month, the color could as easily have come from the heat of his fires. Raymond just had to trust it had already been blackened when the troops from Elcan arrived. He shivered as the nymph's words ran through his thoughts. *Something has woken for the first time in sixty years, and it is not small or benign.*

"For that alone"—Wilber's tone made the hunter's attention snap back to him—"I should burn down your island; villages, towns, fields and woods. But I look for no war with you. Not now."

"No." Raymond grinned slightly. "War with us could be devastating."

"Continue pretending you know nothing about Ansky's prince, however, and your homeland *will* suffer the penalty. Why are you training?"

"In case you try to inflict slavery on us. You say you're hunting someone who came this way, but—forgive us—we don't believe you. That could easily be an excuse to slip your troops inside without suspicion. Except that we are always suspicious."

"So you have not seen or heard anything of a young man—a boy, really—and a stallion?"

"No."

"Forgive me, but I *don't* believe you," Wilber mimicked. "As wily as your answers have been, you have left something unanswered. The very fact that you avoided it justifies my disbelief." He paused.

"What did I leave unanswered?"

"You might be able to train yourselves, Islander, but how could you train for field strategy when you have no experience?"

"What gives you the idea that we were trained in any of that? We slipped past your watch and broke into groups. Nothing more."

"So you could surround the place if need be. What then? Would you try to line up and take us down with a row of undefended archers? You must have had some form of strategy. Or are you suggesting you are arrogant enough to attack us without a plan?"

Wilber took a small step back. "Now, as enjoyable as this contest between sharp minds has been, it is time for seriousness. I have stated why I am here. You know I tell the truth, since you have obviously met Evan Maxwell. You fear conquest. He will bring it. Sneakier still, he will steal hearts and souls with a humble, benign smile. He will soon have everyone's family and friends within his sway, and they will hand him their freedom without question. Before they even realize what has happened, they will be slaves with no escape."

Raymond's face drained of color. Resisting the urge to insist on the opposite, he shook his head. "If we had seen such a person, we'd never allow him to smile benignly."

Wilber laughed. "I will give you until sunrise to answer honestly. If you continue to lie, I will do as I threatened. Each of your companions over there, I will order burned alive or hanged before you."

When Raymond fell into a tight-lipped silence, the king crouched to eye level.

"You could, of course, all go free. Just hand over Evan Maxwell and the horse he stole. Once that is done, we will leave you alone, with not a trace of our presence remaining."

Refusing to glance at Evan, over in the unmoving heap of islanders, Raymond said nothing.

Wilber turned to the knights behind Raymond and gave one of them the gag. "Watch him, and do not put him with the rest." He disappeared inside the tent.

Thankfully, the knight only tied the cloth back around his captive's mouth instead of shoving it down his throat. Allowing himself to glance toward the heap of other prisoners, Raymond trembled. Scared gazes stared back at him. Evan was still unconscious.

In the darkness, having assumed that the prince would never emerge from hiding, the knights had not looked twice. That could change at any moment.

Despite criticism from the other islanders, Charlotte's flock was not the only one that used the mountain. It was true, though, that none but she dared to take their flock all the way up to Castle Mound. Although twelve-year-old Barth and his older brother, Tahan, had found that the closer to the mound their flock wandered, the softer the wool. So, from the western side of the island, they dared to lead their sheep into the woods and part way up the mountain early every morning to allow them to graze on various wild shrubs.

That night, some Elcan men had prevented them from leaving the mountain. No one was to go up or down. So they sat in the dark, huddling beneath their cloaks, listening for the sounds of predators and grumbling about the discomfort.

Barth jumped, realizing someone stood at his shoulder. In the light of the lantern he held up, he recognized Charlotte. She was enveloped in clothes much too big for her; hair wrapped around her head. Through their shared profession and use of the mountain, they had come to be fairly good acquaintances, as much as anyone could be with her.

"Charlotte," Barth gasped. "What's going on? Are you stuck up here too?"

"I need assistance." The nymph's tone was curt.

"In what way?"

"There's no time to explain fully. The entire island's in danger, and I need someone to help me release my companions from the Elcan king on Castle Mound."

"Castle Mound?" Barth squeaked.

"It's dangerous. The question is, will you help? I can't bring anyone else up here. Too many paths are being watched at this point."

"I suppose we will help. For the island's sake."

"Good. Then here's what I need first..."

Dawn came. The unconscious prisoners stirred, and their half-aware attempts to free themselves earned them a beating.

When Wilber returned, the guards dragged Raymond to his feet. "Now, Islander," the king demanded. "What is your answer?"

"My answer?" Raymond stalled. "You've forgotten something. I hunt animals for a living. That requires a certain degree of cunning and the ability to read their intent. In this case, your honesty—or lack of it—is irrelevant. Once you have what you want, you will come to conquer us. You live for conquest. We have not seen the threat your prince poses, but we *have* seen yours. Therefore, you are the one we must deal with now."

His face darkening, Wilber hissed, "You speak of conquest as if you know what occurs in Elcan."

"We are being frank with each other, no? I trade with Summos Valley. It trades with Ansky. The rumors travel."

To the side, Evan was subtly inching toward the prisoner behind him—Tevin.

"Hold it!" someone shouted. Both king and captive glanced over. A knight had grabbed the prince beneath his chin and was twisting his head back and forth, studying his features from all angles.

Raymond paled, looking back toward Wilber. Meeting his gaze, the king smiled knowingly and stepped toward the other captives. "What have you found?"

"Is this not your neph—?" The knight's question ended in a scream as an arrow flew from the trees and landed in his chest. Before anyone could move, two more knights fell to the ground, shafts sunk deep into them.

"To me!" Wilber called to his remaining seven knights. But in four more heartbeats, all lay dying upon the ground. After another moment, the king's right hand had been pierced by an arrow. With his uninjured hand, he angrily seized Evan's throat.

"This ends here," he exclaimed as the prince squirmed beneath his strangling hold.

"It does," a cold voice snapped. Charlotte stood at the edge of the mound, only a few paces from the heap of prisoners, her bow taut and an arrow pointed at the king's heart. "For you. If you don't let him go now."

Menace filled Wilber's eyes as he reluctantly released his nephew and retreated. Gasping, Evan collapsed against Tevin's back. "The choice is yours, Evan," Charlotte said, without a note of gentleness. "Should I kill him?"

The prince closed his eyes weakly, and the maiden's bow tensed. Then Evan shook his head.

Two boys joined the maiden, knives drawn. They quickly began freeing the captives. Covering the king, Charlotte scoffed, "Be grateful you have a merciful nephew. Barth, bind the filth and gag him. We only have a few moments."

While the other islanders joined in freeing each other, Barth and Tahan tightly bound the glaring king. Once he was free, Evan joined them, snapping the arrow in the king's hand and pulling out the two ends. As he ripped a strip of cloth off Wilber's tunic, the king studied him balefully.

"You have grown, nephew. Yet for all your maturity, you forgot one thing. Never leave an enemy at your back."

Wrapping the wounded hand, Evan looked up. Bitterness, even hatred, briefly cooled his gaze. "You are Evfel's king, but you are also my uncle. I would prefer not to fight with you. Our two countries need the peace treaty to stand. If not for..."

He left the rest unsaid. After Barth gagged the king with another strip of torn shirt, the prince grabbed Wilber's tied feet. "Help me find a place to hide him in the tent. It may give us some more time."

The prince, the two shepherd boys, and their captive disappeared into the tent nestled among the ruins of the old castle.

"We're wasting time!" Tevin gasped, "The train might be here any moment."

"I'm sure the prince will see to it," Bounen soothed. "But we wouldn't want that beast of a king to overhear what we plan, or even what we know."

Shortly, Evan reemerged. "Find your weapons and take the swords from the fallen knights. I still have mine, thanks to Lisya, but we will need all the help we can gather. Charlotte, is there a way to make it to the tracks without running into any patrols?"

"They will already be on their way here, if they heard anything. But I'll lead you." She turned to gather weapons while the prince crossed over to Raymond.

"Thank you, Raymond," the prince whispered. "I am sorry."

Trembling, the hunter turned away. "Are you? You do realize that, had it not been for Charlotte, your attempt to free Tevin would have killed us all?!"

Noting the torture in Raymond's gray eyes, the prince sighed. "Did you expect me to just watch, with no concern or care, no attempt to help someone escape?"

Raymond refused to meet his gaze. "That's what kings do, out of necessity."

"Well, I am only a prince."

Trudging away, Raymond joined in assisting those gathering weapons. Passing a dead knight, he stooped to seize a sword from lifeless fingers.

As he looked back toward the prince, his breath caught. Charlotte stood beside Evan, her hand in his while her lips moved. Raymond dropped his gaze, but his ears strained to catch their conversation.

"Don't let Raymond bother you, Evan," he distantly heard the nymph say. "There's a lot he's struggling with, and he's going to have to figure it out himself. I know he will stay beside you, though."

Raymond glanced up to see Evan slip away with a tight-lipped smile. For a second, the hunter wondered if Charlotte was wrong—but inside, he knew she was right. Out of duty to righteousness, Raymond would protect and stand beside the prince. But his heart felt cold, dead.

Tahan left to guard their sheep. Barth, although the younger of the two, trailed along with the small force that crept behind Charlotte. Sometimes, she led them to jump across thin gullies. At other times, they stayed motionless in thick underbrush while knights dashed past.

At last, they arrived at the southern tip of the island, where its cliff overlooked the ocean. There, the train tracks shot from a spur of land extending from the island's mountain and disappeared into the distance. A knight stood in the islanders' way, looking out to sea.

Hunched behind the underbrush, Evan whispered, "We can grab this one and knock him unconscious."

"Do you not intend to bind him, at least?" Charlotte hissed.

"Find some vines. I want him alive, if we have a choice."

"I can grab him," Tevin volunteered.

On Evan's other side, Raymond cocked his head. "Just don't make it too theatrically obvious."

Grinning, Tevin nodded. "Check." He slid out of hiding and walked up to the knight, hefting a decent-sized stick.

"He's going to make a blunder," Charlotte muttered.

With childlike patience, Barth patted her hand. "Have some faith."

As Tevin drew closer, the knight became aware of soft footsteps. He turned toward the sound.

The would-be ambusher hastily hid the stick. "Is the train here yet?"

Looking at him suspiciously, the knight dropped his hand to his sword. "Your market is farther up the mountain."

Charlotte nocked an arrow. Beside her, Evan shook his head, before looking back up.

With a shrug, Tevin inched closer. "Oh, I don't want to trade anything. I was just hoping its arrival would mean you're leaving."

The knight began to draw his sword. He had barely touched it before Charlotte's arrow sank into in his throat. "Oh, help..." Evan sighed.

"We had no time to do anything else," the maiden retorted, pushing herself to her feet and hastily joining Tevin. Reluctantly, Evan followed. Behind him, the rest of the small band rustled.

At the edge of the slope down to the spit of beach, they all paused to look out across the tracks. Gazing at that vastness, the group's task seemed impossible. Evan was the first to break the despairing silence.

"We need to weaken the bridge by cutting the pylons. When the train comes, its weight will drop it into the ocean. We can set up an ambush for any survivors."

"We're short on arrows," Charlotte commented.

Sliding his own quiver and bow off his back, Raymond turned to the woods with the others. "Then we have no choice but to make do."

Evan turned to the nymph. "Charlotte, as soon as we are done rigging the bridge, would you take Barth home?"

Though fire danced in the nymph's eyes, she said nothing. To Barth, the prince said, "Will you stand watch for the train?"

"Sure!"

Evan Maxwell was proving more cunning than Wilber had thought him. The tent had been erected around what appeared to be a deep, old water trough—crumbling but stable. The king had used it to support half of a tabletop, instead of bringing in a complete table. In the trough, the prince and his helpers had found a convenient prison.

Since hearing the islanders leave, Wilber had been struggling to free himself. Cramped as he was, he could not seem to find purchase anywhere. The sturdy wood of the tabletop resisted any of his attempts to shoulder it aside or kick it with his feet. If he had use of his arms, he could push the covering off the top.

Freeing his hands, however, had proved difficult, if not impossible. Those brats had known what they were doing. His attempts to wriggle out of the ropes only pulled them tighter until his hands were complaining of the struggle necessary to force blood into them.

Curse them! They had warned him as well—"Don't pull and you'll be fine," the younger scrap of an islander had said as they hauled the tabletop back over the trough.

Now he was forced to wait for someone to find him. Meanwhile, Prince Evan Maxwell could be plotting anything.

It seemed like forever before a concerned voice called, "Sire? Sire, are you here?"

Twisting to remove the equally obstinate gag, Wilber hollered through it. There was no reply, so he tried another muffled cry.

Feet pounded through the tent flap. "Where?"

The king cried again, and the tabletop thudded as hands seized it. A moment later, it was lifted free. Quincy and his ten Anskonians peered down at him.

"Quick," Quincy ordered. In moments, Wilber was freed.

After a reviving sip of cider, he answered their questions. "The islanders are in league with Prince Maxwell. He was with them when more islanders ambushed us. All those dead out there—that was them. He refuses to return the stallion. He wants war."

"Why did he leave you alive?" Radnor asked.

"Maybe for the humiliation." Shaking his head, Wilber placed the goblet on the table. "Maybe to make a point. I only know his response to my inquiries—war."

Sharing a defeated glance with Radnor, Quincy sighed. "Prince Maxwell has fully betrayed us, then."

"We have no choice but to accept his declaration," the king announced. "Tonight, whether or not our reinforcements come through, we need to weaken his forces. We will start on the southern tip and burn every dwelling to the ground. Evan Maxwell has chosen for us."

The Anskonians bowed.

Once outside, Radnor lowered his voice. "What does this mean for Ansky?"

Quincy shrugged. "Our future king, Evan Maxwell, has chosen a horse over his throne and declared war with our neighboring kingdom to do so. What can we do but stand with the more righteous?"

Looking around them at the many Evfelian knights, Radnor whispered, "We could claim our king, whether or not he likes it, and fight Wilber now."

"Prince Andrew resides back at Castle Ansky. Some Anskonians will claim him as king rather than accept an abdicating horse thief. We would divide Ansky for good, and she would never survive the bloodshed."

The older knight could only nod in agreement.

Chapter 14

Death's Joy

Evan stood alone on the sand, guarding the many archers who remained on the cliff behind him at the ready. The horn of the train sang overhead as the wheels clacked toward its doom. As the front engine's weight reached the last of the bridge's supports, a crack split the tracks and a screech rose from the train's horn as it smashed downward, coach after coach spilling behind it.

As if in a storm, waves burst upward and pounded across Evan. Then the saltwater washed back into the sea. Silence followed in an unnatural calm. Tension shimmered along the cliff.

A figure hauled himself from an upturned window. Barely had his torso emerged before he toppled back inside with an arrow through his chest.

Now the train erupted. Swarms squirmed out all at once. Arrows rained from the sky. They were not a force of thousands, but at least half a hundred had avoided death or major injuries in the crash. Against the islanders' pitifully armed twenty, those relatively few knights were still enough to crush their defense.

Below the flying arrows, Evan drew Lisya's sword from his side. The white ore gleamed in the sun, but no blinding flash betrayed it. It was afternoon, and the sun was almost at its zenith.

Knights surged forward. Some had grabbed shields from the wreck and thrown them over their heads as protection from the raining death as they dashed for the prince. Five men clashed against Lisya's sword.

It was a challenge greater than Evan had foreseen. All the hours he had practiced before leaving Ansky were helpful. The drills against the islanders had also certainly paid off, but assailed on all sides, he would soon be defeated.

Abruptly, the knight facing him dropped and turned to block another slashing sword—and failed. Raymond had joined the prince. "We're empty," the hunter gasped above the cries of the injured and dying.

Evan nodded. "As we planned, then."

"As we planned," Raymond agreed. Indeed, their plan had been carefully laid out. The other islanders would watch for the moment to draw their newly procured swords, then slide down to join the beach defense. Evan just had to drive the enemy back toward the sea for a moment—he and Raymond had to, rather.

With the renewed strength of desperation, the twosome increased their attack. Through the flash of blades, Evan realized Raymond certainly knew how to fight with skill. He might not have had the best sword technique, but he was fleet of foot and shrewd of eye.

For a split second, they forced their opponents back, taking the opportunity to spin around to where the other islanders gathered at the base of the slope. With a nod from Evan, the islanders charged as one and broke abruptly to the sides.

Despite the craftiness of their attack, the knights hewed through them. Cut off from the rest, Evan fought his way to the seaward side of the shore. Should they remain ashore, they would all die. Knowing that most, if not all, of the knights feared open waters, the prince called, "Quick! Into the ocean."

Bleeding, stumbling, eight of the islanders broke through the press and waded out. At first, Evan stayed to guard the retreat. Once the others had all left the field, though, he grabbed Tevin, who had collapsed at his feet, then turned and dashed into the sea with the invalid.

The knights only followed them a few feet into the water. After all, fighting was impossible in depths greater than the ribcage. They had made it out once. It was unlikely they would go back in.

Turning, they instead finished any islander who so much as twitched on the ground. A moment later, the remaining thirty or so knights had disappeared into the woods.

The prince panted, holding Tevin's head above the water. Blood covered the islander's face, flowing from a gash on the top of his head. Crimson dyed the waves as they washed ashore.

Assessing those in the water with him, Evan noticed Raymond and the others seemed to have fared better than Tevin, at least. Still, the bedraggled group clung to portions of the train as if unable to stand on their own anymore.

"Come if you can," Evan sighed, splashing salt water over Tevin's wound. He could feel thin scratches on his own cheek and wrist, but they were nothing in comparison. "If not, I will be back for you."

Weakly, Raymond turned to help the islander next to him. As he moved, his left shoulder rose above the waves. It was covered in blood.

As the remaining eight islanders all but crawled ashore, a figure appeared at the top of the cliff. Evan tensed—but it was Charlotte, worry creasing her brow. As the injured dropped to the sand, her face turned white. Silent as ever, she dashed down the trail, straight to Raymond's side. Not only did blood cover his shoulder, but a long slice ran along his ribcage.

As the nymph's hand fell upon his shoulder, Raymond stirred. "No," he breathed. "Take care of Tevin. He's the worst. I'll be alright."

Dropping his gaze to the form in his arms, Evan agreed. Although he could feel the faint stirring of the ribcage beneath his hand, Tevin showed no signs of consciousness.

Breathing hard, Charlotte joined the prince. "Evan, take Raymond's shirt, rip it into strips, cover his wounds, and stop the bleeding."

With a faint smile at her concern for the man she "hated," the prince slid out from beneath Tevin, leaving him to the nymph's care.

As he ripped the seams along the scarlet-stained shirt, Raymond gasped in pained laughter. "Matalaide will have you flayed."

"Why would I care?" Charlotte retorted, bending over Tevin. "Besides, with those gashes, there's no saving the shirt. She'd need to make a new one, even if we didn't rip it to shreds. Anyway, we're just finishing the job your captors started with their makeshift gags. I notice they left our prince's clothes alone, though."

Briefly, she glanced up at Evan searchingly. He shrugged. "Lisya made these. Maybe they were too tough to rip."

Neither Raymond nor Charlotte replied. After a moment of silence, during which Evan and the nymph wrapped the islanders' wounds, the prince said, "We have to bury the dead and move from here soon, Charlotte. We could be attacked at any moment, and even I, in my uninjured state, lack the endurance to continue. Do we know how many knights survived?"

"No, but leave the dead for now," the nymph whispered, stiffly standing with a wince. "Transporting these few will be hard enough, and I need to gather some herbs from the woods before any of them die."

The prince nodded as his gaze fell on Bounen's bodiless head, lying a few feet away. He shuddered. "War," he commented. "I never understood Wilber before, but I understand him less now. There is no glory in war."

Loose strands of hair billowing about her face, Charlotte stared sightlessly at the train. It shone now in the orange glow of the late afternoon sun as it lay washed in the auburn-tinged tide.

"Charlotte?" Evan asked.

"The Mound rejoices tonight in the blood shed here," she murmured. "I wonder how many of us will live to see it sleep again."

Shaking his head, Evan sighed. "Come on."

Earlier, Charlotte had shot another six escaping knights in the woods. Now, the group of wounded islanders silently passed the bodies, the stronger limping along on their own and the weaker being helped. Evan nearly carried Tevin, who had only slightly regained consciousness.

They had not yet reached the safe place Charlotte had in mind when even that thin level of awareness slipped away. Evan laid him on the ground. "Charlotte, we have to take a break."

With a sigh, the nymph let her charge rest against a tree. "Very well. I'll fetch some water. We'll give them an hour. This is a main trail, and we must move on."

Though she was not gone long, Tevin passed from quiet unconsciousness to feverish tossing. Concerned, Evan placed both his hands around the islander's bandaged head, trying to keep it still. When Charlotte returned with a wet cloth and a large folded leaf filled with water, Evan sighed. "This trek is too much for everyone."

"There's nothing we can do right now." Passing the prince the wet cloth, she nodded to Tevin. "Try to calm his fever with this." Then, lifting his wounded head, she dripped water down his throat. "Shh, Tevin, help us. The herbs I need aren't in this part of the woods. Come back, so we may reach them."

Placing the wet cloth against those burning cheeks, Evan watched the gentleness of the nymph. "Will he make it?"

With a soft smile, Charlotte looked up. "He's Tevin. He would refuse to die on principle. There's no one to fill his shoes back home as the worst heckler of them all, to say nothing of the trouble he used to make. He is growing out of that, at least." She gently placed Tevin's head back on the ground.

With a slight smile of his own, Evan changed the topic. "You know, I tried to order you home."

She looked up at him, an expectant smirk on her face.

"Well, I guess I am glad you disobeyed. I have no skill in this, and..." He blushed at her smile, unable to finish.

"We're free, Evan. Of course I disobeyed. There was no one I was duty-bound to obey." Chuckling, the prince accepted the leaf full of water and moved to the next wounded man.

Still whispering, Charlotte continued to run the wet cloth down Tevin's hot cheeks. The water and her voice were all she had to give at the moment.

"Charlotte," Raymond rasped from where he lay propped against a tree behind her.

Sighing, the nymph joined him. "You should be sleeping."

"Charlotte, he's a prince."

"What?" Receiving no answer, she tried again. "What are you trying to say, Raymond?"

In response to the irritation in her voice, he only closed his eyes. After waiting a second, Charlotte took a guess. "Is that jealousy? If it is, you're absurd. I told you I would never marry. I meant it. And regardless, jealousy ill becomes you."

His eyes shot open. "I'm not absurd. You should see your smile when you're talking to him. Moreover, you're smiling at a male. By your own standards, heaven forbids you to smile at a male."

In disgust, she turned away. As she did so, her gaze fell on the prince, who was helping one of the wounded islanders drink. Fondly, she shook her head.

As if Raymond could read her thoughts, he weakly pushed himself onto his elbows. "See!"

"Raymond, you're a beast. You wouldn't want me to care about any male at all unless it's you."

"That's not true. I'm concerned." Yet Raymond avoided her accusatory stare.

"You know better. I have no interest in Evan except as a friend. We have too much in common not to be so. Anyway, he's a wonderful young man."

"Boy," came the mutter.

"Well, he acts mostly like a man, which is more than I can say for you." With that, Charlotte returned to Tevin.

Heartlessly, Evan and Charlotte woke Tevin as the sky darkened. Although they allowed their progress to slow, they pushed the wounded until they reached a stream surrounded by thick brush.

"No one will see us here," Charlotte panted, having nearly dragged her charge for the past few minutes. "Start a small fire by the water's edge, Evan, where it won't catch on the brush. I'm going to find what we need."

The prince did as she asked and then sat to tend the fire. Around him, the flames highlighted the paleness of the wounded and the feverish flush tainting more than just Tevin's face, whom Evan had carried for the last stretch.

Finally, Charlotte returned. Neither she nor Evan spoke as she mixed what she'd found into a paste. Then, with the prince's help, she went around, covering wounds with her concoction and dripping herbed water into the islanders' mouths. Moments after swallowing, they each slipped into a calm sleep.

Since Raymond had been the most alert, they went to him last, but even he was now trembling with fever. He didn't respond as Evan unwrapped his wounds and brushed Charlotte's paste over the torn skin.

Lifting the hunter's head, Charlotte pressed her water-leaf to his lips. "Drink," she whispered. When he failed to reply, she trickled the liquid into his mouth. Slowly, Raymond's breathing changed like that of the other injured islanders, its tortured pace easing in sleep.

Evan looked up once he'd finished rewrapping the wounds. Surprisingly, Charlotte was running her hand over the brown curls in her lap as she stared down at her charge.

"See," the prince whispered. "All your hatred of him is an act. You do love him."

Her hand halted as she met Evan's pointed expression. After a second, she sighed, "He's my brother, Evan, in all but blood. Even *by* blood, we're cousins somewhere up the line. No, I never truly hated him, although I'm frequently furious at him. Occasionally—this might only be the second time it's happened—I realize I do care. Under it all, he's always giving of himself and fairly wise for a male. Or for anyone, for that matter. He was there for William when we lacked a man of the house. He's *always* been there, Evan, even when I'm horrible. And if I'm honest with myself, yes, I love him. Not the way he wants me to, but I love him."

Gently lowering Raymond's head to the ground, she went to wash her hands in the stream. Next, she ate some of the little scraps of edible plants she had gathered while searching for herbs. Following her, Evan did likewise. Though the food only awoke his hunger, he paused. Around him, the forest sang with the chirp and hum of insects, while the stream gurgled, glinting with fire and moonlight. Rustling in the light breeze, trees swayed overhead.

Charlotte's dark eyes watched him, reflecting the night. Her black hair also shimmered with soft light, and her fair skin shone. She was at once invisible, as part of the night, and visible, as if it merely mirrored her beauty.

"Was the Mound's castle built by the enchanters?" Evan asked to break her mesmerizing gaze.

"No, not according to our legends. The dragons also dwelled in it, but it's unlikely they built it. Dragons don't build things as a rule. Did you notice the crumbling statues on the way up, and the stone stairs in some places? Those are not enchanter-made either, but our history is unknown before the horror of the dragons."

"I heard the island was once the tip of a mountain called Mount Jade. Do you know anything about that?"

She smiled with a small inhale of amusement. "Did you hear that from Lisya? No, I know nothing of a Mount Jade."

When he turned back to the night, she asked, "Did you love your home?"

"Castle Ansky? No. It is four walls, an iron gate and a lock."

She laughed. "I love mine, despite our short history."

For a second, the prince was quiet, listening again to the music of the untamed night. "I also love yours," he said at last.

"I know."

They fell silent and let the sounds of nature wash over them. Evan wondered how much she knew. As a spy, did she just know he loved her home? Or did she know his heart yearned for the freedom and soothing wildness it offered? Were her two soft words an acknowledgment of his ordained sacrifice?

If she knew his thoughts, she passed them by. "Your uncle charged you with having grown. He might only have meant the ability to lead in battle plans and small forces, but he is right. Continue as you are going, and you will make a fine king—the one they need. At least, I will support your reign."

Turning to her, Evan searched her gaze and found only seriousness. He looked away, blushing. "From you, Charlotte, who purportedly hates all men, such support is worth that of all the rest put together."

From the corner of his eye, he saw her glance down. Abruptly, she stiffened, her chin lifting as her gaze went to the sky. "What is it?" the prince asked.

"Smoke from a large fire."

"Do we need to move?"

"No..." Charlotte's voice trailed off. When she said no more, Evan resigned himself to waiting.

As Lazarus took Charlotte's folded dress back to Talliaha, he searched the wood line for any movement. He stopped as something black burst from the shadow of the trees. Darkfire was racing toward the village.

Rearing before the fisherman, the great horse cried, "Wilber is burning every dwelling, and he comes this way! Grab what you most need and flee to the cover of the woods!"

Gasping, Lazarus raced into action, pounding on the nearest door. Behind him, Darkfire's clarion call broke the evening peace—a shout of warning. Then the stallion shot by.

"Where are you going?" the fisherman called.

"To slow them!" After flinging his nose into the air, the stallion increased his pace.

Shaking his head, the fisherman continued to the next door. "Wilber comes to burn our village! Take what you need and flee to the woods!"

All around, the alarm echoed. It did not surprise him to see Talliaha rush toward him. "Is there word from Raymond or Charlotte?"

"No." Shoving Charlotte's dress into the lady's arms, Lazarus rushed back to his own home. "Take what you need and leave!"

Heeding his own advice, he grabbed his fishing pole, his box of carving knives, and the remaining seaweed cakes. He took a last look around his beautiful home, then with a stab of grief, he fled. There was nothing else to do.

Just a few feet from him, Matalaide held a basket of wool. Peeking through all the white was something shiny and blue, but Lazarus hardly dared ask. What was important was that she, like him, had left much behind that she cared about. With his carving knives, at least he could make her a drop spindle within an hour.

With the entire village evacuated, he knew every inhabitant felt the same pain, and the same determination to assist each other. As foretold, riders appeared with torches just as the sun turned red. Hidden beneath the forest's trees in case they needed its protection, the villagers painfully watched their homes burst into flames, staining the surface of the pond with an angry glow.

After a night's rest and Charlotte's care, most of the injured were able to shuffle along behind the nymph. Evan carried Tevin across his shoulders, hoping it wouldn't exacerbate the islander's wounds.

Strangely, they encountered no patrols. With growing trepidation, they continued on. The smell of smoke grew. At last, they came to a small clearing that allowed them a wide view—and all stared down in horror.

Alleluia Lake remained and a few charred hut frames. Other than that, the village was gone. Nothing moved except a thin tendril of smoke still drifting from the gutted structures. Glancing at the colorless faces around him, the deadness in their eyes, Evan whispered, "There are no carrion birds down there. Perhaps everyone escaped."

"Or they were all taken captive," Charlotte muttered under her breath.

"Only the witch could be heartless enough to put that into words," one of the wounded groaned.

"Quiet!" Raymond snapped, his voice breaking.

The prince laid a soothing hand on the hunter's arm before turning to the nymph. "Charlotte, I can stay here to guard them. See if you can find anyone."

Raymond shook his head. "No! I'm well enough to stand guard. Both of you go."

"If a patrol runs across you—"

"Don't argue," Charlotte pleaded, grabbing Evan's arm. "Just leave Tevin here and come. I don't think there are any patrols out anymore. They're probably returned to the mound and their main camp. If they have captives, they will expect us to attack." Looking back at the remains of her home, she whispered, "Or perhaps they expect an attack, regardless."

Considering the pride and independence of the islanders, she was probably right. If there were survivors, individual battle plans were likely coming together all over. Evan only prayed they knew what they were doing.

He propped Tevin against a tree. "Are you sure you will be alright?"

There was no answer. He looked up to see Raymond leaning against another tree, hunched over, an arm across his bandaged ribs. "Raymond?"

When he stepped near, the hunter grabbed his arm. "I am sure of one thing, Evan. I don't want Charlotte going alone. Please. I know she's capable, but with all this... It's no longer a matter of spying."

With a sad shake of the head, the prince pulled the clammy fingers off his arm. "Overnight, war has broken out," he agreed. "Take care of yourself and them, Raymond. Hopefully, we can find somewhere you will all be able to heal."

With a slight smile, Raymond nodded his farewell. "Charlotte will know how to help us once you return."

Nodding, the prince turned to follow the nymph. Hopefully, nothing would bother the wounded, not even wild animals that sensed dying prey. Not one of them had argued against Evan's leaving, but he wondered if they were in more danger than they admitted.

The rest of the way down the trail passed in silence. With each step, Charlotte appeared paler. Knowing she was imagining all the evils that could have befallen her loved ones, Evan took her hand and gave it a squeeze. Though she left her hand in his, it was as if she was too far away to notice.

Abruptly, she stopped, listening. Straining his ears, the prince waited. Seconds ticked by. Then a soft *crunch, crunch* of feet sounded down the trail of stone steps on which they stood.

The nymph jerked Evan off the path and around a thick tree. Before the prince even saw anyone, Charlotte gasped, leaping down the steps and about a rocky bend. "Vilo! Larry! Is everyone alright?"

"Charlotte!" the voice of the fisherman exclaimed. "Where are the men? What happened?"

Evan was already rushing to join them. At the sight of him, the fisherman turned grave. Nevertheless, he opened his arms for the prince's embrace. "We were looking for you. What happened, Max?"

"There are eight wounded up the hill. We came to find out what happened to the village."

"We're all fine, thankfully. There are eight wounded? Where are the other twelve?"

Charlotte whispered, "Their remains lie on the shore beneath the tracks."

"Would it have been more heartless to say they're dead?" Vilo asked.

"Never mind that now," Evan interrupted, waving his hands. "We need to meet with the rest of the village and gather enough people to bring in the wounded before *they* join the dead."

"The others are by the stream, right at the edge of the woods." Slapping the minstrel's arm, Lazarus started upward. "You two go down. We'll find them. Are they off the trail?"

"They're on my overlook," Charlotte called back. As the men disappeared around the turn, she dashed off in the other direction. Evan followed.

As Lazarus had said, the entire village was sitting around a series of small campfires. No one looked happy. Huddled with a group around one fire, Gwenre was sobbing, "I worked so hard on that festival dress, and I had to leave it behind."

Next to her, another young lady patted her back. "But you were so much better than that. You took blankets and food for everybody."

But Gwenre was not to be comforted. She pillowed her head on her knees and sobbed. "I hope Tevin's alright."

Biting his bottom lip, Evan walked by without comment. In their despair, no one seemed to notice him or Charlotte. The nymph, too, was scanning the crowds. Then, with a cry, she grabbed one of her baggy pant legs—she was clearly more accustomed to skirts—and dashed over to another fire.

There, Talliaha jumped up. They met in a tight, relieved embrace that caused Evan a stab of loneliness. "Charlotte, thank God you're alright! No more adventures, please."

Charlotte just held her mother, promising nothing. At last, Talliaha backed up. "Where's Raymond?"

"We need some more men to fetch him along with the rest of the wounded," Evan said, speaking up as he drew level with Charlotte again. The entire camp seemed to turn toward him. "There are eight wounded villagers up there. Vilo and Lazarus already went to keep them safe, but there should probably be two men and a blanket for each, if you have them. They've walked enough as it is."

A brief silence followed. Apparently, no one wanted to ask who had died. Finally, twice the number of men needed stood and began gathering the blankets readily held out for them.

Those eight could be any of their sons or brothers, since they refused to ask. Other sons and brothers had seemingly perished beneath the tracks. The eagerness to assist in any possible way was palpable.

The men were soon off, and Talliaha placed a hand on Evan's shoulder. "I think you and Charlotte could use some sleep and food yourselves. Did no one see to your wounds, Evan?"

She was looking at his face. Self-consciously, he rubbed at it.

"Don't do that," the lady sighed. "You have dirt and dried blood all across it already. Honestly, if you weren't still standing, I would swear you're more grievously wounded than you obviously are."

With a slight smile, Evan relented to Talliaha's motherly ministrations. He was too exhausted to think anymore. The desperation was past. Others could see to everyone's immediate needs.

Chapter 15

A King Strong Enough to Rule

Evan was asleep by the time the men came back with the injured. All he remembered was sitting down by a warm fire and maybe eating something. Then he was waking to dawn light shining through the tall trees. A blanket was wrapped around him.

All about him, the camp had settled into a quiet watchfulness. The wounded had been returned to their families. Not twenty yards away from Evan, Talliaha sat beside Raymond. Although his cheeks were flushed, he slept peacefully. Charlotte also slept, still in Lazarus's clothes, with her head pillowed on her mother's legs. It was almost childlike how she had pulled the fisherman's sleeves over her hands for warmth and let the pant legs cover her feet.

Soft but heavy footsteps approached. Evan looked up as Lazarus's shadow fell across him. "Charlotte told us what happened," the fisherman said wearily, crouching. "Do you think your uncle will attack again?"

Sighing, Evan pushed his blanket off. "I expect him to."

"What's your next move then?"

"We have to find the islanders from the other villages before they try to attack individually. Some might need medicine or shelter. And as a large, organized group, we can do more than as separate assemblies. We should also move this camp to a better concealed position."

"Very well." With a stiff groan, Lazarus rose. "I can gather small groups to search. Is there anything else?"

Glancing around the camp, the prince nodded. "Have you seen Darkfire? He said he would keep watch, and I expected him to sense the danger. Charlotte did."

Coughing, the fisherman bobbed on his toes. After a moment, he coughed again. "Have you wondered how we all escaped?"

"Someone saw them coming?"

"We escaped with supplies, Max. Darkfire alerted us at least an hour before the attack came." He paused.

After waiting a second, Evan pressed, "Then where is he?"

"There's been no word of him since he left to distract the attackers."

The prince's heart chilled. Warmth fled his body as his gaze drifted to the open sky between the trees. After a moment, he whispered, "Then he is dead."

A gentle hand, wide and powerful, dropped onto his shoulder. "We don't know that, Max. They claim this whole thing started because you stole the king's charger. I find it more likely that they took him captive. He'll be alright. As a stallion, they'll treat him well."

Evan shook his head. "Wilber intended to slaughter him if he refused to submit, and Darkfire will never do so again. He did temporarily, as an act, but there is no act anymore. They might have captured him at first, but in his rage, Wilber will keep his word."

With another soothing pat, the fisherman slipped off to gather search parties. Pulling his legs close, Evan buried his head in his arms—a shell to block out the rest of the world.

Bit by bit, islanders from other villages joined them, bringing with them more pain. Charlotte was grinding herbs when her closest cousin in age, Renssin, shuffled into camp with a crowd of other equally beaten islanders. His six-year-old girl clung to his neck, as he clutched her to his chest.

Talliaha, who had been sitting beside Charlotte, jumped to her feet. "Renssin!" she called.

Shifting his daughter's head to his right shoulder, Renssin searched for the voice. Finding it, he sighed and walked over. "Great-Aunt, I'm glad you escaped the attacks." But he sounded far from glad. Deadness choked it. His girl's stare was vacant, sightless amid the shine of tears.

Placing a hand on his arm, Talliaha asked, "Is the rest of your family safe?"

In the ensuing silence, trees rustled. Gently, the lady motioned for her great-nephew to take a seat by their fire. "I will bring some water," she sighed.

As her mother left, Charlotte returned to her task. "Holding it in won't heal your pain," she advised. When he remained silent, she added, "What happened?"

Finally, Renssin caved, slumping to the ground. Still holding his daughter, he brushed her brown hair out of her face. "We were sleeping when they came," he gasped. "I heard screams. The fire."

Seemingly struck dumb as well as blind, the girl patted for her father's hand, wordlessly wrapping both of hers around it when she found it. At the festival just the year before, she had exchanged stories with other girls her age and seen as well as any of them. Now, horror and smoke had robbed her of some of her greatest gifts.

Charlotte set aside her work in sudden sympathy, placing her hands about the knot of fingers. "Your newborn as well?"

"All the rest," Renssin choked. "My beloved... with the baby. The knights cut them down. And Jacob and Yahin. I never found them afterward. Just Myrryl here. I was carrying her."

Charlotte had no words. A moment later, her cousin continued, "The next morning, I tried to go back. Everything was in cinders. I didn't find a sign of them, not among the remains of our home, not in the streets..."

Changing the subject, the nymph asked, "Were you able to save any of your pottery tools?"

The only answer was a pained shake of his head.

Sadly, Renssin's woes were shared by many. Family members had died. Survivors bore terrible burns and long slashes from swords. Wounded in heart and body, many of the men swore they would take Wilber down. Even some women echoed their vengeful emotions.

Wilber had attacked like a thief in the night and not everyone had been prepared. Due to Barth's warning, the people in his village had escaped unscathed, but it was only one of a lucky few. They were even able to bring their sheep with them.

The islanders hid their flocks with Charlotte's in the shallow cave midway up the mountain that had served as a fold since the time of the enchanters' darkness. Twice a day, Barth and Charlotte slipped away to check on them and would then close the heavy door hidden behind the ivy, muting the sound of bleating from any searching knights. In this way, the islanders' hidden camp remained invisible.

"It is a sad state when people only know how to kill and how to make plans for killing more," Evan admitted, following Charlotte about as she helped treat the many wounded. He carried supplies while she worked, fetched replacements if she ran out, but otherwise only followed her.

"Stop feeling guilty," Charlotte advised, spreading ointment over one child's burns. "In the first place, it's not helpful. In the second, you at least know you're not duplicitous."

Rolling his eyes, the prince snorted. "Oh, that makes it so much better."

"Certainly. I bring lambs into the world. When they stumble, I heal their cuts. When they sicken, I nurse them back to health. Then, with the same hands, I slaughter them for dinner. Some in my family have kept their tenderness despite that. I haven't."

She continued her ministrations, now binding cloth around the child's hands. After a little while, she shrugged and whispered, "Perhaps it has more to do with other factors."

"Such as your inability to find friends?"

With a small smile, she dipped her chin. "I have found one."

As Evan's thoughts drifted to Darkfire, his own first friend, he dropped his gaze.

Little by little, Tevin recovered. Raymond moved about the camp, weak and pale but on his feet. The health of the other six members of Evan's small force ranged between being unconscious and slow of mobility. When all the remaining islanders had come together and many were back on their feet, Evan asked Vilo to gather those he knew were wise, as well as the young men hungriest for battle.

They met by night in the tunnel at Whistler's Falls, where at least most of the sky was blocked. Although Evan had spent days helping the islanders, he doubted people from the neighboring villages would agree to anything but his death once he revealed who he was. Likely, only the bright light of Lisya's sword—the undeniable proof of her support—would keep him alive.

But the sword had its own dangers. If the sudden brightness alerted knights to their meeting, they would need to move swiftly.

Still disguised as an islander, Evan followed Vilo and Lazarus. He knew Charlotte was trailing them only because he could see her, shadowed beneath her cloak, when he looked back. In silence, the crowd of forty slipped through the woods, stopping only once the mountain rose on either side of them. There, with the stream rushing by their toes, Vilo held up his hand. "The noise of the water will cover our voices here, but first, Evan, do you wish to come forward?"

Licking his lips, the prince pushed down his hood. Around him, a low murmur of angry suspicion filled the air. "You!" one of the islanders hissed as the prince joined Vilo before them. "We ought to have known. You sounded like one of them."

Not daring to move, Evan waited as hands tightened on bows. Hopefully, the fact they had not yet drawn arrows suggested he could reason with them—as long as he trod carefully.

"I do apologize. I never intended harm to come to your island, but I can't change that now. Lisya sent me here, and my only option is to help you in any way I am able during this sudden war."

"Ha!" another voice croaked. "In the first place, I doubt you've ever met Lisya. In the second, your only option is to turn yourself in. Where's the horse you stole?"

Under his cloak, Evan placed his hand on his hilt. "Dead. But as to my proof that Lisya sent me..."

The stars, including Resplandecer, vanished as the sword's night-shattering light finished his sentence for him. An audible wince of pain rose from the islanders.

"As for turning himself in..." The low voice of Charlotte came from behind the prince as he returned Lisya's sword to its sheath. She had kept in step with him when he joined Vilo before the large group. "It is too late for that. The king of Evfel has lost his fear of the magic here, as he would have eventually. Ansky, as a free kingdom, is the only thing standing between us and his conquest of our home. In that, Evan Maxwell, king of Ansky, is our friend and ally, with or without our enchantress's intervention."

Begrudgingly, the islanders nodded. Whether or not they liked Charlotte, it appeared they bowed to her logic. As they straightened, one said, "Very well, we'll hide you while we gather strength to slaughter the invaders from Evfel with her king."

"Is that your response?" Evan demanded. "I have no desire to kill any more than necessary, and if we can force Wilber to give his word, that will be best for the peace of Elcan."

"Then what is your plan to rid us of them?"

"The king has not moved from the heights," the prince informed them. "He is well prepared for a straight attack."

"So starve them down," one man spat.

At the prince's elbow, Charlotte shifted. "We could box them in. Several trees reach above the mound. We used them when some of our own were captured recently. If we block off their escape, we can pick them off little by little."

Lazarus shook his head. "The strongest of us are too heavy to scale those trees. That would leave the task to maidens like yourself and to children. Also, they will be sure to fire back once they're aware of our plan. We can't put you at that sort of risk."

Crossing her arms, Charlotte glared. With a sigh, however, Evan agreed. "I think a siege is our best option. That said, they will try to force through. Our injured, elderly, women and children should stay farther down the mountain. Charlotte, I was hoping you would take charge of the camp. They need you to protect them."

The nymph stared at him. Her thoughts were hidden beneath her dark gaze, but her fingers touched and parted, arching like spiders' legs. As if reading his unease, she pressed her palms together and looked away, still without comment.

Leaving her for the time being, Evan bowed to the gathering. "This is your home. You know best where to set up your fortifications and where to ambush those trying to break through. I leave the rest of the planning to you. Know that Wilber will probably be expecting this move. You must proceed with utmost caution.

"For now, we should leave this place before someone finds us."

His part of the debate complete, he walked away from the gathered men, increasing his pace to allow the islanders time to speak without him. Charlotte stayed at his side. Despite her wordless support, she left his request unanswered for the rest of the night.

Darkfire would never submit. Be that as it may, tied by a cruel war bridle to a stake on Castle Mound, his head pulled almost to the ground and hobbled by two of his legs, his self-imposed dehydration had taken a toll. Yet the stallion's gaze still burned with fire as Wilber passed a few paces away.

Darkfire made no movement; all struggle vanished with the night. His captors had won, temporarily—his defeat made more complete by the fact they had seen the nature of his hooves. Of course, they had failed to realize the truth. They assumed the islanders had altered him somehow. But Wilber correctly concluded that the stallion was incapable of being tamed.

Which only made his continued survival more ominous.

"Sire." One of the knights, Quincy, had stopped before the king. "There has been no sign of the islanders."

"Have you seen any at all?"

"No."

Tapping his fingers on his arm, Wilber muttered, "That is what concerns me. If you saw anyone, we could watch them at least. Yet, they have disappeared. If we could evacuate to the mainland, making sure they followed, that would be another matter. But they have stranded us on their turf."

He whirled angrily. "I refuse to fight them in their woods. It would be our slaughter in their homeland. Here, it is open. Here, we have the high ground. And their wrath will bring them here, if we wait."

"They could besiege us," Quincy warned.

Wilber's lips curled upward as he glanced at Darkfire. "They could, but would Evan Maxwell besiege his own stallion? He has invested too much time in training it to obey only him."

The islanders closed in around the mound slowly, one group and then another slipping up the mountain. A day after the first group had left, however, an islander returned with a scrap of paper he had found nailed to a tree and handed it to Evan.

Before opening it, the prince warned the islander, "This can only mean they are aware of your plans. It would be best if you closed off the mound at once."

"We already thought of that." So saying, the islander left.

The note was short.

Evan Maxwell,

If there is the slightest hint of a siege, we will sacrifice your stallion. You have tried to make him useless to me. So be it. I can still find a purpose for him.

Wilber Dalacort,
King of Evfel
Regent of Ansky
Current Protector of Cyra

Crunching the note into a tight ball, Evan exhaled. "That serpent."

"Tell him it won't work." The soft voice at his elbow made the prince jump. Charlotte stood there, concern on her face. "If his threat has no power over you, he won't do it. You can easily say you can't hold an animal's life above those of hundreds of people."

"No," Evan sighed. "If he has Darkfire at all, he will carry out his threat. If only out of spite, he will do it."

"Do you want me to confirm he speaks the truth?" Her question was accompanied by a touch on his arm.

Meeting her concerned gaze, the prince placed his own hand over hers. "No, I believe him. I have no reason to, perhaps, but I do. He would have guessed it would come to this, and he would have prepared multiple ways."

"What are you going to do?"

"I have to be the one to rescue Darkfire. There is no other way. But your siege must take place."

"How would you go about rescuing him?" The nymph's tone was skeptical. "Wilber is just as likely to expect that response."

"What else can I do?"

"I think a king would put the mission first." Charlotte's voice was tinged with sadness. "Should you try to rescue Darkfire, you're not likely to return. Ansky's throne will be forfeit to Evfel."

Staring at her, Evan shook his head. "I never want to be the sort of king who puts worldly goals ahead of individuals. Some would say I am selfish, emotional or weak, but if I betray my friends…" Voice trailing off, he shook his head.

Charlotte dropped her gaze to the ground. "Yes, putting the protection of friends above everything else might be selfishness. That is why I said nothing when you asked me to take charge here." He waited in silence. After a while, she whispered, "I want to make sure… you come back alive." She raised her head and again met his gaze. "My mother says she's selfish. I too have lost loved ones, and in my loss, I have found a friend. But I know what you're thinking. If an attack breaks through your forces, I will be able to defend the camp. Perhaps I'm the most qualified to do so. Should I abandon that responsibility to guarantee your safety?"

For a moment, Evan was quiet, studying her. Then he stubbornly promised, "Whatever I do, Charlotte, I will do alone, without impeding your siege. You have my permission to kill Wilber if he endangers your home. I will do my best to make sure your actions will not bring harm to the island."

"So you sacrifice the very purpose for which you decided to become king. You will leave Ansky to Evfel in order to rescue Darkfire."

Yanking away, Evan muttered, "Never." He stormed off, shame heating his face.

His conscience pricked him no less when he stole away late that night for Castle Mound. The cold breeze of approaching fall blew about him.

It was early dawn when Wilber woke to a surprise. Four Anskonian knights were escorting Evan Maxwell up the mound, one on every side of their captive. They passed the wild stallion, stopped before the king, and fanned out into a semicircle.

Had the prince truly wanted war, he would never have surrendered. His mere presence brought that lie to a crashing end. Hoping the knights failed to realize that, Wilber chose to brazen through. "What convinced you to surrender, Evan Maxwell? Dare we fear some trap?"

"You said this ends here. It does. You want Ansky. I want you to release the stallion and leave the island."

"Ah, if I did want Ansky, I could take it now." To emphasize his words, the king seized his sword hilt.

A grim smile touched Evan's face, brimming with a ruthless cunning that even Wilber had never expected to arise from all the hatred and bitterness he had cultivated. "You could *die* now," the prince warned. "Kill me without my consent, and you will sever your own heads. The islanders' mercy hangs on mine. They are content, for now, to give me final say. If I choose to take your life or if I die, not one of them will hesitate to kill you. I came for an Evfelian challenge."

A stillness followed as the knights gathered around. With an amused snort, Wilber regarded the young prince. No longer was he the boy the king could subtly wrap around his thumb. Indeed, he was no longer a boy at all. Not only had he gained a few inches since spring, he had made too many of his own momentous decisions.

"What are the terms?" the king asked after a moment.

"Ansky. The winner claims the throne." The prince paused. "And the stallion. And if I win, your immediate departure from this island."

There was only one reason Evan would count Ansky's throne among the stakes, Wilber knew—to make sure he agreed to the challenge. Odd that the prince was that confident of... What? He would never win. "Are you forgetting an Evfelian challenge is to the death, to prove the strength of the victor?"

"I see no need. If the winning strike is a killing blow, that is one thing. If it only wounds enough to end the duel, killing your opponent is something else entirely."

Feeling the gazes of the Anskonian knights, Wilber shrugged. "I will leave the island either way. With the war ended, the debate over possessions is resolved."

His Evfelian knights stepped forth from the smaller tents.

"I ask one thing, Evan Maxwell. Do you truly wish to wager your throne? It will be an inevitable consequence if you die, but if we are to remove that requirement of the challenge, then you may keep it. This challenge would only decide the owner of the stallion."

Evan's blue eyes, filled with distrust, quietly regarded the king. He was marked dead in Wilber's opinion, who had made that last statement only to keep the Anskonian knights in the dark. Wilber was the far better swordsman, even with a slightly tender right palm; Evan Maxwell was history.

"If you will settle for that, Uncle." Evan's tone was now marked by the familiar bitterness. Clearly, he knew the real thoughts behind Wilber's words, but for some reason, he let them remain unchallenged.

Stepping back, Wilber motioned for the knights to create a wider circle for the duel. Then, drawing his sword, he nodded to one of his men. "Pass him a blade."

"No need." Throwing off his cloak, Evan revealed his own weapon. From the black scabbard at his side, he drew a white blade.

Grinning, Wilber bent his knees. He could afford to play with this sapling, to draw his opponent out before the killing lunge.

Their blades touched. The king attacked, blocked the return, and stepped back, circling.

Lips compressed, Evan copied his attack, parry and retreat. Around them, more knights gathered to watch.

Again, Wilber advanced, faster this time. Hastily, the prince retreated, blocking the attacks. His face had drained of color. Over sixteen times the blades clashed together with a speed that caused the mound's clearing to ring with the sound. Evan's breath came in short gasps now. He had made the last mistake of his life, and his face reflected that knowledge.

Desperately, Evan planted his feet, striving to gain the advantage. But with smooth ease, Wilber continued to keep him on the defense, forcing his panting breaths to shorten.

Sweat poured down the prince's face. At last, his block faltered. Laughing inwardly, Wilber lunged.

And then the unexpected happened.

Evan did not try to block the death stroke. Switching hands, he angled his body so the king's sword stabbed into his right arm. With his left, meanwhile, he twisted his sword over the king's recovering blade and sank it into his opponent's shoulder. All along, he must have known he lacked the skill to win. It seemed he had only been waiting for that moment, braced for the pain. And so, he had skillfully built his uncle's overconfidence.

As Evan withdrew his sword, the king cried in agony and the white blade, blood trickling over it, touched his throat. "Yield, Uncle."

Looking up into that determined face, flickering with its own pain, Wilber considered doing just that. But yielding would cripple his rule forever. It already had, by his standards. By Dalacort tradition, Evan Maxwell had proven strong enough to rule. Almost—he had purposely not driven the sword through his opponent's heart.

As Wilber considered the young man panting before him, he spotted archers above the mound—islander archers. They had snuck up while the knights were distracted.

"Attack!" He shouted. "It was a trap!" To his surprise, Evan did not swipe off his head even then, instead springing back as knights surged toward him.

Ducking aside, Wilber called, "The crossbows!"

Shouting, the islanders charged.

Chapter 16

CHARLOTTE'S GIFT

WITH A SHAKE OF HER HEAD, Charlotte crept the rest of the way up the mound while Lazarus led the islanders' charge. Forget the siege. The island would go up in flames and blood. It had already been set in motion. There was no stopping it now. Instead, she was there to loose Darkfire.

After shooting the guard assigned to watch the agitated stallion, she snuck forward. Darkfire was straining against the rope around his head when she reached his flanks. With a small knife, she cut his legs free, whispering, "Stop. You're only making it tighter." Then, slipping her blade beneath the war bridle, she sliced it in two. Tossing his head, Darkfire released a furious scream. Even as it echoed, he broke into the growing fray.

Releasing her breath, Charlotte pulled her bow off her shoulder and crouched down, striving to tell friend from foe. She spotted Evan a few feet away, at the near edge of the battle, faltering terribly as he blocked a knight's sword with his obviously untrained left hand. His right hung uselessly at his side, blood running down his sleeve.

Repositioning herself, she felled his opponent with an arrow. Instantly, another knight charged the prince, but before she could remove that threat, she saw the crossbowman.

Behind an outcropping of ruins, a knight leveled his crossbow at the prince's back. Crossbow bolts could move with the force and speed of a dragon. Unless something intercepted it, Evan was dead. Charlotte could not deal with the threat from where she stood, not while the ruins protected the man.

So, even as the knight battling the prince forced him to stay in harm's way, Charlotte moved. The crossbow bolt embedded itself in her side; only its feathery end protruding. Almost simultaneously, the archer dropped to the ground, her arrow in his throat. Pain swept over the nymph, and she crumpled, gasping.

Most of the islanders knew there was something darkly magical about the mound, and Raymond had even told them that the grass was growing up black. Despite the dangers, though, Vilo was willing to risk an experiment under the circumstances. He did wonder why Wilber would ever set up camp here. Perhaps it was just because he figured the whole island was similarly unnatural. But that question was irrelevant to the needs of the moment.

Fighting through to the middle of the mound, he lowered himself to the ground. Though the top was now barren of grass, he had ripped some from the sides, roots and all—indeed, particularly the roots.

Crawling, he found a log that had been set aside for the campfire and sawed at it to create friction. Every scream, every thump of a collapsing body caused him to cringe. At last, though, his efforts released a small flicker. Blowing the flame into life, he tossed the grass roots into it, swiftly ducked back to prepare for whatever might happen—and hoped something would.

There followed no magic explosions, but instead of the usual hiss of wet weeds hitting flames, the roots let off a screech, which continued to grow. Vilo covered his ears, wishing as he stood exposed to that painful sound that he had been smarter.

Then there came a crackle above him, joining the long wail. Looking up, he saw roots pop into the air from the heat. They burst as they did so, showering particles of light, then seemed to grow wings and fly off.

Darkness swooped around Charlotte. The heat of flames burned inside her. Someone shouted her name.

And then she was staring up at Evan's anguished face as he bent over her.

Weakly, she reached for his hand. "My king needed a rescuer." Speaking made pain shoot up her sides, as did every breath she took. Darkness rolled in swiftly once more as the pain seared into her, but she pressed on. "Watch... Moth—"

She did not know if she finished her thought.

Only half-conscious, she felt the ground quiver. As if one with nature, she heard a cackle gathering in strength below. Then came a deep hiss, as if hundreds of creatures slid through the grass. Screams and gurgled cries followed.

Fighting the pain, she looked around. Evan had collapsed beside her, his blood staining the ground, his breathing shallow, like one near death.

Beyond them, spots of light fizzed through the air. The rooted blades of grass had taken a life of their own, writhing about men's feet and yanking them down. What happened to those men once they lay on the ground, she could only guess from the mound's glee. None of the islanders still standing were touched nor was Evan, beside her. The grass folded away from them, as if stung.

Then, abruptly, the sky darkened. With growing weakness, she strove to prop herself up on her elbows and wrap Evan's arm. But she could not move—not until something soft slipped under her shoulders and she imagined the brush of warm wings carrying her away.

When the last root in the flames shriveled entirely, the mound stilled. Not a single clang of battle sounded.

Popping his head up, Vilo looked around. None of the knights were still standing. Very few of those scattered across the mound moved at all. Grass was entwined around the necks of the dead. A few living knights trembled, curled into balls and holding their ears.

Some islanders remained on their feet, slowly releasing their own ears. Lazarus caught the minstrel's eye. Anger shone in the older islander's face, yet he also looked unsurprised.

Helplessly, Vilo shrugged and shook his head. "I won't do it again."

"I thought you had more sense than that! Did you even know what you were doing?"

"No."

Looking heavenward, the fisherman groaned. "It would be worse if you did. Next time, don't try to take miracles into your own hands."

There was nothing Vilo could do or say. The remaining knights were rounded up, all their pride and fighting spirit gone. He could hardly remember a time when he had felt more foolish.

A cool wind whipped across Evan. Shivering, he woke to find himself on a pile of blankets. Darkfire lay curled beside him, soft snores emitting from his cavernous throat. Far overhead hung a tent canopy.

"Max…" The whisper caused him to jump. Lazarus was crouched beside him, holding out a steaming bowl. "Drink this. It's just a salty broth."

Pushing himself up, Evan cringed as his right arm throbbed in pain. "What happened?" he asked as he accepted the bowl. "How long has it—?"

The fisherman held up a hand. "We're cleaning up the mound, disentangling the dead knights from the grass. This is Wilber's tent. We've turned it into a healer's shelter. You gave us quite a scare. Darkfire found you crumpled beside—"

"Charlotte! Is she here? Will she survive?"

Sighing, Lazarus said, "We found her beside you. She's gone already. We are still gathering the dead, but tomorrow morning we'll hold a burial."

Devastated, Evan could only stare.

The fisherman touched his arm. "She's in a better place, Max."

"But… There was a crossbowman. She stepped in his way." Shaking his head, the prince strove to sort through flashes of guilt, denial and pain. "I think she purposely blocked it. It should have been me, Lazarus!"

Sighing, the fisherman placed a hand on Evan's arm. "She probably did. I've no doubt she snuck up here for you in the first place. But I'm not going to sit here and say you did a very foolish thing and should have paid for it, nor that you should have done this or that. There's no room or time in this world for that. You did what you had to do. She did what she had to do." A chuckle escaped him. "Vilo, poor Vilo, did what he had to do. The rest is history. Learn from it and move on."

Darkfire shifted, bumping his nose tenderly against the prince's back. Evan took a deep breath. "And the Lady Talliaha? Does she know yet?"

"It's evening, Max. As soon as Wilber's forces surrendered, one of us went to tell them the news."

Evan dropped his gaze. The fisherman patted his shoulder. "It could have been a complete slaughter. As skillful as some of us are, as proud and determined as we are, we are untrained. They *were* trained, although we outnumbered them quite a bit. With what happened, there are only fourteen men in the little tent we designated as a prison. And Wilber himself, of course."

For a moment, the fisherman waited. When Evan failed to speak, he sighed, "Max, those are your captives, your uncle. It's up to you to decide what to do with them. You have a few days. Your uncle's currently feverish. I don't know how much he'd understand or remember, but don't let guilt clutter up your thoughts. We all make our choices."

Evan nodded, but no life returned to his chest.

Darkness fell around the mound. Unwilling to camp there, many islanders had returned to the site farther down the mountain. Raymond and Talliaha had come to help clear out the battle site while it had been light, but when he saw her leave with most of the other ladies, he followed. In silence, he joined her for a small supper.

Although no tears glistened in her eyes, they remained distant. For hours, she sat erect but vacant, as if the mound had cursed her into stone. Beside her, Raymond dozed wearily.

He woke sometime later. Black quiet surrounded him, hailing the early hours. Talliaha no longer sat nearby.

Painfully, Raymond pushed himself to his feet and shuffled off in search of her. It was her broken sobs that guided him. She had curled into a tight ball by the river that fell into Whistler's Falls. With a sigh, he knelt before her and wrapped his arms around her, thinking how tiny she suddenly felt.

Without argument, the lady buried her head in his shoulder. It took a moment before she whispered, through her weeping, "I waited so long, Raymond. An eternity, really. Then I had three children... No mother was prouder."

"No mother could be prouder, my lady. Your children were the best on the island, and no one can be as proud as you. Charlotte..." He swallowed. "Gave everything in her death."

"I don't care!" Talliaha's fist pounded into Raymond's shoulder—thankfully, the healthy one—as her sobs increased. "Evan should be dead! Wilber should be dead!"

"Shh... You do care." He received no answer from the broken woman in his arms, so utterly human in this moment. Sighing, he tried again. "Lady Talliaha, you have had Charlotte for sixteen years. That's a long time, in reality."

She vehemently shook her head, never removing her face from his shoulder. Although his heart agreed with her, he went on, "Those in the next life deserve their time with her, and she deserves to be home. Let her go."

Moments lengthened as Talliaha trembled against Raymond's shoulder. Finally, he heard her breathe, "I had so long to imagine children, I had them all pictured. My daughter was wise and noble. She had bright auburn hair and eyes as blue as the sky. I wanted that daughter. I never pictured her to be as wonderful, as beautiful as Charlotte, as... Nor that she would bear such pain."

When she quieted, Raymond asked, "Are you still proud of her?"

Talliaha sighed brokenly. "I don't think I could be more proud of anyone, Raymond." A brief sob escaped her, and he gently rocked her back and forth.

"Just remember that. Remember, all pain has forever left her. Our nymph is dancing alongside the deer in the most beautiful wood there ever was."

They both left the subject there, listening to the sounds of the forest around them. Charlotte, her bitterness and loneliness a ghost of the past, was dancing in the woods for which she had been born.

Dawn came, along with the cold breeze of autumn. Cold or not, it hardly mattered to the islanders, who were digging a great pit. The families of the dead placed the individual bodies in their care beside the hole they had dug. Some islanders even retrieved bodies from beneath the tracks. The dead knights, for their part, were shoved unceremoniously into the hole once it was finished.

At a distance from the proceedings, Evan stood beside Darkfire, his gaze fixed on Charlotte's body. Her mother had dressed her in her green gown. She had brushed out her long hair and threaded bright flowers through it. In peaceful slumber, the nymph lay stretched out on her green cloak, ready to be lowered into the hole.

Talliaha herself stood by her daughter's head, somehow erect, somehow able to assume the regal stance that had earned her the title "Lady." Yet, her eyes sparkled with pain. Raymond stood with his arm around her, staring at his feet.

Vilo's stringed gourds swelled, strumming a farewell while the bodies were gently lowered. There was both peace and longing in the tune. Then the dirt came, scattering itself over its new charges, covering Charlotte's serene face. Unable to watch her disappear beneath the turf, Evan turned away. Darkfire's soft hooves followed him.

"Have you decided what to do about your uncle?" the stallion asked.

The prince made no response.

Evan was sitting on a fallen tree, peeling the bark off an old twig, when Talliaha found him. Nodding to Darkfire, the lady pulled herself up beside the prince. He still said nothing, and she sighed. "I don't blame you, Evan. Yes, I..." She halted her words with a grim smile. "Well, it will be better if I don't say that."

"You would have preferred it if she let me die. There is no need to hide it. I feel that way myself."

Talliaha was quiet for a second. Then she shook her head. "No. I don't know the future, Evan, but I do know there's a kingdom that needs you. I wanted Charlotte near me, but maybe the world needed her to do as she did, in terms of both who she saved and her selfless example." She smiled. "When you save a king, the ripples are sure to be large."

"I'm a prince," he muttered.

Abruptly, she laughed. "'I'm,' is it? It seems you're an islander too. I suppose that's to be expected when everyone around you speaks the same way for months." Lowering her voice, she leaned close. "Move on, Evan. Do you want us to build a small boat for you to return home?"

He looked up at her. "What do I do with my uncle?"

Searching his eyes, Talliaha said nothing at first. After a deep inhale, she asked, "You don't expect him to surrender, do you?"

"If I cannot trust him, I must have him executed."

Pushing her wisps back beneath her veil, the lady compressed her lips. Then she slipped off the tree. "Maybe you can choose to trust him and see where love takes you."

In the end, Evan asked the islanders to build him a boat. It took another ten days, however, before Wilber was well enough to see anyone. In the meantime, Evan decided to speak to Radnor alone, or relatively, considering the many watchful eyes on them. "For ten months," the prince began, "I would like you to be Ansky's regent while I help the islander's repair the damage Wilber has done."

The knight only barked a laugh. "You must be insane."

"No. I have no other choice. Whether you love me or not, you do love Ansky greatly, and your years give you wisdom and experience. There are no other qualifications, but so few who can meet them."

"Indeed. The first wise choice would be to make sure you never took the throne."

There was only one response Evan could give. "You will do what you think best for Ansky."

Radnor folded his arms. "And you think you, a horse thief and friend of islanders who can command grass to strangle others, should ascend a throne?"

"Are you willing to give it to Wilber?" Evan asked instead.

Pausing, the knight stared back. At last, he growled, "I cannot be *your* regent. I will fight to the death to keep Ansky free from Evfel, but I would begin a coup if I thought we were strong enough to withstand one."

"You cannot?" When Radnor simply glared, the prince sighed. "If you refuse, I must put it into effect without your consent."

If it were possible, the knight's eyes cooled even more. "Then there is no purpose to this conversation, O *King*."

Slowly, Evan nodded. There truly was nothing more to say but that Ansky needed Radnor. And he had decided not to listen.

Three days after that conversation, Wilber returned to longer stretches of consciousness. Stepping into the prison tent, Evan paused by the entrance. Three islanders were stationed inside at all times, swapping with others every few hours.

Most of the prisoners were unbound. Quincy, however, apparently unyielding despite the passage of time, was bound hand and foot.

Knowing Wilber himself would have been in that position were he not lying there so pale and weak, Evan cautiously stepped over. A grim smile twisted the king's face. "So, Evan Maxwell," he croaked, "king of Ansky, master of your charger, and protector of Cyra. Do you intend to go further and add more titles?"

Returning the grim smile, Evan replied, "You must not feel well or you would hardly be so passive. No, I have no intention of going further." Despite the ghost of Jeffrey's plea to conquer Evfel, the prince continued, "This is my offer. Several islanders and I will escort you and your men back to the main street of Ansky, where you will confess all you have done. Then I will claim my rightful throne and name Sir Radnor as Ansky's regent. Afterward, the islanders and I will return here until next summer. That allows Aunt Lorene to have her child before your journey and plenty of time to guarantee safe passage to Evfel when you leave Ansky forever."

Several gasps sounded behind Evan and a brief cloud of anger passed over the king's face. "Is this part of keeping peace with Evfel?"

Straightening, Evan lifted his chin. "No. This is part of giving you a second chance, something all men are born with and are duty-bound to give each other. Every other option results in one of us dying. I could banish you to Evfel immediately—and you would return, marching through the gorge, with an army far larger than anything I can gather. I could banish you to the Calmar Mountains— you would slink back and raise Evfel in arms. I could send you to sea—you would die. Or I could simply kill you now."

Wilber said nothing, but Evan nodded as if he had answered. "I will give you your second chance. In a few days, you will be brought to the south shore. The islanders are building a boat large enough to carry you, your men and a horse for each of you across the channel with us. You had better make good use of this opportunity. I will not give you a third." With that warning, he swept out.

The prince had made his choice, and announced it without consulting anyone beforehand. His silence was not from a lack of courage, but from his doubts about whether he was making the right decision. But now, with no option but to request assistance from the islanders to accompany Wilber back to Ansky, he knew he had only made it more difficult for himself.

Perhaps even worse, Vilo approached him on the subject the next day before he had officially told anyone except the Evfelian king. Joining the prince, the minstrel sighed. "Did you tell anyone what you intended before now? You know islanders were just outside. They heard everything."

"I told Darkfire, a little." Evan could not stop the reddening of his face in shame.

"So, you won't have any islanders going with you? That was a lie?"

"No, I need to ask for volunteers. I... Vilo, I must be honest. If anyone had echoed my doubts before I made the choice official, I could never have done it."

There was no condemnation in Vilo's gaze. Rubbing the side of his nose, he simply said, "You know Ansky and your uncle better than any of us. But we know our reputation, particularly after what happened. If we go with you, Wilber could promise the grass is green on this island, but they would never believe it. They will always be sure it is blackened all year.

"In their minds, we are manipulative, powerful enchanters, more likely trying to take Ansky for ourselves than to expose the truth."

"What then, Vilo? Wilber will see to it that I die if I go alone."

"I cannot gainsay mercy, Evan, but I must warn you of the image you will leave of yourself. I know you need our help to carry this out, but with our presence, they will say you saw the chance to rid yourself of responsibility and keep Darkfire. If not that, then that you've become one of us with our magical ways. That is our prediction."

"Perhaps, but it might wake a few to the truth—if only a few. I have no other hope."

Three more days passed. After loading the horses they had pilfered from Wilber's cavalry, the islanders gladly rounded their prisoners together. From the camp, they marched them to the broken tracks, where Evan and the ten men who had volunteered to accompany him—including Raymond and Vilo—joined them.

Wilber leaned on Quincy's arm as they walked past the place where Evan stood beside Darkfire.

Watching the prisoners board the boat, Darkfire asked Evan, for perhaps the twentieth time, "Are you sure I cannot join you on this trek?"

"Stay, Darkfire. We will be back soon. I want your company, in all truth, but I fear your presence will give the people of Ansky another cause to believe I have forced Wilber to swear to a lie before them. They think I stole you. How would I answer to their suspicions that I took all I ever wanted, particularly as I go backed by islanders?"

"And you want to give Wilber until next summer to leave Ansky? I think that is too much time."

Sighing, Evan patted his friend's neck. "Depending on the greed of the valley, they might have a train up by next year. That will make the journey faster."

"Great. I loved the ride they provided."

Bumping his shoulder into his friend's large side, the prince shook his head. "If I am to give them any time at all, traveling next summer is the logical choice."

"I think you will walk straight under a headsman's ax."

"Darkfire! Choose trust. What else can we do? As I said, even if he does try something sinister, perhaps his confession now will win Ansky for me."

"Maybe. As long as you are not doing this for your own sake."

Staring up at the stallion, Evan repeated, "My sake?"

"You would sooner place your head on the block than return to the castle and ascend the throne."

Evan looked away. A slight prickle of doubt wormed its way into his chest. True, his heart had settled here, where autumn glinted on the forest leaves and finches tittered overhead. Back on the mound, green was again spreading across the ground—proof that the evil had departed the island. Although death would always continue striking, the willful killing on the mountain had ended. The same would not be said for his reign in Ansky.

At last, Evan shook his head. "I have to go. But Darkfire, come what may... famine, our deaths." He smiled and added, "Quincy becoming a crony of the king of Evfel—"

"Quincy? Why Quincy?"

"Because he is a stubborn and arrogant young man who is headed that way already. He will do anything to prove himself in Wilber's eyes, including fight his island captivity."

Snorting, Darkfire shook his mane. "Then be all the more careful."

"That is why the islanders are coming. For good or bad, this cannot happen without them. But I am not returning for myself. Should we leave right now, leave all these islanders to deal with the carnage we started and remove Wilber's second chance?"

Dipping his head, the stallion said, "I will see you off at least and wait for your return."

Evan had no desire to move, but he did. Hopefully, Wilber's forced confession would make a difference in Ansky and open the path to Evan's peaceful ascension to the throne. But when everything was said and done, all anyone had was hope. To that, the prince would cling. He had no other choice.

Epilogue

(In Nomacir)

ARM, HUMID AIR—a false summer in the midst of the cool spring—was a blessing. It enabled Arnacin to open the window without chilling Valoretta or Tenacius, their infant son. Contentedly, he watched his small family from the windowsill of the upper room in Makarios and Kassandra's house.

Valoretta roamed in a circle, humming her Miran tunes to the child in her arms. "He's so fragile, Arnacin," she breathed. "It's still unfathomable."

The sound of hooves pounding into the yard outside the door wiped away the parents' smiles. Arnacin sprang off the sill, where he could be seen by the riders, and flattened himself against the wall, Valoretta at his elbow. There, he watched the street.

Ten men reined in their horses in front of the house. Five dismounted. One of them, their apparent commander, banged on the door, snapping an order in the Nomacirrian tongue. A creak sounded from the door as it opened. No one stepped into view, but a small voice replied, echoing Arnacin's sense of foreboding. Amid his angry speech, the commander pointed to the harbor. Even without understanding the language, the islander was certain they were talking about his ship—and consequently, its occupants. A month was long enough for any rumor to circulate and for numerous people to have seen him about.

Valoretta's warm fingers slid into his. Carefully shutting the window, he stepped farther away from it while the men filed into the house below.

"Are they really here for us?" Valoretta asked, speaking in the old tongue of Mira.

"It's likely." The islander's own tactic to avoid being overheard was simply to drop his voice. His old Miran was broken, his understanding of the language more adept when reading or hearing another speak it.

Smoothing the black wisps of hair on the baby's head, he forced himself to continue. "When Channing came to visit three weeks back, you heard him admit the people of Nomacir were fearful, particularly of Tenacius, 'the new son of Zedelious.' If—"

"No. We can sneak out. I could use more time to rest, but I'm not so unwell that I can't leave now if necessary."

"If they are here for us, Valoretta, they will already have men by the ship."

"Then we can find temporary passage aboard another, if you sneak on."

"You know why that's not an option, *Mira*. You are no more safe aboard another vessel than I am."

Her eyes flashed, despite the worry in their depths. "Whatever you're thinking, I know it's not an option, either. At least Isholt is a ruling queen. If necessary, I will speak with her."

"At what cost? In any case, you're assuming she will grant you an audience under an alibi. Announcing yourself in order to approach her would likely be suicide."

Valoretta's expression remained unmoving, but her compressed lips suggested she saw no alternative.

Arnacin exhaled. "I hope they don't know of Tenacius's birth, but if they do, and if they are as afraid as Channing believes, the only way they might leave him with you is if they remove the chance that I could raise him."

"It's not right," she hissed, her gaze on the ground. "You're not a Zedelious, and you didn't do anything wrong."

Kissing her forehead, the islander pulled away. "Stay here and keep him safe. Bolt the door behind me. Please."

Valoretta's long stare was all the answer he would receive, but he could not risk staying any longer. From the end of the bed, he pulled a rough shawl, even as he wished he could take his cloak, which lay beside it. That garment, however, was a disguise that cast him in shadow and mystique. It would only fuel the soldiers' fears. Instead, the shawl's homespun brown length, only covering his shoulders, would still give warmth, but would lack the appearance of a phantom.

Tenacius released a short cry as Arnacin slipped into the darkened corridor—a lament for a lost loved one. The slight click of the door's bolt sliding into place sounded its finality.

Stealthily, Arnacin crept to the landing at the top of the stairs. The conversation below was clearly audible, although that made little difference—even after a month, he knew only a smattering of Nomacir's language. He could tell from the voices that the lady of the house, Kassandra, was debating fiercely on her own. Her husband, Makarios, if he was present, said nothing.

As the islander strained to understand the conversation, he picked out their words for "refuge," "queen" and some verbs. However, it was the lady's spoken word, *geno*, that spurred the islander into movement. He had heard her fondly call Tenacius "Little Gen" or "Geno" enough times to know it was him she was discussing.

Arnacin's approach was so soundless, it took a moment for anyone to realize he had stopped behind Kassandra in the vestibule's archway. Then the commander's gaze turned to him. The islander's mouth went dry as he stared into surprised eyes, but he counted three heartbeats before the suspicious armored man growled in the common speech, "So, the feared Black Captain comes to surrender? What do you hope to gain?"

Speaking the truth would hardly serve his purpose. Arnacin only twitched his head, a "nothing" that refused to come.

Kassandra stepped between them. "I say again, he wouldn't be here at all if it weren't for the dying mother, so you have no right to hang him!"

"No right?! He shouldn't have even been in our waters, according to the judgment Captain Adhelmar took the liberty of making! We just eliminated his vermin of a family. Now he thinks to bring it back and with a son to be the new scourge of the sea, once grown."

Menacingly, the commander decreased the space between them. "Now step aside before we arrest you as well."

Footsteps behind Arnacin caused him to jump.

Makarios brushed by. "No need for that. We all want justice, I believe. Did the queen actually send you?"

The commander's face reddened. "Our captains are on the verge of mutiny, complaining about the mercy given without cause to this... this... pirate! They are enraged that Adhelmar's impudence went unpunished, for taking such a weighty decision into his own hands!"

The commander pounced, seizing Arnacin's arm.

Makarios moved toward the door, as if to block any escape, but the soldiers gathered more closely around it. Instead, Kassandra's husband turned to the commander. "There was no proof he was a pirate! Until recently, no one even knew of Adhelmar's action. You turn this into a scandal without any more proof of a crime than there was originally. Captain Adhelmar only granted partial pardon for service to our queen. Without Arnacin, *Isholt's Revenge* might have sunk, and we never would have brought an end to the Zedelious line at all!"

The commander looked down at his prey. "If necessary, I'm authorized to offer one compromise. Out of respect for our own then, I ask you, pirate, give us possession of your little family. Do that and you're free to leave."

Arnacin's chin rose. "Never."

He winced as the commander nodded and hauled him toward the soldiers. His stomach turned, but he allowed them to fasten the restraints—the metal that bit into his wrists, secured so snugly a skeleton could not slip free.

In the silence that followed, Makarios removed a scroll from his belt. "You didn't come from the queen, and you are to leave this family alone. They depart tomorrow, anyway."

The soldiers paused their search down the islander's legs as their commander stared at the scroll for a moment. Then he snatched it and ripped away the binding ribbon. There was no seal on the outside, but Arnacin saw the dark stain of dried wax when it was unrolled and involuntarily stepped back. Makarios had been in contact with the queen.

After skimming the document, the commander's gaze locked on Makarios and his wife. "What trick is this? Why would you hold on to this until now?"

"Trick? With Her Majesty's own seal and signature? I can assure you, it's no trick."

"Then why not reveal this order at once?"

Makarios bowed his head in apology. "Her Majesty commanded us to keep it secret, unless it became absolutely necessary to reveal it."

"Yet this says she has proof of his innocence. I doubt she would ask you to hold on to that secret."

Kassandra shrugged. "She would prefer to keep it to herself until they have left. That is all she told us."

"Strange, is it not?"

"We are but loyal servants to Her Majesty, as I am sure you are. She gave no reason, and never once did we ask for one."

At last, the commander huffed, "Fine, but they better be gone by tomorrow, like you said."

He motioned to his men to release their prisoner. "After that, if the queen's grand secrets fail us and there's a coup, we will have to tell the captains we were about to bring justice when the criminal escaped."

With a last glare at Arnacin, the commander led his men back out the door. The islander's heart did not stop pounding with their exit, however. He trembled.

"Hey," Kassandra soothed. "We'll have you off by tomorrow morning. You'll be fine."

Arnacin shook his head. "We're leaving tonight. I don't trust them, or your queen." Looking back and forth between the two, he asked, "Who really wrote the order?"

"The queen." Makarios pulled another scroll from inside his coat. "Here. She wrote a letter to you and Valoretta as well."

The islander did not move to accept it. "I can't read it."

"She wrote in the common tongue."

"But did she write in Mira's characters?"

"Oh."

In Makarios's ensuing silence, Kassandra asked, "Shall I read it to you?"

When Arnacin gave no response, she took the note, unrolled it, and began.

Mira,

My deepest condolences for the loss of your home and regards to you and the Black Phantom. I am very glad to learn you escaped, and perhaps even more glad to know it was the Black Phantom who rescued you.

That knowledge spurred my quest to discover his heart and his innocence. I must apologize to him. I have succeeded in piecing together secrets he would have died to keep.

To protect you both, I will wait until you leave to divulge the testimonies of Captain Adhelmar, Noel Butter and Maco.

I must also apologize for my artifice. I have met both of you under the guise of a local friend. As two of my harbor informants and my faithful administrators to those needing aid, Makarios and Kassandra helped with the ruse, but do not fault them. They but do what I ask.

If ever you have the opportunity, Mira, to speak to me of your reign as a fellow queen, please do. But if not, I understand.

Wishing you and your family the best of futures,

Isholt

Arnacin fled back up the stairs. Whether Nomacir's queen had lied, he would not stay to discover.

A pale Valoretta met him on the landing. "I saw them go. What happened?"

"We're leaving as soon as you're ready."

"Will they let us leave?"

Arnacin nodded weakly as his wife embraced him. Unresisting, he tucked his head into her shoulder, soothed in that she also trembled—he was not alone in his fear.

One thought gradually strengthened him, however. His mother, Charlotte and Will awaited him. At long last, the bow of his ship would be turned to the west for good.

Thanks for reading *The Island Siege*. If you've enjoyed reading this book, please leave a review on your favorite review site. It helps me reach readers who might enjoy more of my books.

Read on for a sneak peek at Book 4 of *The Black Phantom Chronicles*, *The Final Drive*, available at emeraldlakebooks.com/drive.

Prologue

LIKE MANY OF THE FORTIFICATIONS within and around Castle Ansky, the dungeons had received the special attention of the masons under King Wilber of Evfel. Even imagining escape was now impossible. But if there was one positive thing to say for it, there was much less dampness and decay—practically none, in fact.

And yet, that was far too generous.

Pulling his thin blanket over his scrawny shoulders, Sir Klement looked up from where he was sitting on the floor as feet clomped down the corridor outside. As he did every afternoon—the only marker of the days—the jailer, Apulion, entered the cell with a bowl of what he called soup. Starved, the prisoner never refused the slop.

The chain connecting Klement's wrists clanked its familiar complaint as he reached up to accept the rough vessel. Blobs of fat and carrot ends bobbed in the greasy-smelling water, but someone had included an actual piece of meat among the scraps. Klement did not know if the meat was included on purpose, but he sipped the soup gratefully while the jailer settled onto the bench he had dragged just out of reach. Chains prevented the prisoner from taking more than three steps in any direction.

"Well?" Apulion asked, folding his arms across his chest. The question was old, but Klement awaited it every day with eagerness. It brought with it company and speech while he drew his meal out as long as possible.

On this occasion, the jailer's lips twitched smugly.

Wondering at the smirk, Klement nevertheless replied, "No true-born Anskonian will ever yield to Wilber of Evfel. Yes, I know his reasons for seizing control again after Radnor died last winter, but submission to Evfel is no better than Prince Maxwell's supposed affiliation with magic." He hid his contempt by taking another sip from the bowl.

The smug smile broadened. "They will in order to protect themselves from hell. Maxwell just disappeared into the Ice Woods without falling."

Choking, Klement looked up at the jailer. "What?" As Apulion stood to thump him on the back, he shook his head. "It must be a lie."

Shrugging, the jailer returned to his seat. "Is it? His claims last fall, forced through Dalacort lips, came with the island-ers' backing. And we cannot ignore the Evfelians that never returned, strangled to death by blades of grass."

Klement kept his lips sealed, even though he lacked a counterargument.

"And this time," Apulion continued, "there are too many witnesses for debate. You yourself should remember the commotion down here just this past week. Summos Valley alerted us that Prince Maxwell was on the way back—"

"Why are they involved?"

"I could not care less, but that is beside the point. Wilber decided to capture him and finally hold an actual trial, one that reveals Maxwell's true allegiances. The capture was easy, but the stallion ran away. Still, I locked our traitorous prince up myself, I did. According to King Wilber's orders, I put him in our most impenetrable cell, chained so as to be unable to move."

The jailer paused, letting those words linger. "He vanished."

Klement shook his head. "Someone helped him."

"The castle gates were immediately barricaded. But, very well, let us assume he escaped with help before anyone could act. Except…"

Impatiently, Klement pressed, "Except what?"

"We had an extra Anskonian knight at that time. He was as untrained as all the rest from town, but no one could remember when he was drafted. In the hunt for Maxwell, no one thought too much of this knight. He was at least ten years older than our prince, brown-eyed instead of blue, blond-haired rather than brown, taller, broader and so forth. The only thing that made anyone pause was that he had a vibrantly red-haired boy as a companion and could ride King Phillip's untouchable horses.

"Now, maybe he was just one of those animal-tamer types. Or so we thought for a week. But when there was no sight of Maxwell, Wilber finally ordered the gates to be opened and a search party to move out. A hundred men rode forth, Evfelians and Anskonians alike. Among them went the animal tamer, for if Maxwell was spotted, no one could ride better than he. Wilber personally selected the party."

Again Apulion paused his story. After a moment, Klement started to rise in frustration. Naturally, he could never reach far enough to shake the other, but he wanted to.

Laughing, the jailer said, "Have patience. I will tell. So, we waited back here. Hours later, ninety-nine men and a hundred horses returned. The animal tamer was gone, and the host was pale as albinos. They said they were in the midst of the valley when one of the knights broke away. Only, it was no longer the animal tamer. Every feature had changed. His blond hair became brown. His build was slighter. To put it bluntly, he had transformed into Maxwell.

"He turned his steed—one of his father's—not toward the mountains, but toward the Ice Woods. As they neared them, they saw something leap from the gate—the stallion stolen from Wilber last year. Maxwell leapt off the horse he was riding, was picked up by that demonic beast, and together they disappeared into the woods. They never slipped once."

Leaning back, Apulion regarded the transfixed prisoner. "Now, if you find that unbelievable, let me tell you about his red-haired companion. Know that no one left after that host. Wilber had the gates closed immediately behind them, but everyone has combed the castle for Maxwell's companion. No one has seen him since the prince left."

A long silence followed. Klement knew his heart beat, yet it seemed detached from his chest. No, he could not believe Maxwell had allied with the evil forces in the Ice Woods.

As if reading his thoughts, Apulion sighed. "The facts are, sir, Wilber has been telling the truth all along. The supposed confession forced out of his lips was the lie, and Maxwell has joined in with evil spirits."

Slowly, Klement looked up. "But why? What would even prompt him to make such a pact? And if the horse is a spirit of the Ice Woods, is it perhaps not more likely that Prince Maxwell was put under some spell when he was trying to tame it?"

Apulion sighed. "You are scratching at the bottom of the barrel. Anyway, it appears to me, sir, you might have until Maxwell is brought to justice. I assume the king is being pressured by Ansky to grant you a second chance, but if you still refuse to accept Wilber as your rightful ruler when he calls for you, it will be the rope that brings your end. To make matters worse, you will have betrayed all of Ansky in your refusal to aid it against a traitor. If our onetime prince succeeds, no matter the cause for his conversion, all of Ansky will fall to the creatures of darkness dwelling in the woods. I would suggest you think about it."

Chapter 1

SHEPHERD OR NOBLE?

ENCHANTRESS ISLAND rose above the small ship sailing toward its eastern shore. The late afternoon sun shone in glimmers, setting behind the tree-topped mountain in a slow descent. Light burnished the peak and flashed across the wind-blown ocean waves. The island itself burned beneath the sun like an emerald emerging from the sea and was no less wondrous than it looked. After five agonizingly long years, Arnacin would be home once his unusually sluggish ship reached the shore.

A light creak of the cabin door, followed by soft footsteps, told him of someone's arrival, yet he did not turn. Joining him at the bow, Valoretta whispered, "You're trembling, Arnacin."

The islander said nothing. No words could untangle the fluctuating web of joy, relief, fear, anticipation and self-doubt.

She waited a beat, then asked, "Are you still concerned about what your family will think of you, a husband and father, without their knowledge of either?"

Finally turning toward Valoretta, Arnacin confessed, "I don't dare ask myself." Beneath her hood, her pale blue eyes met his, and he changed subjects. "Is Tenacius asleep?"

"For now. When will we reach shore?"

"Not soon enough." His words came out in a sigh.

Valoretta said nothing for a long moment. Then she lightly touched his arm. "You should help me with Tenacius when he wakes in another ten minutes, or it's going to be a long afternoon."

Arnacin shook his head. Nothing could rip his focus from his home at that moment.

Valoretta's gaze remained fixed on him. "When we arrive, I'll stay here with Tenacius until afterward." She had no need to define *afterward*.

Arnacin did not take time to lower his sail or drop the anchor. As soon as the water turned shallow, the islander jumped over the bow. While the wind pushed his flat-bottomed ship onto the sand with a deep grinding hiss, he raced into the village along the shores of Alleluia Lake.

Now, as he approached the dancing water, the fact that the lake was really only a medium-sized pond was jarringly obvious. Once upon a time, he had thought it immense and second only to the ocean. Still, despite its actual size, it drew the eye, and its familiarity buoyed his spirits.

Before reaching the village, however, he slowed. No sounds of chatter or children greeted him, no yapping dogs, no boys splashing each other in the pond. As he entered, he noticed that half the doors were shut despite the summer humidity. Not only that, but he thought he remembered homes in different places than they were now. Though a few women sat in the distance, working outside their doors, they did so in silence.

As a dog wandering down the street suddenly perked its nose in the air, took a sniff, and then growled softly, Arnacin pulled his hood up against the deep cold that seeped into him. The soft patter of paws followed him before apparently losing interest and wandering away.

Reaching his home, Arnacin stopped. Its wood appeared unweathered and the door was shut, as was that of the neighboring home, which had been Raymond's. Yet Raymond had never been inside, and *still* he had never shut the door.

Quickly turning back to his home, the islander knocked. No response came. As his heart stopped for a beat, Arnacin numbly pushed open the door. The house was dark, and the curtained alcove that had once given privacy to his parents' bed was no longer there. A flat wall stood in its place, fresh and subtle and giving no hint as to the family who had once lived inside. The only signs of occupancy were a single pallet, a small table, one stool, and a pot and ladle hanging in the dead fireplace, though a light dust spoke of the owner's absence.

Slowly, sensations returned. Wind from the water rushed through the open door, around the room, and passed him—a mournful, cold and dying sigh.

Arnacin's skin crawled. Studying the barren scene only a second longer, he shut the door on the darkened interior with a snap. The sun's light suddenly became thick and depressing.

Pushing aside his dread, the islander trudged down the street, searching desperately for something, anything, that would put his greatest fears to rest.

Back past Alleluia Lake, where some of the homes sat on their legs three feet above the ground, past hundreds of memories that now snickered at him, he wandered until someone carding wool under her eaves captured his attention. "Matalaide!"

Matalaide's head snapped upward at his relieved cry, yet she stared at him without recognition. Then, abruptly, she leapt to her feet and strode over to him. She did not greet him or smile. Seizing his arm, she yanked him toward her hut.

She nearly threw him inside and shut the door behind them. "What do you have to say for yourself?" the weaver finally barked.

Catching himself on the loom, Arnacin whirled back toward her. "What's happened?"

Anger flashed in Matalaide's eyes. "First, you leave in the dead of the night! You desert everyone, every responsibility, and then you dare return?"

"I had to!"

"Oh, ho! Is that your take on it? I would think five years was long enough to come up with a good apology."

The weaver still stood with her back pressed against the door. Trembling, Arnacin expected the hut to begin shrinking in on them before waking to find it all the worst nightmare yet. "Matalaide," he whispered. "What happened?"

In the dim light of the nearby candle, he saw tears appear in the weaver's eyes. As if realizing how clearly he could see her pain, Matalaide fixed her gaze on something not far from Arnacin's shoulder. Cautiously taking his gaze off her, the islander glanced that way and then froze. Silk lay over the back of a chair—deep blue silk with some emblem in the middle and fire along the bottom. The exact insignia was unclear. Only black lines faced him, but it would not matter if those lines depicted angel wings. It was a mark of nobility.

Matalaide approached it and ran her finger along the brilliant blue cloth. "There was a battle on our shores, Arnacin. All the able-bodied men who survived have gone to help finish the war. Your mother left with them." When Arnacin didn't respond, the weaver added, "I'm sorry to say your brother and sister are dead. Will died two years ago of food poisoning—at least, that's my assumption—and Charlotte died of an arrow in the battle. She wasn't supposed to be there, but..." Matalaide shrugged. "She was Charlotte."

The air buzzed sharply in the ensuing silence until Arnacin forced some response from his tongue. "None of those things ever happen here!"

"Call me a liar, then!" Matalaide whirled back toward him. "Face it, boy! You needed to be here, and you weren't!"

Arnacin shook his head in horror, and the weaver sighed. The pity on her face was far worse than her flash of temper.

"Many things change in five years." As she pulled the banner off the chair, a dark, fiery horse revealed itself in the falling folds. "And it is likely we have claimed a king. Charlotte herself deliberately took the arrow meant for him."

"No!" Arnacin dashed through the door and fled for the mountain. Yet his denial had been automatic. He knew, by the blue standard alone, that Matalaide spoke truly. Charlotte was not wandering the mountain, nor would she ever again. His nightmares were reality. The island had lost itself.

Subscribe to my newsletter at
emeraldlakebooks.com/blackphantom
to be notified when the next book in
The Black Phantom Chronicles
is released.

Acknowledgments

To the Crafter of Dreams, for making not one, but two, dreams that shaped this story. Evan, Darkfire, Lisya, Jeffery and Charlotte are your creations, sent to me to meet and develop.

To my family, from my sister, who always listens to my wild dreams and brainchildren, to my uncle, who correctly told me I had too many plot holes in my first version to keep his attention. I completely ripped it apart thanks to you and my own maturity. But even you couldn't make me give up.

To Buck, Gail, Margi and Mark, my horse trainers. You helped bring Evan and Darkfire to life.

To Kathy. I went to you for my first coaching/pitching session, just to wet my feet. Although I won't flatter myself as being the most awkward writer seeing you that day, I can imagine how left-footed I was while we discussed world-building.

To Carol, for pulling me into a writers' group, and to Tara, for keeping that group going for so long. Those were good years.

To Emerald Lake Books. This would still be a WIP without you.

To those of Oddball Newt. You allowed someone so fixedly in love with the medieval into your steampunk world. It's always great fun.

To Scott and Becky. You do so much for us speculative writers.

To the Black Phantom's readers and supporters. This could not happen without you.

And lastly, to all the people I haven't named. My editors, beta readers, and general champions. Your names are here in invisible ink. To you all, I say thank you.

About the Author

ESTHER WALLACE is an award-winning author and freelance illustrator. She started her journey as a homeschooler, telling stories to her younger siblings.

Her favorite books and movies are the ones that challenge the reader as well as the protagonists—the tales so driven by character, those heroes and heroines stay with one through all the hardships and joys of life. Figures like Frodo Baggins, Princess Eilonwy of Llyr, Taran Wanderer, and Harry Potter leap off the page, as they should.

Her largest jolts of inspiration appear when reading, watching or reenacting history or joking with her large family around the dinner table.

To learn more about Esther and her work, visit her website at theblackphantomchronicles.com.

Esther enjoys hearing from her readers. If you'd like to contact her or invite her to your next book club meeting, visit emeraldlakebooks.com/wallace.

For more great books, please visit us at
emeraldlakebooks.com